Pleasure Beach

Pleasure Beach

P.J. MELLOR

APHRODISIA

KENSINGTON PUBLISHING CORP.

http://www.kensingtonbooks.com

APHRODISIA BOOKS are published by

Kensington Publishing Corp.
850 Third Avenue
New York, NY 10022

All Kensington Titles, Imprints, and Distributed Lines are available at special quantity discounts for bulk purchases for sales promotions, premiums, fund-raising, and educational or institutional use.

Special book excerpts or customized printings can also be created to fit specific needs. For details, write or phone the office of the Kensington special sales manager: Kensington Publishing Corp., 850 Third Avenue, New York, NY 10022, attn: Special Sales Department, Phone: 1-800-221-2647.

Aphrodisia and the A logo are trademarks of Kensington Publishing Corp. Kensington and the K logo Reg. U.S. Pat. & TM Off.

ISBN 0-7582-1440-5

First Kensington Trade Paperback Printing: February 2006
10   9   8   7   6   5   4   3   2   1

Printed in the United States of America

Contents

Pretender   1

Same Time Next Week   91

Jack of Hearts   189

To Mary Law, English teacher extraordinaire, wherever you may be.

To my parents, "Mac" and Virgie McAllister, for their lifelong love and support.

And to my husband, Michael, my prototype for what a hero should be and my oh-so-willing research partner. I love you!

Acknowledgments

Thanks to my wonderful agent, Sha-Shana Crichton and fantastic editor, John Scognamiglio.

Thanks also to Romance Writers of America and my critique partners, past and present: Cheri Jetton, Linda Barrett, Pat O'Dea Rosen, Jesica Trapp, Babette Dejongh, Peggy Hamilton-Swire, Karyl Van Wageningen, Terri Dunham, Judythe Hixson, Janet Clementz-Garza, and Sharon Mignerey.

Pretender

1

Her lawyer turned and strode away without a backward glance, obviously confident his orders would be followed.

And, of course, they would. She was great at following orders.

"Who'd believe you're a woman on the run?" she asked her reflection in the rearview mirror. "McCall Lindsey, honor student, Girl Scout, all-around boring and blah." Even the highlights she'd recently added to her shoulder-length, wren-brown hair hadn't helped. Instead, they gave her the look of a demented skunk.

With a sigh, she headed her beat-up Escort toward the parking lot exit. The air conditioner spit out stale-smelling, hot air while she waited for a break in traffic.

She blinked back tears. "How did you get yourself into this mess?"

Fund-raising may not have been a career she'd aspired to, but she'd been danged good at it—well, until Sunshine International charged her with embezzling the multimillion-dollar funds from the Summers Group and fired her. Now it was a safe bet she'd never work in that field again.

Seeing a break in traffic, she pushed the little accelerator to the floor mat and zipped into the flow, ignoring the squeal of brakes and honk of several horns.

Against the steering wheel, the key her lawyer had tucked into her hand bit the tender flesh. A week at the beach might not be too bad. Labor Day was over. Maybe a little seclusion was just what she needed. Time to regroup and gather her thoughts about what she'd do with the rest of her life. She gave a watery laugh.

Or to plan her suicide.

Derek Summers broke his pencil in half, then threw it at his legal advisor.

"Hank, you told me it was a legitimate and worthy cause, a good tax write-off. I hate publicity! You know that! That idiot attorney has subpoenaed me! Me!" He threw his hands up. "I don't even do interviews. No way in hell am I appearing on every tabloid by going into a courtroom!"

"Now, don't get your shorts in a wad, Derek," Hank Connors soothed. "I'll see what I can do about getting you out of it."

Derek regarded the man who'd been legal counsel for the Summers Group for three generations. The man looked older than dirt, but if he said he'd do something, it usually got done.

"Why don't you go home, now, Mr. Summers?" Hazel, his almost equally ancient secretary, asked from across the room. Hazel had been Derek's father's secretary and knew more than he'd ever care to know about the family business. "Have you taken your blood pressure medication today?"

"Damnit, Hazel! Don't coddle me! And for your information, I went off the pills almost a year ago. So stop asking. I'm fine."

The two employees exchanged looks, which set him off again.

"I saw that! You two think I'm overreacting."

"Mr. Summers, calm down." Hazel flipped through the appointment book she always carried. "You were scheduled to leave for your beach house this morning." Through the magnified lenses of her rhinestone-encrusted glasses, her brown eyes stared meaningfully at him. "Why don't you head on out before the traffic gets any worse?"

His shoulders slumped, all fight gone. "Whatever." He jumped to his feet and jerked his navy sports coat from the back of his desk chair. "When I get back next week I expect you to have things worked out, Hank."

"I'm already on it, boss," Hank assured him. "I'm checking into the background of the prime suspect." He looked down at the paper in his hand. "A Miss McCall Lindsey."

McCall's *service-engine* light blinked on by the time her car wheezed to a stop beside the rental beach house on South Padre Island. Trying to ignore its possible implications, she focused on the house looming above her.

Made of redwood and glass and surrounded by decks on each level, it was easily three times the size of the little house she rented in the Heights section of Houston.

Her ring snagged the side of her best skirt when she climbed out of her car. Dang. Why hadn't she changed before heading out?

She looked down at her hand. Her eyes filled with tears. The miniscule diamond was missing from the promise ring Joel had given her three years ago.

It hadn't been all that valuable, and Joel had long since moved on and even married someone else. But that tiny gold ring had meant something to her. It meant someone had once thought enough about her to promise to think about proposing. Not much in the grand scheme of things, but it had been all she'd had.

And now it was gone. Along with everything else in her life.

Listless, she tugged the ring from her finger and stuck it in the zipper compartment of her nylon wallet. When she found her next job, she would see about replacing the stone. After all, besides the diamond studs Hattie Brubaker gave her, it was her only other piece of jewelry that was worth anything.

The handle broke off her rolling suitcase when she attempted to drag it from her cramped trunk.

"Great," she grumbled "No job, no husband or even a significant other, no good jewelry and now this. On a scale of one to ten, I'm a minus."

Unzipping the bag enough to slip the tips of her fingers inside, she dragged it through the sand toward the steep steps that led from the parking area to the back deck. When that failed, she yanked on the suitcase until she came to the steps.

Drag, plop. Drag, plop. Dang suitcase wasn't going to defeat her. It was slow going, but she finally reached the deck.

"Wow." Waves rolled to shore, their sound soothing her. In the distance sea gulls called. A faint tinge of pink showed on the horizon.

She looked around the spacious deck. In the far corner, closest to the sliding doors, sat a hot tub that would easily hold six adults. She peered into the churning water, impressed by the thoroughness of her lawyer's preparation.

"Death by hot tub. . . . No." She shook her head. "All that hot bubbling water would bloat my body. It would be nice to leave a good-looking corpse."

After fumbling with the key, the heavy glass door slid open on its well-oiled track.

The cool darkness of the interior greeted her. When her eyes adjusted, she took in the decor—well, what there was of it.

The large room held an array of massive furniture, some leather, all overstuffed. Great fieldstone fireplace, although who would build a fire at the beach? She shrugged and walked into the kitchen.

"Nice," she noted, liking the way the sunset gleamed off the stainless-steel appliances. "Good to have in case I'm overcome by a Martha Stewart moment."

Dragging her suitcase to the curved staircase, she dragged the bag up the stairs until she walked into what had to be the master suite.

"Oh, my gosh." Her fingers released their death grip on top of the suitcase. It fell with a soft thud, spilling its contents across the plush sea-blue carpeting.

The curved outer wall was entirely glass. She picked up a remote control and pushed a button. With a soft whir, the glass parted, allowing the surf to echo, giving the illusion of being held within a giant seashell.

The huge, round brass bed beckoned her. Taking an uncharacteristic hop backward, she sprawled on it, rubbing her hands and now bare feet against the raw silk spread. The warm dusky-peach color of the spread glowed in the impending sunset.

Feeling hedonistic, she rose to strip off her sensible business suit and fling it across the room. Her serviceable white cotton bra and underwear followed. Of course she would just have to pick them up and put them away later, but for right now, she would live her fantasy.

Being a good girl never got her anywhere. It was time to discover her inner wild woman.

She opened the bottle of sleeping pills Hattie insisted she bring with her and popped two in her mouth. So what if they always made her sleep like the dead? What did she have to wake up for, anyway? There was no job to get to, nothing and no one to meet.

Naked, she padded to the open window and looked over the stretch of beach to the Gulf. Below her was the edge of the lower deck, some rocks and sand. Lots of sand.

"Death by sand diving. . . ." She rubbed her arms and stepped back. "Too abrasive," she said to the sunset.

A huge yawn escaped her. Stretching, she walked to the bed and climbed onto the sinfully decadent spread, wondering if it had satin sheets.

She yawned again. The long drive caught up to her, causing her muscles to ache, eyelids to droop. The sound of the surf beckoned her. A sunset swim before the pills took effect would be great.

Maybe she'd just rest a few minutes before she put on her bathing suit.

Her hand stroked her nudity from breast to hip and she smiled. No one would believe goody-two-shoes McCall Lindsey was experiencing her wild side.

"Yeah," Derek spoke into the mouthpiece of his cellular headset as he flipped on his turn signal. "I'm turning in right now." His Porsche Boxster purred to a stop in the garage of his beach house. He turned off the ignition and scrubbed his face with one hand while he stretched. "Jack, I appreciate the thought, but I'm beat. I had a long drive and traffic was a bitch."

He stepped out of the car and popped the trunk. "My birthday isn't until next week, but thanks." He set down his suitcase and sighed. "What's the hurry about me getting the birthday present you left at your place?"

A push of his remote button turned on the exterior and interior lighting of his house. A soft click told him the doors unlocked as well.

He dropped his suitcase inside the back entry hall, then punched the LOCK button. "Okay, if it's that important, I'll head over there now and pick it up before the renter gets there.

The master bedroom. Got it." He walked back toward the car. "Key still in the same place? Thanks, pal, I'll give you a call when I wake up."

Another beep unlocked his car door and he threw in the phone before heading down the beach toward his friend's place to pick up his gift.

"Oh, Jack, my man," Derek whispered from the doorway of his friend's master suite. "You have outdone yourself this time."

When his fiancée broke their engagement, Derek had been relieved. Unfortunately, his friends thought he was desolate and took up a crusade to find him a replacement.

All had failed.

Jack was the only friend who hadn't tried to fix him up over the past year, for which he was profoundly grateful.

Derek rested his shoulder against the door jamb and grinned.

And now Jack had given him . . . this . . . for his birthday.

He'd been celibate for way too long. Jack must've known he was ready to experience something new.

To walk on the wild side.

His eyes caressed the nude perfection of the woman spread before him on Jack's *orgy* bed while he stripped with more eagerness than he'd felt in longer than he cared to remember. He snagged a handful of condoms from the mess on the floor on his way to collect his birthday gift.

Good old Jack, he thought as he climbed up on the bed with his personal nymphette.

He bought me a hooker.

2

McCall squirmed in the throes of the most delicious, erotic dream. Lying on a silken bed within a giant seashell, her personal love slave kissed and licked every inch of her nude body. Wet pressure set off shards of excited pleasure in spots that had not been touched by a man in a very long time. Her love slave had a very talented tongue.

She purred, tugged him higher, and rubbed her erect nipples against his firm chest while she returned his passionate kiss.

His hot erection throbbed and gently bumped against her stomach and upper thigh.

Restless and aching, she pulled him to her, indicating with her spread position that she was his for the taking.

And he took her.

A dim recess of her mind marveled at the realistic quality of the dream, the hot hardness plunging in and out of her wet sex.

Her fantasy lover gently bit the hard tips of her nipples while his hand reached between her legs to fondle her nub, his thrusts becoming harder and faster.

Her breath hitched; multicolored fireworks exploded behind her eyelids as wave after wave of pleasure washed over her, drowning her in sensation.

Above her, he shouted his completion, his magnificent body stiffening.

Swimming toward wakefulness, only to drift back into the undertow of deeper sleep, she sighed. Tender hands petted her from lips to toes before covering her with the soft bedspread.

She sighed again.

Death by orgasm.... She smiled drowsily. *What a lovely way to go.*

After locking Jack's door, Derek shoved his hands into the front pockets of his jean shorts and set off toward his own beach house.

A sappy grin curved his lips, he knew, but he couldn't stop smiling. Jack really knew what he needed. It was the perfect birthday gift to take his mind off the horror of the upcoming trial with the fund-raiser from hell.

His smile faltered as he climbed the steps to his deck. He knew she was a hooker, but while he'd been fucking her she'd felt more like a lover.

He shook his head and walked through the darkened house toward his bedroom. He'd just been without a woman for too long. That was why she'd had such an effect on him.

But why did he wonder what color her eyes were?

"Hi, Hattie, it's Mac," McCall said, balancing her cell phone while she finished emptying her suitcase early the next morning. "I just wanted to let you know I'm at the beach house. It was so thoughtful of you and Tucker." Tucker, her lawyer, was also Hattie's grandson. "And thank you again for paying my legal fees."

She hung up one of the brightly printed sundresses the old woman had insisted on buying for her last week. "I know I'm not guilty, but it's great to know other people feel the same.

"Yes, I slept wonderfully. Like the dead." She shrugged and tossed a handful of underwear into the dresser drawer, then glanced at her nudity in the mirror.

And gaped.

Dang, she glowed. Absolutely glowed! The sea air was really doing wonders for her. Either that or it had been one heck of a dream.

"I'm fine, Hattie. I told you, don't worry. Yes, I'll be careful. I—"

The neon-colored condoms Hattie had insisted she take during their last visit were strewn out next to her suitcase. Something wasn't right. She walked closer. One, two, three . . . Omigosh! One was missing!

Maybe it hadn't been a dream.

"Ah, Hattie?" Her heartbeat pounded in her ears. "Could I call you back later?" Shoving the remaining condoms back into her suitcase, her gaze fell on the wrapper of the missing one, lying on the nightstand. "No, nothing's wrong." She laughed to reassure her friend. "No, I'm just trying to unpack and it's difficult to hold the cell and work at the same time.

"Oh! Tuck said I should turn off my phone and let my voice mail pick up. So if you can't reach me, leave a message and I'll get back to you. Great. Thanks again. Bye, Hattie."

Her shaking thumb depressed the power button.

She picked up the wrapper and looked out over the beach, the air swirling around her suddenly heated skin.

Death by mortification. . . .

Derek woke slowly and reached across the bed. His hand connected with nothing but the cool sheet and he remembered.

She hadn't felt like a hooker—not that he'd really had any experience. Maybe that's what made her a professional, her ability to make her client feel as though she cared about only him.

That thought brought him down from the euphoric, sensual haze he'd enjoyed throughout the night.

He swung his feet to the floor and sat on the edge of his king-size bed. Maybe he should take a run and go by Jack's place. Just to make sure she hadn't taken anything when she left.

Maybe she'd still be there.

The thought brought instant arousal. Hard and throbbing, he stepped into a cold shower, then donned his running shorts. After a quick coat of sunscreen, he brushed his teeth and was out the door, running down the beach.

His steps faltered a few yards from Jack's deck.

Bright sunshine reflected from alabaster skin. He watched her lower her perfect nude body into the hot tub, his cock throbbing and eager, despite his earlier decision to just check on Jack's house.

Before he realized it, he stood on the edge of the deck.

Her head was turned up to the sun, eyes closed. Her long, light brown hair glowed with health and streaks of blond, making his fingers itch to run through the silken-looking strands.

The sun had already turned the fair skin on the tip of her nose and cheeks a becoming shade of pink.

"You really should apply sunscreen if you plan to stay out here for long," he told her in a low voice.

She jumped and screamed, the motion giving him a tantalizing view of pert, raspberry-colored nipples on a world-class rack. Beneath his shorts, his erection pushed against the liner.

Sinking beneath the churning water, she backed to the far side of the tub. "This is private property," she said through tight-looking lips; he imagined those lips around the part of his anatomy that literally jumped to attention. "In fact," she continued over the sudden roar in his ears, "this is a private beach."

"I know," he managed to say, fists clenched to keep from dragging her out of the tub and plunging into the wet heat he knew existed just below the water level. He motioned with a jerk of his thumb. "I'm staying at a place down the beach."

"Oh." She still kept as far away as possible, her arms crossed protectively over her breasts.

He wished she'd drop her arms. His mouth salivated for another taste of her delicious tits. But right now he'd settle for a look.

"Are you a friend of Jack's?" At her puzzled look, he clarified, "The guy who owns this place?"

"Oh, ah, no. I'm a friend of his brother-in-law."

"Tucker?" The sorry son of a bitch who took on the case of that scum-sucking fund-raiser, McCall Lindsey. When the hooker nodded, he schooled his expression and gave what he hoped was a friendly smile. She couldn't help the poor choices her friend Tucker made.

"So, is Tuck your lawyer?" She nodded and he wondered why she needed a lawyer, then remembered her profession. "Well, he's one of the best." He bared his teeth in a parody of a smile.

The woman glanced nervously at the door, back to him, and then back to the door, probably gauging the distance to safety.

His mind scrambled for something to say, some kind of introduction. But he'd have to come up with an alias. Given her line of work, it would be financial suicide to reveal his identity.

"I'm Alex," he said, using a shortened version of his middle name so it really wasn't a lie. He stepped closer to the hot tub, extending his hand.

Her hand trembled within his, her eyes wide. They were

blue, he noted. Such a light shade that they almost disappeared against her pale skin. Her blond-tipped eyelashes did nothing to add color to her pallor.

"Mac." Her voice was low and husky. Shards of desire ripped through him.

"I'm sorry, what did you say?" He leaned closer.

"Uh, my friends call me Mac." Tucker had advised her to lay low and not advertise her identity. Of course, she doubted he'd envisioned her being in quite this position.

"And Mac would be short for what? Your last name? Or is it your first?"

"Last." Why hadn't she prepared for something like this?

"It's your last name?"

She nodded and he grinned, revealing a perfect set of blinding white teeth and killer dimples. "So, I guess, after last night, I can consider myself one of your *friends*, Mac?"

Numbly, she nodded again while flashes of memory tumbled through her mind. They'd been together last night? Reality hit her.

It was no dream.

Her gaze traveled from the top of his tousled, sun-kissed blond hair to the bottom of the running shorts, which was as far as she could see due to the edge of the hot tub. Sunshine gleamed from the smooth, golden-tanned skin of his very impressive chest.

Oh, wow. If she was going to step out of character as she obviously did last night, she couldn't think of a better person to do it with than the splendid specimen before her.

Hattie's words about enjoying a fantasy life filtered through her mind. Why not begin living the fantasy right here, right now?

"What do you charge for dinner?" he asked.

She blinked. Huh? "I'm sorry, I think I misunderstood you. What did you say?"

Alex looked slightly embarrassed. He glanced down at his feet, then met her gaze. "I'm not in the habit of, well, this kind of thing. I'd like to take you out for dinner, but I thought I should ask what it would cost me."

She blinked again. Was she missing something? How could she possibly know in advance what it would cost him to take her to dinner? "I guess it would depend on where we went."

"Is that right? Huh, I didn't realize that."

How could he not realize that? she wondered. Gorgeous as he was, was he somehow mentally deficient?

It didn't matter. She'd decided to explore her wild side, her inner temptress, during her enforced vacation. And she couldn't think of anyone she'd rather do it with than the man standing on her deck.

But the man was turning to leave.

"Wait!" She jumped up, then immediately sank back under the churning water. Why had she come out here naked? There were two perfectly good bathing suits in her bedroom.

He stopped at the steps leading down to the beach and looked over his shoulder.

"Um . . ." She licked her lips and tried one of the come-hither looks Hattie had been advising her to use. "What's your hurry? Why don't you join me?" She motioned to the other side of the tub. At his obvious hesitation, she added with a smile, "No charge."

He smiled and strode back across the deck, wasting no time in shucking off his miniscule shorts, and then climbed in with her.

The old Mac would have averted her eyes, but during her stay at Pleasure Beach, she was determined to be the new, improved version. McCall Lindsey, wild woman.

She looked across the bubbling water at the hunk and fought down her feeling of tenderness. She'd always been a sucker for the down-and-out. A champion of lost causes. She had a good handle on reading people, and this guy was a snap. So concerned with cost, he obviously was barely scraping by to survive in this area.

Poor Alex.

3

As soon as Derek was submerged in the hot water, he reached for her—his personal bath toy.

She came willingly into his arms, her face turned up for his kiss.

Man, the way she looked, all sexy and sun-kissed, knocked him out. He wanted nothing more than to plunge into her wetness and explore what they'd begun last night.

But he couldn't. At least, not yet. He wanted their time today to last, wanted her to want him as much as he wanted her.

She was a pro, he reminded his eager body. Did he have what it took to turn a hooker on? If the almost painful hard-on was any indication, probably not. But he was willing to give it his best shot. Or die trying.

He traced the outline of her lips with his tongue. She moaned and edged forward, obviously wanting to deepen the kiss. He held back, blowing softly against the wetness before nibbling at each corner of her succulent mouth.

Beneath the water, his erection pulsed with each beat of his heart, telling him he was a fool to try to give someone like that pleasure before taking his own.

But it was suddenly the most important challenge of his life.

Mac's bones took on the consistency of warm Silly Putty, her muscles melting. Still, her flesh-and-blood fantasy lover continued his sensuous torture.

Big, hot hands spanned her waist, raising her above the water until her nipples were directly aligned with his mouth. Before she had time to decide whether she should be embarrassed at the exposure, his mouth closed over one distended tip.

Each deep draw on her breast created an interesting tingle between her legs, an answering ache in her womb.

She wanted to reciprocate, but her body refused to follow her orders. Instead, she hung there, limply suspended above easily the most gorgeous man she'd ever seen, while he suckled at breasts that became heavier and more sensitive by the second.

Maybe she'd suffered a minor stroke, which would explain her inability to move or form a coherent sentence. Pleasure rushed through her. Dang, it felt good!

She whimpered when he lifted her higher to perch along the lip of the tub, instantly missing the warmth of the water and his voracious mouth.

But not for long.

He spread her legs with a gentle hand on each knee, holding them open when she attempted to protect what little modesty she had left.

Lightly, he blew on the feminine folds all but bare from her recent adventure in bikini waxing. The effect sent delicious shivers coursing through her.

She tried to clamp her legs together, but he wasn't allowing it.

"So pretty," he whispered, "all pink and plump." He leaned forward to kiss the pink skin, then leisurely lapped at her folds.

All thoughts and sensation immediately zapped to that one area, centered on the feel of his hot tongue. Like warm, wet velvet, the tongue caressed each petal before concentrating on swirling around and around her ultra-sensitized nub, driving her wild.

It was a short drive.

McCall moaned and rested her weight back on her arms, spreading her legs wider.

The sun shone down on her, kissing the tips of her breasts, warming her upturned face. The constant Gulf breeze gently wrapped around her, holding her in its sensuous embrace.

Behind her, the sounds of the waves and seagulls faded to be replaced by the echo of her own heartbeat. When he drew the nub into his mouth and sucked, her breath hitched and her heart stumbled as wave after wave of pleasure washed over her.

During the throes of her climax, she clamped her legs together, imprisoning his head. It wasn't until his fingers took up where his talented mouth left off that she relaxed and her legs fell open.

Alex smiled up at her, his heated gaze caressing her from the top of her head to the spot his hand touched so intimately, and back.

"So responsive, so slick and pretty," he praised. One, then two fingers slid in and out of her heat, driving her slowly toward the edge again.

When his tongue replaced his fingers, she felt orgasm number two cresting.

Before she caught her breath, he pulled her back to him and into the hot, bubbling water. With a forceful thrust that made her eyes widen, he filled her.

His mouth took hers on her gasp, his tongue mimicking the other part of his anatomy. Her bones dissolved.

Body limp, she rode the rise and fall of the water while he plunged in and out. Each stroke of his sex pulled her closer to the brink of another climax while its echo tugged on her heartstrings.

It was all she could do to keep her eyes open, wrung out from such violent pleasure. Yet her eyes widened when climax number three washed over her.

Alex's shout of completion echoed in her ear where her head rested against his hard-planed chest.

For several long moments, he held her, his hand stroking and petting while his lips trailed gentle kisses along her hairline and temple. The hot water churned around them, its action rubbing her breasts against his chest.

Derek heaved a sigh and looked out over the water. He held a bit of heaven in his arms, but he reminded himself it was an illusion. The woman he held so possessively had shared several, perhaps hundreds, of encounters such as this. Just because it felt so unique and special to him, didn't mean he should get carried away.

But, damn, she felt good in his arms. Right. Like she was made to be there.

Dangerous thought.

"What do you do, Mac, when you're not . . . um, dating?"

She pulled back and stared up at him with those pale eyes. She was good, he'd give her that. If he didn't know better, he'd swear she had no idea what he was talking about.

She shrugged. "I don't date all that much." He valiantly ignored the effect her nipples had on him. "I had a serious relationship a while back, but it's over now."

"A John?"

She frowned, looking genuinely puzzled. "No," she said after a moment, "his name was Joel. I—"

His mouth covered hers. It was his only hope. Learning

more about her was too personal. He didn't want to hear about her life with anyone else.

McCall couldn't believe her luck. The hunk was kissing her socks off—had she been wearing any. Maybe her luck was about to change. After all, how could something that felt this good be wrong?

She deepened the kiss, straddled his lap and smiled. He was up to the challenge. Again. His engorged sex prodded her eager opening. She wiggled closer.

He groaned into her mouth, the sound vibrating against her teeth.

"I want to fuck you," he said on a growl, "now!"

"Yes!" She threw back her head and laughed up at the sun. He plunged into her again and again, causing wickedly lovely sensations to dance through her, quivering her muscles.

The fantasy was alive and well. And doing the humpty-hump in a hot tub, right out in the open.

McCall Lindsey, wild woman.

4

On wobbly legs, Derek stepped out of the tub and carried Mac into the house. She protested sleepily about them tracking in water.

He didn't care.

Wild with lust, all he cared about was slaking said lust with her on Jack's sin-with-me bed.

His rock-hard cock bumped painfully against his thigh with each agonizing step. Hell, he'd never make it to the bedroom.

He took a hard right and entered the kitchen that ran the length of the right side of the house and laid his birthday present on the granite island countertop.

Her eyes flew open, but before she could protest, he covered her lips with his hungry mouth. She immediately became boneless in his arms. How the hell did she do that? It drove him wild.

Of course, she was a pro, so if anyone would know how to drive a man wild, it was her.

"I want to eat you," he said. He knew he was being crude

and blunt, but surely she'd heard worse than that in her line of work.

He spread her limp legs and admired the sweetness of her pink cunt. Rosy from the hot tub, it was swollen and pouting.

He leaned down to give it a quick nip. She gasped and bucked off the counter, and would have fallen had he not anchored her.

"Shh, shh," he whispered against her moistness, then placed a tiny kiss on the unbelievably soft petals. "I just can't wait any longer, baby." He forced his tongue to go slowly as it dragged the length of her, then traced the outline of the distended nub.

She whimpered, her knees falling open. His hands stroked the velvet smoothness of her inner thighs before gently holding them open to stroke her with his thumbs while his tongue delved in and out of her sweet wetness.

The muscles in her thighs began to vibrate against his palms. Her movements became jerky, almost frantic. Her hands grasped his head, yanking painfully on his hair. It wasn't hard to read her body language. She wanted him inside her. He wanted that, too. But first he wanted this.

He softly blew against her trembling flesh. "Easy, baby, easy. Let me love you with my mouth first." He took a nipping sip. "Come for me, sweet thing. Let it go." His tongue lapped her again. "That's right. Relax. I can taste your excitement."

He lowered his mouth again to suck on her nub, his fingers plunging in and out of her wetness. His steel-hard cock bumped against the side of the oak cabinet, sparks of achy pain shooting through his groin. He didn't care. Nothing else mattered except getting her off, watching her face when she came in his mouth.

And she did.

McCall tried to clamp her legs together against the gush of pleasure, but Alex was having none of that. Gentle hands cupped her knees, keeping them firmly spread wide, while he licked and sipped every bit of her moisture.

Despite the cold stone counter at her back, sweat trickled beneath her breasts and beaded her lip.

No doubt about it, she had a full body flush going on—big time. She tried to calm her racing heart and willed the heat from her cheeks. She was McCall Lindsey, wild woman. She had to keep that in mind.

At least for this moment in time. This moment out of her ordinary, boring life when she dared to let go of all inhibition and simply live for the moment.

To her surprised delight, she found arousal building again.

"Alex," she said to the top of his head, while he placed butterfly-light kisses between her spread legs. "It's my turn."

Her inner wild woman found the strength to push him back and swing her legs around the edge of the counter to hop down.

She stroked him from shoulder to knees with just the tips of her fingers. If she lived to be one hundred, she'd never forget the feel of his smooth, hot skin over hard, flexing muscles.

With a nudge, she pushed him back to sit on one of the bow-back oak kitchen chairs, and knelt between his spread legs. His erection jutted up from the chair and she paused.

The guy was definitely well endowed. How had she ever taken all of him? Memories of how well they had fit together, how deeply he'd embedded within her, had her squirming as she reached for him.

The head of his penis was so engorged, it was purple. Her tongue swiped the tip, tasting the saltiness of his skin. Within her grasp, he surged. Beneath her left forearm, his stomach muscles clenched.

She stopped to pet his abdomen, relaxing the bunched muscles, while her other hand gently cupped and petted his sacks.

"Let me love you now," she whispered as she leaned to take his hardness into her mouth.

His thighs gripped her ribs, his hot hands clamped her shoulders, holding her in place.

She smiled against his slick hardness and he groaned. She slid her mouth up and down, her tongue swirling around his shaft, constantly moving.

Within the quiet of the kitchen, his breath grew ragged, echoing from the walls. His hips began to pump.

She paused. Now what?

His hands bit into her upper arms as he dragged her up his body and plunged into her as soon as they were aligned.

Delighted trickles of sensation filled her. Groaning, she clamped her legs to his hips and met him stroke for stroke. She couldn't stop smiling.

Score one for the wild woman.

Derek stood, still deeply embedded within Mac, and ordered his legs to hold their combined weight until he made it up the stairs and to the master suite.

Damn, he was horny! He honestly couldn't remember such an all-consuming need, even as a teenager. No doubt about it, Mac knew how to turn him inside out.

His steps faltered on the way across the great room. Of course she did. She was a pro.

"Alex? Is something wrong?" She leaned back within his arms, her blue eyes wide. Her lips, swollen from his kisses, had a pouty look that caused his sex to stir with renewed interest. Her eyes widened more. "Again? So soon?" She giggled and plastered her breasts to his chest. "You're extraordinary!"

His chest swelled with pride, along with other parts of his anatomy, as he said, "I aim to please, ma'am."

She giggled again and he could have sworn he felt it all the way to his heart.

Ridiculous.

He dropped her on the wide mattress, enjoying the view when she spread her arms and legs to regain her balance.

God, she was gorgeous. Perfect from head to toe.

Her tousled shining hair gave her the appearance of just-finished lusty lovemaking. Which was true.

Her blue eyes sparkled, her smile forming tiny laugh lines at the edge of her eyes. The slightly bruised skin on her swollen mouth glistened, showing off her sexy teeth. Teeth that had nipped him in such an avid display of raw sex that he'd wanted to howl along with his raging hormones.

Delicate shoulders gave way to a rack that would put a centerfold to shame. While he watched, the raspberry-colored skin of her nipples drew into tight-looking peaks. His mouth salivated.

His gaze continued its downward path, past a narrow waist. The curve of her hips flared out nicely and he remembered clutching the pert, rounded bottom. His palms itched to do it again. And again. No doubt about it. She had a world-class ass.

Fascinated, he watched her almost-bare femininity, also swollen from recent activities. Moisture glistened on the distended labia. He clamped his jaw to keep from falling on her again and licking away every drop of moisture. What had gotten into him?

Her thighs were full and firm. Perfect for holding him close while he fucked her.

Her legs tapered nicely to small ankles and no doubt the sexiest feet he'd ever seen.

Unable to resist her a second longer, he climbed onto the bed and picked up one of her delicate feet.

McCall felt his lips brush her insole, followed by the gentle swipe of his tongue, and resisted the urge to jerk her foot back. Feather-light kisses touched the tip of each toe, zipping warmth up her leg to center at her juncture.

He picked up her other foot and repeated the process, causing her breath to become shallow and rapid.

His warm mouth settled on each knee, sucking and kissing. The kiss behind her knee elicited a giggle that immediately turned into a moan when he gently sucked the sensitive skin, causing her toes to curl.

Warm hands stroked her thighs, making her wish she'd lost those twenty pounds she'd found since her last sexual encounter. Pounds that took up residence in her thighs and butt.

"Your body is beautiful," he said in a husky voice as though he read her thoughts. "Perfect." He placed a lingering kiss on the inside of each chubby thigh, which made her wish she could suck them in as easily as she did her stomach.

His talented fingers stroked the moisture between her legs. How did he know just where to stroke her to make her wild with lust?

Before she could ask, he turned her to her stomach. She frowned. What was he going to do now? All she could see was the bedspread and the curve of the bottom of the pillows. Darn. She wanted more time to see his beautiful face. Besides, the idea of him looking at her fat backside was a definite turn-off.

McCall twisted in an effort to turn back over, but he held her firmly flat on her stomach.

"Don't," she whispered when he dragged his tongue along her left cheek, embarrassment heating her face.

He smiled against her skin and repeated the process on the other cheek, then placed gentle kisses from the curve of her bottom to her waist.

He took little nips along her rib cage, working his way around to her breasts. The action rolled her over. He took the tip of her breast into his mouth and suckled. She felt each pull deep within her belly and arched her back, filling his mouth more completely.

His hard chest flattened her breasts when he raised up to align his mouth with hers.

"Don't try to hide your body from me," he said against her lips. "Ever." His hands left a fiery trail when he skimmed her sides from breasts to hip, then back up to cup her possessively. "It's perfect. These," he bent his head to kiss the tip of each breast, "are perfect. *We're* perfect. Together."

With that he shifted his hips and pushed deeply within her. They sighed. He brushed his lips on the tip of her nose in a fleeting kiss.

Gazes locked, he began deep, lazy thrusts, occasionally dipping his head to lap at her nipples. Each lap caused a spurt of excitement, clenching her inner muscles and eliciting a groan from Alex.

The groan caused inner tremors in McCall, which triggered the entire sequence again.

He released her breasts to cup her face. Nose to nose, if felt as though he could see into her soul. Did he suspect she wasn't the wild woman she pretended?

"I want you," he stated in a strained voice.

She dragged one hand away from his perfect buns and reached up to push back a lock of golden hair from his tanned forehead. In the muted light of the bedroom, his eyes looked more gold than green.

"You have me," she whispered back and clenched her inner muscles, milking another groan from him.

"I didn't mean just to fuck," he said, his thrusts gaining momentum. "I want you." Pant, pant. "In every way possible." He groaned and pumped harder. "For the entire week. I want you whenever and wherever. However much—" His neck arched, the cords standing out against the smooth skin of his neck. Deep within her, his penis surged. Her breath caught as her muscles clenched, her heart tripped. His release heated her abdomen, eliciting a deep, answering response.

Alex collapsed against her. She welcomed his weight, clutching him tightly to and within her.

Tears burned her eyes. Orgasms like that were rare, draining. That had to be the reason she felt so deeply, so wrung out, so . . . exposed.

No. That was wrong. She felt . . . complete.

Dangerous emotion for a wild woman.

5

Derek reluctantly withdrew from the wet warmth encasing him. Sitting on the side of the bed, he looked down at the brightly colored condom tightly sheathing his cock and resented the hell out of it. Resented anything that kept him even remotely separated from the woman on the bed behind him.

What had she done to him? It was idiocy to harbor thoughts like the ones he'd had since seeing her again on the deck.

To resent using a condom was flat-out suicidal.

He glanced back at her. Naked and panting, she lay with her eyes closed, killer legs still parted as though inviting—or daring—him to dip within her sweetness again.

She looked so innocent. Almost pure. He swallowed a snort of laughter. Pure she was not. He knew that for a fact.

Another fact he needed to remember was that she was a pro.

He reached back to trail his finger over the erotically smooth skin on the tip of her breast and smiled when it immediately puckered. His smile grew wider when she made the soft purring sound that drove him wild and curled toward his hand.

Between his legs, his sex stirred with renewed interest. Damn! The woman made him insatiable.

His smile faded. But more than wanting to plunge into her again and again, he wanted to hold her and feel her skin next to his skin, her heart beating against his heart. He wanted to know her inside and out.

He wanted to hold her, claim her as his and never let her go. Damn.

McCall rose slowly from the boneless lethargy and stretched. Beneath her, the silk spread gently rubbed along her skin. Sea air from the open window caressed her sensitized nipples.

Being a wild woman definitely had its rewards.

She skimmed her nudity with the tips of her fingers, remembering Alex's touch. Moisture pooled, surprising her. How could she be aroused again so soon?

The sound of the shower running drifted into the bedroom. McCall cupped her breasts and pinched the nipples, mildly irritated that Alex had deserted her.

Wait. She was a wild woman. At least, for the week. Why couldn't she be the aggressor?

Before she could think of about a zillion reasons not to, she jumped off the bed and all but ran into the adjoining bathroom.

The sight stopped her in her tracks.

Sunlight beamed down through the skylight, illuminating the god standing within the clear glass, double-shower enclosure. Mist from the surrounding showerheads rose around his magnificent body, while a wider opening close to the ceiling formed a mini-waterfall to add to the dazzling effect.

Eyes closed, he tilted his head up to the sun, revealing his perfect profile, the strong column of his throat. Water sluiced from well-honed broad shoulders and cascaded over firm pectorals and washboard abs to caress his very impressive package before streaking down long, sleek runner's legs.

Her mouth dry, while other places were definitely wet, she grabbed the door handle, opened it and stepped into the steamy warmth.

If he was surprised to have her join him, he hid it well. Her feet scarcely touched the wet warmth of the tile before his arms pulled her tightly to him.

"Hello, sleepyhead," he drawled right before his mouth covered hers.

Senses on overload, she'd vowed to be the aggressor, yet felt herself begin to melt beneath the potency of his kiss.

While his tongue stroked hers, his hands explored her body with a devastating thoroughness that caused instant response.

His hands cupped and squeezed her tender breasts. She lightly bit his nipple.

His hands slid to her waist, then downward to cup her derriere with possessive intent.

She cupped his testicles, felt them harden while his penis jutted against her ribs.

Before she realized what she was doing, McCall found herself climbing her sensual playmate like he was a human sexual jungle gym.

His hands grasped her waist when she gripped his shoulders, and with one downward plunge, she impaled herself on his hard shaft.

Feeling deliciously wicked, she wiggled her bottom. He groaned and, deep within her, his penis flexed. She wrapped her legs around his waist, feeling him almost totally withdraw, then lowered her bottom again, loving the feel of him pushing against her womb. Cascading warm water added to the eroticism. She rubbed her nipples against his and groaned along with him.

"Not yet!" His voice growled above the sound from the multiple showerheads.

She whimpered and tried to regain her erotic seat when he pulled out of her with hard hands gripping her waist.

"Trust me," he said against her ear. "Hang on!"

He lifted her until she sat on his shoulders, her thighs on each side of his head, his hot breath low on her abdomen, then lower, against her aching folds.

Clutching his hair, she closed her eyes to better absorb the sensation of his hot tongue licking and suckling her most intimate parts, while water from the wide overhead opening sluiced over them in an erotic waterfall.

Had she been thinner and younger—not to mention more limber—she would have attempted to hang down his body while he pleasured her with his mouth, and returned the favor. Assuming she could reach him.

She peeked down through her eyelashes with one eye. Way down. Definitely not doable. At least not for her.

The thought caused an ache in her heart.

She blinked back the sudden onslaught of tears and gripped his hair tighter, holding him closer. She couldn't bear the thought of being this intimate with someone else or him doing this with another woman.

Some wild woman she turned out to be.

Derek knew the moment he lost her. One second she was a wild and willing participant, then the next her body stiffened, her thigh muscles tight against his ears. Had he been too rough, gotten carried away?

He lapped at her nub and felt her stiffen again as though she only tolerated what he was doing. Hey, maybe that was it. After all, it was what she did for a living. If he had to do things like this with anyone who walked through the door, the thrill would be gone in a New York minute.

The last thought sobered him. He nuzzled her one last time, placing a kiss on her opening. Her thighs immediately relaxed. Taking the invitation, he swirled his tongue around, darting in and out in quick, strong strokes.

She obviously liked it, by the way she slumped against him, widening her legs to allow for greater access.

He held her in place with one hand while the other reached up to palm and tweak her breast.

He groaned, her moisture tart on his tongue. More thrilled and excited than he'd ever been, he wracked his brain for anything mundane to keep his climax at bay while he pleasured his partner.

It was suddenly his goal in life to bring the beautiful woman in his arms to the most earth-shattering orgasm of her life.

McCall couldn't say when things had turned, but suddenly she had trouble dragging air in and out of her lungs. Every muscle in her body vibrated with pent-up passion. Between the water coursing over them and the wetness between her legs, she was surprised Alex didn't drown.

Every nerve ending in her body was centered around the spot where his mouth worked its magic. His talented tongue swirled erotic patterns over her engorged sex again and again, occasionally dipping deep within her. When his hands joined the sensuous siege, fondling and squeezing her breast, it was almost sensory overload.

Her climax crested again and again, then finally washed over her with wave after wave of release. Had Alex's hands not held her firmly aloft, she'd have fallen to the shower floor in a sated, boneless heap.

"My turn," he whispered as he lifted her down.

She nodded and tried to get on her knees before him, but he wouldn't allow it.

"Much as I'd love your mouth on my dick, I can't wait for that now."

He pulled her up, her feet leaving the floor. The sea-blue granite tile felt cold against the heated skin of her back. She'd scarcely touched the wall before the hot tip of his penis probed her, then shoved its way into her receptive body.

"Wrap your legs around me, babe," he said against the hair next to her ear, "and hang on."

With that, he placed her limp legs around his waist and pounded into her. Had it not been for the solid wall behind her, and his weight pressing into her from the front, she'd never have remained upright.

She began to drift, enjoying the experience, the erotic sensation of skin against skin and warm water washing over everything, without having to do any of the work.

Hell-o! He bumped against something that flipped some kind of internal switch. Suddenly she was back in the game, meeting each thrust, trying to pull him deeper, her breath coming in short, choppy pants.

His hands gripped her ankles and pulled her legs up on his shoulders, widening the sensation, allowing deeper penetration.

After only a few thrusts, she heard herself scream while her orgasm gushed in a tidal wave of pleasure.

His muscles rock hard, he thrust deeper once, then stiffened, head thrown back, a primal growl emerging from his throat.

Wow.

He gently brushed strands of hair from her face as he lowered her until her feet touched the tile. His lips brushed hers, but it took too much strength to open her eyes. In fact, had she not locked her knees, she would be in a puddle on the floor of the shower.

The slick feel of soap glided over her. She sighed at the sensation. One would think she'd be on sensual overload by now, yet the feeling of his hands gliding over her, slick with soap, was stirring a renewed awareness deep within her.

With her eyes still closed, she rubbed her soapy breasts against him. "I'm sharing the soap," she explained.

The low rumble of his laughter echoed against the tile; combined with the steam, it added another layer of intimacy.

Her eyes popped open when a slick soapy finger probed her.

Alex smiled down at her, his teeth gleaming white, his eyes slumberous. "We need to make sure you're clean, inside and out." Another finger entered her. Slick with soap, it caused an interesting sensation as it stretched her, gliding in and out.

When she was thoroughly soaped and thoroughly aroused, he reached behind him for a handheld showerhead and proceeded to make sure the soap was thoroughly rinsed away.

Weak in the knees from her recent release, she sighed with relief when he wrapped her in a soft bath sheet, picked her up and carried her from the bathroom. Did wild women take naps?

The woman was addictive, Derek thought while he carried her down the stairs. But the truth was he was wild for her. Again.

He tossed the handful of condoms onto the floor by the sofa and made a mental note to buy more. Maybe a case. He looked down at her, sleeping soundly where he'd placed her on the sofa. His cock reacted to the sight. Make that two cases.

How much of her time had Jack paid for initially? It had to be up by now. Well, whatever it cost to keep her here, with him, it was well worth it. What good was being filthy rich if you couldn't buy simple pleasures? Great sex was definitely one of those pleasures.

His yawn surprised him. Maybe he'd lie down for a few minutes. Holding Mac while she slept would be good, too.

The big sofa easily accommodated both of them, especially with his playmate's small stature. He pulled her close and snuggled down for a nap.

A feeling of contentment washed over him. He felt happy . . . complete.

McCall snuggled closer to the warmth, enjoying the feel of skin on skin.

Skin on skin.

Her eyes opened to the heated gaze of her flesh-and-blood fantasy lover and she smiled. "What a wonderful way to wake up."

"You ain't seen nothin' yet," he drawled.

As their gazes locked, he lowered his head to take one plump nipple into his mouth. The effect of his suckling took her breath away and made her toes tingle and twitch.

He reached behind him and then rolled back, several condoms in his hand. "We're down to just these." He waggled his eyebrows. "We need to restock."

"We do?" she said with a squeak.

"Yep." He nodded. "Darlin', I'm gonna fuck your brains out. I need lots of protection."

He raised one of her legs onto the sofa back, leaving her exposed to his avid gaze.

"I love your pussy," he said in a husky voice, then licked her with slow, obvious intent. "It's so pretty and pink and responsive." He petted *it* and it, indeed, responded.

A wave of heat washed over her, burning her face. Sweat popped out along her upper lip.

"Don't move," he ordered, getting up and walking backward toward the kitchen. She heard the refrigerator door open and ice rattle.

Within seconds, he was back, crawling on the sofa toward her. He held up a piece of curved ice. "We need to cool you off a bit."

The feel of ice dragged over her nipples made them almost painfully erect. From there, he drew an outline around each breast, then down her stomach to her naval.

He leaned down to sip the moisture from her belly button, then continued his trek.

He sat up and dragged the ice down the inside of each thigh, causing her to jerk.

"Shh," he crooned, petting her thighs wider. "It's okay. It's just water. Do you remember what we did with water in the shower?"

She could only nod, the flames of arousal licking at her as surely as her lover would lick the moisture of the ice from her.

He grinned, looking unbearably sexy, then focused his attention between her legs.

He pressed the tip of the ice cube to her nub. So hot, it immediately melted some of the ice. Cool rivulets trickled down her folds to pool at her behind.

"We're getting the couch wet," she felt compelled to point out.

He shook his head of gloriously mussed golden hair, a soft smile on his kissable lips. "Nope. You're still lying on the towel."

Slowly the ice moved downward, slicking across, up and down each fold, driving her mad with lust. Just when she thought she couldn't take another second of the delicious torture, coldness invaded her portal.

Her breath hitched. Her nipples tightened to painful peaks. Her eyes widened when she raised her head enough to watch him slide the now sliver of ice in and out of her, the thumb of his other hand lazily flicking back and forth over her engorged nub.

"Oops," he said and grinned up at her. "Slippery little devil seems to have fallen in. Don't worry, I'll get it."

He lowered his mouth, his hot breath a wondrous contrast to the frozen ice. His tongue felt doubly hot when it speared into her and rotated.

With a cry, she arched her hips off the sofa, clutching at the heated skin of his shoulders, while waves of rapture carried her away.

His hands shook, she noted, when he ripped the condom open. Seconds later, he filled her. With her left leg still up on the back of the sofa, it gave an interesting angle of penetration while allowing him room to continue the wonderful movement of his thumb.

Unbelievably, her second climax was stronger than the first. Must have been the years of abstinence.

She brushed his hair from his forehead and placed a soft kiss to his temple. Tenderness clutched her heart.

Then again, maybe it was the man.

6

Derek gathered the limp woman close and pulled her onto his lap, then nibbled her earlobe. Her unique scent wafted around him. He inhaled greedily, marveling at the effect she had on him.

If he lived to be one hundred, he'd remember the way she smelled. The way she felt. The way she responded, along with about a million other things about her.

Emotion he refused to acknowledge clutched his throat, tugged at his heart.

He couldn't keep her indefinitely. They both had other lives to lead. The thought of the life she led caused a red haze of jealousy to descend.

His heart skipped a beat at a sudden thought. Why couldn't he keep her? Hell, he had enough money to be her exclusive customer for the rest of their lives.

What was he thinking? If the debacle with the fund-raiser from hell didn't ruin his reputation, hiring a full-time hooker would. And what would that do to his parents?

He toyed with her plump breast, smiling when the nipple

responded. It was better to just enjoy her company while he was there, then forget about her when he rejoined the real world.

Why did that thought make him want to clutch her to his heart and never let her go?

McCall stretched within her lover's arms and pulled down his frowning mouth for a kiss.

"What's wrong, Alex?"

He looked down at her for a moment, then smiled. "Do you like to dance?"

"I love it, but why would that make you frown?"

"Do you like seafood?"

She wondered if he realized how turned on she was getting as his hands absently caressed her breasts.

"Yes," she said in a strangled voice.

"Great! I know a place not far from here that serves the best crab on the Gulf Coast. And they have a great band."

He obviously mistook her come-hither look for concern, which wasn't all that surprising, now that she thought about it. It happened a lot. She wasn't very good at flirting.

"Don't worry about what you wear. It's casual."

"I'm not worried about what I'll wear," she assured him, reaching for the last condom, slightly shocked at her overtly sexual behavior. She ripped open the foil pouch with her teeth, careful to maintain all-important eye contact, and discreetly tongued the piece of foil from her teeth. "It's what you're *not* wearing that has me a little worried."

Thrilled to see he was "up" for it, she made quick work of sheathing him—first with the condom, then with her body.

Wild woman rides again.

Derek let himself back into Jack's house and jogged up the steps to the master suite with his garment bag and nylon duffel slung over his shoulder.

It was stupid to keep running back to his place for clean clothes. If he was going to stay with Mac, he may as well move in for the rest of the week.

He tossed his gear into the walk-in closet. "Mac? I'm back. You about ready?"

She walked out of the bathroom and his breath whooshed out of his lungs.

The bright, multicolored print of the sundress would fit perfectly with the apparel of the other patrons in the restaurant. What there was of her dress, that is.

He suspected it was really a top, since Mac was short and it still struck her above midthigh. The plunging neckline scooped so low, he was sure he detected the edge of her nipples. Before he could mention that fact, she turned and bent to put on her shoes.

His heart skipped a beat, then raced at the amount of skin before him. The damned dress was practically backless; nothing but strings—crisscrossed from the flare of her hip to her shoulder blades—held it together.

"Take it off," he finally squeezed out.

She whirled to gape at him. "What? What are you talking about? I thought you wanted to go out!"

"I'll order in."

Her eyes narrowed. "What's the problem, Alex?" She sauntered toward him. He backed up a step and shoved his hands in the pockets of his khakis.

"Your dress," he blurted. At her wide-eyed look, he continued. "It's practically nonexistent! I'd spend the entire evening fighting off other men." He shook his head. "I'd also be sweating bullets because I know exactly what's under that sin-with-me dress. I'd be so hard, I wouldn't be able to swallow a bite."

"Maybe we need to fix that little problem . . . before we go." She sidled up to him and unbuckled his belt, then popped the button at his waist. The zipper echoed in the quiet of the room.

His fists clenched tighter in his pockets to keep from reaching for her. "We can't," he said in a strangled voice.

"Sure we can." She nudged his hands out of his pockets and smiled up at him while she dragged his pants and boxers down his legs. His cock sprang free, ready for action—which seemed to be its constant state since he'd met Mac.

"It occurred to me, while I was showering all alone, that we need to explore some of our fantasies." She stood and reached for the tie behind her neck. "This is one of mine." She hesitated and he nodded his eager approval.

Her dress fell to her waist.

Like a Pavlovian dog, he began salivating. Breathing became difficult.

She knelt before him, rubbing the engorged tip of his rock-hard cock over and around the smooth skin of her nipples, driving him insane with lust. Lust was the only reasonable explanation for his reactions to this particular woman.

"I think there's a name for this, but I can't remember what." She pushed her ample breasts together, sliding his cock in and out of her cleavage.

"Tit fucking," he supplied in a tight voice.

"Do you like it?" she casually asked. Before he could answer, she was on her knees, flicking her tongue across the purple tip until he thought he'd scream before she took it into her hot mouth.

He groaned. Obviously, coherent speech was not an option at that moment.

She set the rhythm. Kiss, lick, suck, rub. He did okay with control until about the sixth or seventh go-around.

Then he lost it.

He wanted to rip the rest of her dress from her and plunge into the wet heat he knew lurked beneath, or at least lift her skirt and shove her panties aside, before he made his deposit.

Instead, to his horror, he spilled his seed all over her gorgeous breasts. Before he could voice an apology, she laughed and guided his still throbbing cock through the slippery mess to stroke her nipples.

Face flushed, she shimmied out of her dress to reveal her total lack of undergarments. Talk about fantasies.

He stood, like a dummy, while she purred and rubbed her magnificently nude body up and down his, making them both slick.

She was his every adolescent fantasy come to life.

Still smiling, she grabbed his hand and pulled him toward the bed. "I don't care if we make a mess. I need you now!"

She pushed him down on the bed then straddled his renewed erection to ride him hard.

At their mutual completion, she collapsed across his chest, her soft panting tickling his arm, her scent enveloping him. Through a sensual haze, a thought niggled at the back of his mind. The thought emerged to hit him with the force of a sledgehammer.

He loved her.

7

Mac sat up, still impaled, and stretched, then smiled down at him. His face felt tight when he attempted to smile back.

"Want to share a shower?" Her smile faltered. "Alex? Why are you looking at me like that? Are you okay?"

I may never be okay again. "Sure, let's take a shower. But it has to be quick, okay? I'm starving." He lifted her from him and walked into the bathroom to turn on the shower.

Of all the stupid things to do. What kind of moron fell in love with a hooker? He glanced at his reflection in the mirror over the double sinks. *Me.*

McCall adjusted the straps on her second sundress and looked in the mirror at Alex's reflection. "Are you sure you want to go out?" she asked again. "It might be expensive. The freezer and refrigerator are both full. I'm sure we can find something here."

His gaze met hers in the mirror. "What? You think I can't afford you?"

Refusing to let him see how his sharp words cut her, she

shook her head. "Of course not. I was just offering an alternative solution."

He walked up behind her and slid his hands up the sides of her legs until he reached the waistband of her thong, high beneath her skirt.

"Leave these here," he ordered, already dragging her panties down her legs.

"Alex!" She made a halfhearted attempt at swatting his hands away, but then stepped out of her underwear. The tingle of excitement, always hovering near when she was around this man, sent a surge of moisture between her legs.

He tucked the scrap of lingerie into his pocket with a satisfied smile. "It's payback time for the shoes, babe."

"What are you talking about?"

Derek felt sleazy for forcing her to go out in public bottomless, but it also excited him beyond reason.

"Don't you know what they call those kinds of shoes?"

She shook her head as she started down the stairs. He followed, keeping a safe distance from her potent charms but close enough to admire the gentle sway of her unclad bottom.

She stopped at the couch and turned to him, hands on hips. "Well, are you going to tell me what these kinds of shoes are called?"

He did a quick inventory to make sure this dress covered more than the last one, and grinned. "Fuck-me shoes."

Unable to resist, he ran his hand beneath her skirt and patted her dampness, then smoothed her skirt back down. "Remember that, Mac. Because that's exactly what I plan to do. Over and over." He leaned to place a chaste kiss on the surprised O of her mouth. "Later."

He turned her toward the door and tapped her bottom. "Right now, let's get something to eat. I'm starving."

She stopped at the base of the beach stairs.

"Do you have a car?" she asked.

He thought longingly of his Porsche, parked in his garage. He had to protect himself, if he ever expected to live past the weekend. He shook his head.

"My service-engine light came on just as I pulled up," she informed him. "I'm not sure my car will make a long drive." She looked so adorable, chewing on the edge of her bottom lip, that he almost caved and threw himself at her feet, begging her to be his and end this charade.

Almost.

"Not a problem, Mac. The Purple Crab is just down the beach a ways. We can walk." His feet sank into the sand. "Hand me your shoes." He put them in his pocket, then took her hand and set off toward his favorite South Padre eatery.

He refused to dwell on how right her small hand felt in his or how happy he felt just walking beside her.

Over huge platters of steamed crab, they indulged in neutral conversation, laughing at silly jokes, making clandestine observations about the other patrons. Too soon, the lights dimmed and came back up, signaling last call.

"Would you like another pitcher of margaritas?" Alex asked, signaling their waiter.

McCall shook her head, feeling a definite buzz from the last two pitchers they'd shared. "No, thanks, I'm ready to go." Ready for him to follow through on his promise-threat. That thought brought on another full-body flush. She fanned herself with her napkin. "Whew! Is it hot in here to you?" She stumbled out of her chair and grabbed his arm for support. "I think I need some fresh air."

While her date paid their tab, she walked out onto the sand and removed her shoes. She'd love to strip naked and run along the beach with her fantasy lover, but even wild women had their limits. At least, this wild woman.

"Are you thinking about your shoes?" he asked, his voice low and intimate, next to her ear.

She frowned. Her lips were numb. "My shoes?"

Instant recall came flooding back at the hot intensity she saw in his eyes. She laughed and skipped away from him down the beach. She must have done something right in her life to deserve a break from reality like this.

He caught up with her within seconds, clasping her hand in his, and fell into step beside her.

"What do you want to do now?" he asked, stopping and pulling her into his arms. His hands rubbed the silky fabric of her dress across her bare bottom.

"I want to make love to you," she answered truthfully, "right here on the beach."

His eyebrows raised almost to his hairline. He glanced all around. "Why don't we wait until we're closer to the house? It's a private beach, so what we do in front of your beach house won't have any witnesses."

"You don't sound very enthusiastic for someone who was bragging, not three hours ago, about how many times we were going to do it." She knew her voice was slurred.

He dropped her hand and put both fists on his hips. "You're drunk."

"Am not." She swatted at a piece of hair that seemed to be super glued to her recently refreshed lip gloss.

"Okay." He shrugged. "Tell me and I'll do it."

"Here and now?"

He nodded. "Here and now. Whatever you want, however you want it." He gave a slight bow. "Your wish is my command."

I wish you'd love me, not just my body, forever. But of course she couldn't tell him that. It would ruin everything. And if loving her body was all he could do for the next week, so be it.

She walked out to an abandoned beach chair and sat down, pulling her skirt up around her hips.

He stalked around to stand in front of her. "Well?"

Feeling more bold and sexy than ever before in her life, McCall hitched a knee over each arm of the chair. Even in the darkness, she could see his gaze locked on the bare sight between her open legs. The poor man's mouth had dropped open.

She brushed her hand over her own wetness. Slowly reaching up to release the top four buttons on her sundress, she allowed her bare breasts to be kissed by the moist sea air. She fervently hoped that's not all they'd be kissed by before the night was over.

"Well?" she asked in the sexiest voice she could muster, and wished she could order the beach to stop moving. Maybe if she closed her eyes for a moment, the world would stop spinning so she could enjoy the erotic fantasy that she'd just set up.

Between her spread legs, the gentle breeze off the water caressed her dampness.

Her muscles relaxed. It wasn't as stimulating as Alex, but . . .

Derek watched Mac's eyes flutter shut. Her spread legs fell wider as her body relaxed.

She was asleep.

Beneath the taut fly of his slacks, his erection throbbed.

Now what?

He couldn't leave her here, asleep with her, um, assets on display. But did he trust himself enough to touch her, while his testosterone surged like a tidal wave, without taking advantage of what she'd offered?

Despite everything, he was a gentleman. He reached down to gently push her legs together and tug her skirt down as far as possible.

As short as her skirt was, her delectable bottom would be exposed while he carried her to the beach house. Besides embarrassing her, he couldn't bear the thought of anyone other than himself seeing that part of her.

With a sigh, he unbuttoned his oxford cloth shirt and slipped it off. The cooler sea air soothed his heated skin, taking his ardor down a notch.

"C'mon, Mac," he said, grasping her arms. "It's time to go home." Getting her up proved to be more difficult than he'd envisioned. Sort of like trying to lift a pile of Jell-o. To make matters worse, a fine sheen of perspiration glistened on her skin. Combined with the lotion that made his mouth water, it made her slippery.

Finally, she stood before him. Sort of. Propping her against his shoulder, he reached to tie his shirt around her slender hips.

There. He surveyed his handiwork. And groaned.

Her bottom was discreetly covered, but her breasts were now totally displayed, due to the dress being pulled down by his shirt. Tugging on the stretchy material proved ineffectual; the only result of his efforts, besides the jungle beat of his erection, was sweat on his forehead and upper lip.

Mac giggled and began slipping downward, eyes still closed.

He grabbed for her and bit back a groan when his hand clutched a warm, bare breast.

Mac purred in her sleep and did a little shimmy he felt all the way down to his toes.

"Mac," he said in a hoarse whisper, "help me out a little here, would you? Here—put your arm around my waist."

Instead, her hand dropped down to his groin, where his hardness surged with interest.

"Not there!" Sweating bullets, he pulled her around to face him. The woman seemed almost boneless. There was no way she'd make the walk back to Jack's place. He glanced longingly at his own house, just a few sections down the beach.

Did he dare risk taking her there? No. It would be better to drag her to Jack's.

Decision made, he lifted her. Her legs immediately circled his waist, her breasts plastered against his bare chest.

Gritting his teeth, he made sure his shirt was still doing its job, then headed down the beach. With each step, her nipples abraded his, her wetness rubbing against his aching cock with nothing but a thin layer of cloth separating them.

It would be so easy to pause and release the confining pressure of his zipper and let his sex slip into her wetness. Did he dare?

"Please," Mac said against his neck. "I need you inside me." She squirmed, turning his erection into a shaft of burning iron.

"You're drunk," he said through clenched teeth, increasing his pace.

"You promised," she whispered above the roar in his ears. "You promised to ... *you know* ... me. Over and over." She hiccuped. "Our time is running out. You *promised*."

How could she do what she did for a living and not even be able to say the word? It wasn't like she didn't know what was going on. It wasn't like she'd never screwed anyone before.

The thought stopped him in his tracks. Surprisingly, he didn't care who'd been with her before. But he desperately wanted to be her last.

And, damnit, he loved her! How sick was that?

She chose that time to whimper and wiggle against him again, causing him to nearly stumble in his haste.

His hands shook while he held her up and fumbled with his fly. An eternity passed within seconds before he sprang free and plunged into her welcome heat in one wild thrust.

They both groaned. Then sighed.

With slow steps, his wobbly legs took them to the edge of Jack's deck. By the time he climbed the steps, all the while deeply embedded, her wetness sucking at his cock with each step he took, he wanted to howl his frustration.

Judging by her increased breathing, Mac was just as frustrated.

"More," she demanded in a breathy voice while he fumbled

with the key in an attempt to unlock the door. "Now, Alex, now! Forget the house! Forget the bed! I can't wait another second!"

Okay, it was unanimous.

He dropped to sit on one of the chaise longues, filled both hands with her breasts and bucked his hips.

Her head fell back, her long hair a silky curtain against the skin of his arms, her beauty illuminated by the moonlight.

His heart hitched. If this was all they could have, he'd take it.

Love was a bitch.

8

McCall must have fallen asleep after their wild lovemaking on the deck because she woke slightly to find Alex gently bathing her. She smiled and relaxed, drifting off again while he paid special attention to soaping her breasts and between her legs. Desire, never far whenever she was near this man, stirred, but she was simply too exhausted to act on it.

She drifted in again while he stroked warmed lotion in every nook and cranny, aroused but too sleepy to do anything other than moan before she slid deeper into sleep.

Sunlight filtered through the skylight, beating on her eyelids, dragging her awake.

She stretched, automatically reaching across the bed for Alex. Naked beneath the sheet, she was alone.

She yawned and stretched again, the faint scent of the almond lotion Alex had used for her massage wafting up to her. Where was he? She couldn't very well be a wild woman by herself.

Or could she?

* * *

Derek whistled tunelessly as he let himself into Jack's house and headed to the kitchen to fix Mac's breakfast tray. Breakfast in bed was no treat for him, but he'd heard women really got off on it. Mac probably would, too.

In her line of work, she was always the giver. He wanted her to be the pampered one for a change. Even if it was only temporary.

He'd just finished loading the tray when he heard it. Faint at first, but growing stronger with each step toward the top of the stairs.

Polynesian music reverberated from the curved wall of the master suite, its heavy beat echoing through his body. Mac stood naked on the balcony, her head thrown back, gorgeous body slick with lotion or oil while she rubbed and gyrated in time to the music.

He set the tray on the nightstand and walked up behind her. She must have sensed him because she paused and looked back over her shapely shoulder.

He smiled and drew one of the suite's upholstered chairs close to the door. "Don't let me stop you." He settled down to enjoy the show.

Mac hesitated, then began her sensual dance again. His khaki shorts instantly grew two sizes too small.

She poured some of the almond lotion he'd used last night into her hand and let it trickle down her breasts, all the while moving her hips to the seductive beat of the music. Her hand cupped her close-cropped pussy and caught the thin ribbon of lotion, then smoothed it all around her flat stomach, the curve of her hip, and then up to join her other hand to thoroughly massage her erect nipples.

He groaned when she poured another handful of lotion and rubbed it lustily into her buttocks, turning to taunt him with the sway of her hips, the sight of her hands stroking the satiny skin.

Then she bent over.

He held the armrests in a death grip, barely breathing, while he watched her smooth lotion up each spectacular leg to her crotch, then finish by stroking it over the exposed plump pink folds, all the while moving her hips to the seductive beat.

Never breaking eye contact, he released the button of his too-tight shorts and let the zipper fall open from the weight of his erection.

She definitely did something to him. He hadn't felt like this since he was a horny teenager, whacking off to *Playboy.*

His hand closed around his pecker, moving up and down while he watched Mac continue her seductive dance.

She grinned, obviously enjoying the show he was putting on for her as much as her own.

More lotion pooled in her hand. "That's right, lover," she crooned, "Harder, faster. Do it for me and Ill do it for you." Her gaze met his. "After all, I'm the professional. I'm the wild woman!"

She poured the lotion over her breasts, squirming to the beat while she rubbed her erect nipples, then slicked her hands down to her pussy.

"Drop the shorts," she ordered, then climbed onto the back of a double beach chair to prop her feet on each arm, legs spread. "You show me yours and I'll show you mine."

More excited than he could remember being in his entire thirty-two years, he shucked his shorts and briefs at the speed of light and resumed his seat, his rock-hard cock jutting up from his lap.

"Wait!" She hopped down from the chair and grabbed the bottle of lotion. "You need lubrication." She walked toward him, pouring a generous amount of lotion onto her glistening tits. "Here, let me." She leaned forward and rubbed her slick breasts against the tip of his shaft, which immediately responded with a will of its own. Pushing her generous globes together, she moved his penis in and out of her cleavage until it was slick with lotion.

"There," she said in a breathless whisper, stepping back into the sunshine, one hand plucking her nipple while the other languorously rubbed between her slightly spread legs. "Let's do it."

With that, she turned up the music and climbed up onto the chair back, resuming her erotic pose.

Through a sexual haze, he watched her pleasure herself, growing harder and more excited by the second, his hand moving of its own accord.

With a gasp of surprise, he reached his peak just as her breath hitched and her back arched, tits erect. Hot semen spilled over his fist, wetting his abdomen, trickling down around his balls.

When their breathing slowed, she tossed him a towel. "Now it's our turn." Moving to the music, she poured out more lotion and began massaging her breasts again. "C'mon, lover, join me. You can be wild, too."

"Right out here, in front of whomever walks by?" Despite his words, he stepped out on the deck, already getting hard at the thought.

She nodded, the sun glinting off the silvery blond streaks in her hair. "It's a private beach. It's doubtful anyone will be walking by. Besides, we're on the second floor." She looked at the edge of the solid wall of the balcony. "And the ledge is higher than hip height. No one can see what we're doing . . . unless we want them to."

"Well, I know what I want," he said, lifting her back to her perch on the chair, then settling himself between her spread legs.

McCall let out a squeak of surprise at the first lap of Alex's tongue on her sensitive folds. His fingers toyed with her while he licked and sucked.

Feeling liberated, she leaned back, resting her arms along the top of the balcony, enjoying the feel of the sun on her face and bare breasts and the talented tongue between her legs. His fingers moved in and out of her wetness to the beat of the music, causing her altered breathing.

McCall Lindsey, wild woman. Exhibitionist. Her breath hitched as her muscles vibrated and contracted yet again. Better make that McCall Lindsey, exhibitionist and *multiorgasmic* wild woman.

Waves of pleasure washed over her while the waves of the Gulf washed to shore. Wow. Who knew? Multi orgasms had always been the stuff of urban legends. Until she'd met Alex.

How would she survive the rest of her dull life without this?

"Okay," Alex said, drawing her back to the present while he drew her down to straddle his impressive erection. "Now we get to do what we started last night."

Last night? She frantically wracked her brain but all she could remember for certain was Alex insisting she not wear underwear, eating dinner and drinking margaritas. After that, everything was a blur. Random impressions.

She vaguely remembered feeling very sexy on their way home and suspected they might have had sex on the deck, but she wasn't entirely sure.

"You issued an invitation to me," he explained. "You wanted me to take you, on the beach chair, just outside the Purple Crab." He eyed her suspiciously, his hands pausing in their play with her nipples. "Feel free to jump in here at any time, if you remember what happened."

"You refused because it was, um, too public," she guessed.

"Right." He nodded and smiled, resuming his sexy, distracting play with her nipples while the heat from his erection made her sex weep for him.

She licked her lips, thrilled to see him follow the movement of her tongue with his hot gaze.

"Well," she said, wiggling her bottom against his stomach, a feeling of sexual pride zipping through her at the instant reaction of his penis. She brushed his lips with hers. "We appear to be alone now." She grinned and kissed the tip of his nose, then raised her hips and impaled herself.

Somehow, during the ensuing wild ride, she managed to divest him of his Hawaiian print shirt and rub her aching nipples against his chest.

Just as her climax was upon her, he stopped and turned her to face away from him. The position allowed him to enter her from a new angle. Within seconds, her climax crested, washing wave after wave of pleasure over her.

Alex joined her, his shout echoing within the confines of the balcony.

Feeling boneless, she relaxed against his chest, enjoying the closeness of afterglow and the way his fingers still toyed with her nipples while he trailed lazy kisses up and down the side of her neck.

A girl could get used to this.

Derek nuzzled the top of Mac's shining hair and lightly squeezed her breasts. *Mine.*

"Do you like your job, Mac?" he asked, lightly pinching a responsive nipple. He was rewarded by her little wiggle and a surge of moisture around his still embedded cock.

"Well, I did until I was fired." She shrugged. "After I go back to Houston, I'll have to hit the streets again."

"You could work for me," he said before he could remind himself of why that was a bad idea.

"It would be a long commute from Houston, but thanks."

"I'm from Houston, too."

"You are? Okay. But what would I do if I worked for you?"

He arched his hips, pushing his sex deeper within her. "The same thing you've been doing, babe."

She giggled and wiggled against him, giving his cock ideas it didn't need.

"You don't have to pay for me to do this," she said in a soft voice. "I'd do it anyway."

Rotating on his shaft, she turned to him, taking his face in her small hands. "Don't you know that by now? I love—um, love making love to you."

He bent to flick the end of a nipple with the tip of his tongue before drawing the morsel into his mouth and sucking deeply. Her muscles clenched his cock like a velvet glove.

After repeating the action on the other breast, he lightly kissed her. "I'd want to pay for your time."

"You don't have to do that," she whispered. "For you, it's always free."

Deep within her, his penis surged. "That's good," he said in a husky voice. "Because the way I'm going, I'd be broke within the year."

He arched his hips and no talking occurred for quite a while.

McCall lolled her head against the side of the bathtub and regarded her human bath toy through her lashes. "Do you think it's possible to wear yourself out with sex?"

At the other end of the tub, Alex laughed, but didn't open his eyes. "Not if it's done right." Beneath the water, he wiggled her little toe. "And, babe, we're experts."

She sighed. "That's true. We're professionals." In a deep voice she said, "Do not try this at home," then laughed.

He joined her, then ran his hand up her right leg, caressing her thigh. "I meant what I said earlier. You can work for me."

"But—"

Gripping her thighs, he pulled her toward him until she

straddled his lap. Wrapping his arms around her, he hugged her close and placed a smacking kiss on the top of her head.

"You're coming to work for me," he said in a voice that brooked no argument. "I wouldn't have it any other way."

"But you don't even know what I do. And I may have some legal trouble, I—"

"Shh," he said against her temple, then trailed tiny kisses to her ear, leaving a fiery trail. "There are no troubles we can't handle. Whatever legal problems you have, my lawyer can get you out of." He leaned his forehead against hers, his eyelashes mingling with her own. "Say yes so I can love you while the water is still warm."

"You mean have sex with me," she corrected, hating how prim her voice sounded.

"No." He grinned down at her. "That would be fucking you. Hell, yes, I want to do that!" He flipped the switch, firing up the jets along the sides of the tub, and placed her bottom in front of one.

She gasped at the sensation of warm water fluttering her swollen labia. In all, it wasn't unpleasant.

He leaned to nip her still engorged nipples, then licked each distended tip.

He moved in closer and fondled her breasts while the jet still worked its magic, then trailed kisses across her face before settling on her eager mouth with a soul-deep kiss.

It went on forever, but not long enough. He broke the kiss and leaned back, his hands never pausing. "You're so damn responsive," he growled, nibbling at her lower lip.

"Only with you," she assured him, then gasped when his fingers entered her.

"You swear?"

For some reason, he seemed to need reassurance. His fingers were doing such magical things, it took a second to form a coherent sentence. She nodded. "Yes, absolutely positive. Alex, I've done things with you, felt things with you, that I've never done or felt with another man. Ever."

He made a gurgling half growl deep in his throat and pulled her to him. As soon as they were aligned, he plunged into her.

She would have liked to continue their conversation, but hormones took over, and within seconds she was as wild for him as he was for her.

Before it was over, he took her in the tub, the shower, against the wall of the bathroom, against the glass door of the bedroom and again on the balcony, culminating on the upholstered chair he'd used during their mutual lap dance that morning.

Sated, they slumped together on the chair, breathing ragged, skin sweat-slicked.

"We need another bath," she finally panted.

Alex groaned. "I don't know if I could live through another bath with you right now."

"How about a shower?"

He groaned again, burying his face against her breasts. Evidently he wasn't as far gone as he'd have her believe, since she felt his tongue lick the tip of her breast.

Her hand felt limp and barely attached to her arm when she tried to swat him away from her breast. "Maybe we should shower separately."

"No way in hell are you getting in that sexy shower stall alone, darlin'," he said. "Just give me a minute to gather my strength."

After a moment, he stood, holding her high in his arms, and strode to the shower. Within moments of feeling his soapy hands all over her, the arousal she'd thought was spent revived.

"I planned to keep my hands," he glanced down at his erection, "as well as other body parts, to myself."

She closed her soapy hand around his hardness and he groaned.

"What is it about you?" he asked, drawing her close to his

arousal. "All I have to do is look at you to get turned on." He nuzzled her neck. "All I want to do is get naked and fuck you."

She pushed him toward the seat in the corner. As soon as he sat, she climbed onto his lap and sighed at the feel of his turgid sex impaling her. "Be my guest," she said, lifting her breast to his mouth.

The feel of his sex surging into her in time with the deep draws of his mouth on her breast brought her to an earth-shattering orgasm in record time.

Just as the last ripple of pleasure subsided, he stood and placed her to stand with one foot up on the seat while he entered her from behind.

Okay, she thought, *I got mine, this one's for him.* She closed her eyes and leaned her head back against his shoulder, enjoying the feel of his soapy hands caressing her breasts and aching nub.

Aching nub? Yep, it was definitely aching with renewed arousal. Amazing.

She whimpered when he pulled out at the last second and turned her to face him. Before she could mention that she wasn't finished yet, he lifted her and plunged back into her, shoving her back against the cool tile of the shower.

"I love to watch your face while I'm fucking you," he explained with a grunt and increased the tempo of his thrusts. "You're so gorgeous when you come."

Well, that did it. Without warning, those words triggered a deep response within her and the mother of all tidal waves of pleasure washed over her.

She screamed—actually screamed—and clutched his shoulders to keep from swooning. Her nails bit into his gorgeous shoulders, but she couldn't make them release their grip.

Over the roar of her climax, she thought she heard him yell something that couldn't be right. It sounded as though he'd shouted, "I love you!" But that would be impossible.

Wouldn't it?

* * *

Derek slid down to sit on the floor of the shower, pulling Mac on top of him. Water rushed over their heads, blurring his vision. He hoped they wouldn't drown, because he had zero strength right now to turn off the water.

Had he really told Mac he loved her? How stupid was that? Especially in the heat of the climax he'd just experienced. Would she believe it wasn't said in the heat of passion?

Feeling above him, he finally located the controls. The water slowed to a trickle, then stopped. Silence filled the shower stall.

Placing Mac away from him, he stood, then helped her to her feet and grabbed one of the thick towels from the heated rack to wrap around her. Time for damage control—and he needed to hide her delectable body as much as possible.

Drying off, he glanced down at his purple pecker and froze, towel in hand. The sight that shook him was not the fact that he'd about worn the poor little guy out. It was the fact that it was naked.

As in, no condom.

How could he have been so careless? He watched Mac bend over and dry her legs, his pecker stirring again. No wonder it looked abused. He'd been in a sexual frenzy since he'd met her. With all the blood pooling between his legs, it was no wonder he'd forgotten a raincoat.

He wracked his brain, trying to remember when they'd last used a rubber. Damn! Last night—no, this morning. Nope. Last night. So they'd been unprotected all day long. He mentally counted up the times they'd made love and groaned.

"Alex?" Mac's hand was cool against his heated shoulder. "What's wrong?"

"We didn't use a condom." He held his breath, waiting for her to freak. Didn't happen. Instead, she shrugged and walked to the dresser, obviously unmindful of what a provocative sight she made.

He stalked to her, grabbing her arm, preventing her from pulling on a pair of the ugliest white cotton panties he'd ever seen. They looked like something his grandmother would wear.

"I said, we didn't use anything! All day!"

"I heard you." She tossed the granny panties back in the drawer, grabbed an equally ugly pink terry-cloth robe from the pile of clothes on the dresser and wrapped it around her. "What do you want me to say, Alex? Do you want me to yell and scream at you? Well, guess what? Not gonna happen." She walked to the window and looked out at the Gulf a while, then turned back to him.

"I know it was irresponsible of us. I know we should have used protection. But I also know I'm disease free. How about you?" He nodded numbly, wondering where she was going with this. Was it because he told her he loved her? Did she think it was okay to make a baby now so he'd be forced to marry her?

Temporarily sidetracked by the vivid mental image of Mac, all soft and round and glowing, with his baby growing safely inside her, he had to blink and swallow around the sudden lump in his throat.

"Alex?" She walked closer to take his hands in hers. "Are you sure you're okay? Look, we're both disease-free, consenting adults. We slipped up, but things like that happen sometimes, in the heat of the moment." She grinned up at him. "And, you have to admit, we've had quite a few heated moments."

"What about the baby?" he asked in a quiet voice. Hell, he'd marry her whether there was a baby or not, he realized with a start. But a possible pregnancy might be a head start on convincing her to give up her life of sin and make a different kind of life. With him.

Her shoulders drooped within the slouchy robe. He made a mental note to burn that robe as soon as they were married.

"Is that what you're afraid of?" she asked, tears sparkling her pretty eyes. "You're afraid you got me pregnant?"

"I wouldn't say afraid, just concerned."

"Don't worry," she said on what sounded suspiciously like a sob, but he couldn't tell because she'd turned back to the window. "I'm not pregnant. So . . ." she spread her arms, "problem solved."

"Are you sterile?" God wouldn't be so cruel. He hoped.

"Ster—no! Well, not that I know of, anyway." She sighed. "Look, it's not exactly romantic, but the fact is, I just finished my period. There. We're safe from unwanted pregnancies." She turned, hands on hips. At least, he thought they were on her hips, but it was sort of hard to tell with that ugly robe. "But just to be on the safe side, we should probably make sure we use condoms for the rest of the week," she said.

"We could get married." Where had that come from? Sure, he'd thought about proposing, but he'd planned to do it right. After he'd revealed his true identity. Candles and roses, the whole nine yards. Not standing in a rental bedroom, wrapped in a towel.

"Married?" She gave a sad little laugh. "You're joking, right? We barely know each other!"

"We know we're compatible," he countered.

"Sexually. Sure. But that doesn't mean we should get married. What if we married and found out we had nothing, other than great sex, in common? I don't ever plan to divorce."

"Neither do I." It would be financial suicide.

"And neither of us even have a job right now!"

"I have a job." He reached for his briefs. Maybe if he wore something besides a towel, he'd have more success in convincing her it was a good idea. "A damn good one," he felt compelled to add.

"Then why are you so concerned about money?"

What was she talking about? "Huh? You've lost me, lady.

What the hell are you talking about? What makes you think I'm concerned about money?"

"When you first came over the other morning. You asked how much it would cost to take me to dinner."

"Well, of course, I did! I'd never been in this type of situation before. I had no idea."

"You're telling me you don't date?"

She looked shocked. Did she think he was in the habit of picking up hookers? "Of course I don't 'date'! This was all Jack's idea." At her widened eyes, he backpedaled. "Not that it hasn't been the best three days of my life. Once we got to know each other, I couldn't imagine 'dating' anyone else. You're a great 'date.'"

She looked confused. "Damn straight, I am. But I have to tell you, I don't usually behave like I have with you when I date."

What a relief! "I'm glad to hear that." He flashed what he thought was a reassuring smile. "I'd like to think what we have is special."

She nodded "It is."

He grabbed the ties of the ugly robe and reeled her in. "I meant it when I told you I loved you."

Her eyes narrowed. "You're sure it wasn't the heat of the moment?"

"Nope." He wrapped her in his arms and rubbed his nose against hers. "I love you."

She looped her arms around his neck and pulled him down for a kiss. "I think I love you, too."

"Then you'll marry me?"

"No." She stepped out of his embrace and crossed her arms.

"But why—"

"Because we don't know each other well enough! If you're serious, you'll understand why it's important that we wait until we're sure."

"I'm sure." He knew he sounded surly, but it was the way he felt.

"No, you're not." She held up her hand when he began to protest. "You're not and you know it. Heck, you may not even really love me. It may be just a hormonal flush, the reaction to incredible sex."

"Thanks," he said, grinning at her. "I thought it was pretty incredible, too."

"Well, before your ego takes over, let's change the subject."

"I'm hungry." It was true. Suddenly ravenous, he realized they hadn't eaten since breakfast.

She thought for a moment. "Me, too." She glanced around the bedroom. "Just let me straighten up and get dressed and we'll see what's in the fridge."

"Ah-ah," he said, walking up behind her and slipping his hands through the lapels of the ugly robe to cup her breasts. "Takes too long. I'm starving. There's a burger place down the beach. Throw on some clothes and let's go."

"But the room—"

"I'll help you straighten up when we get back."

She sighed. "Okay. Just give me a minute."

He sat down in the chair, suddenly in no big hurry to leave the intimacy of their—and, yes, it was their—bedroom. At her raised brow, he grinned. "Just settling in to watch the show."

"I thought you were hungry."

"I am. Doesn't mean I can't enjoy the view while I wait."

And what a view it was, he thought as he watched her shuck the ugly robe and slip a baggy sundress over her head. Normally he disliked baggy apparel, especially on women with bodacious bodies. But he kind of liked baggy stuff on Mac. Maybe because it might help keep other men from noticing her. That, he amended, and the fact that she apparently favored not wearing underwear with baggy dresses. A definite advantage, where he was concerned.

Thinking of sinking deeply within Mac's welcoming heat caused him to think of the condom situation. With a start, he realized he preferred not using a condom. He wanted nothing to be between Mac and him when he was inside of her. If she became pregnant, so be it. Then she'd have to marry him. He watched her slip into a pair of nearly there sandals, admiring the sexiness of her toes.

Yep, barefoot and pregnant suited him just fine.

9

McCall glanced sideways at the man beside her and wondered for about the millionth time when the bottom would fall out of her happiness.

It would happen. It always did. And, this time, her happiness was totally off the charts. Therefore, the big let-down could happen at any moment.

They'd pigged out on hamburgers, fries and shakes so thick you had to wait a while to drink them. Alex had refused to let her order a mixed drink. He said he wanted her to remember what they did when they got home. Home. What a lovely concept.

While she would have loved nothing better than to spend the rest of her life with Alex, she struggled to be realistic. Besides the fact that they barely knew each other—except in the biblical sense—she had that pesky problem of possible incarceration. She couldn't very well say, "I love you, too, Alex, and yes, I'd love to marry you . . . in ten to twenty years."

Alex put his arm around her and drew her close to his side. She wrapped her arm around his waist and savored the contentment of walking close to him. With his arm around her, she felt protected, valued, cherished. Loved.

She didn't kid herself. More than likely this was for Alex a beautiful illusion, an interlude out of time. Once the week was over, they might see each other a few times. But it would be awkward. He'd call less and less. The dates would dwindle. Eventually, he'd move on with his life, with or without any excuses of how his life had taken him in a different direction, how they'd grown apart or a thousand other trite excuses men had for dumping you.

And she'd be left to pick up the pieces of her heart and try to get through the rest of her miserable existence. Some people weren't cut out for marriage. Maybe she was just one of the unlucky ones.

She glanced up at Alex and wished it weren't so.

Derek looked out over the waves and planned his strategy. In hindsight, springing his proposal on Mac had been a bad idea. Proposals should be carefully planned, romantic, not just *"Hey, how about we get married, huh?"* spoken immediately after sweaty sex. He gave himself a mental kick. He was smarter than that.

Whatever he did, it had to be soon. They only had tonight and tomorrow night if he wanted her to leave Pleasure Beach a reformed and engaged woman.

"So," he said, "when do you want to have the wedding?" Damn. Smooth, real smooth.

She must have thought he was a lunatic because she stopped and pulled her hand out of his.

"Alex, I have . . . um, issues. I can't even think about marrying anyone until I get them straightened out."

"Issues," he repeated dully.

She nodded and swallowed.

"I thought the issue was love," he said.

Moonlight glistened off the tears in her eyes. "I do love you, Alex. More than you know. It's just that, well, I seem to have gotten myself into a little trouble and, well, until it's straightened out, my life is not my own."

"This trouble, does it require legal assistance?"

She sniffed. "Yes," she said in a watery voice.

"Do you have a lawyer?" His legal team would make mincemeat out of whatever charges she faced.

"Yes. Tucker, remember?"

Ah, yes, Tucker, the unscrupulous sleazoid who insisted on defending the fund-raiser from hell.

"Tucker is a fine lawyer, I'm sure, but I've heard he hasn't been too particular lately about who he represents. I could put in a call to my lawyer for you."

"Thanks, Alex, but I got myself into this, I'll have to get myself out." She raised on tiptoe to brush her lips against his cheek. "It shouldn't take long. I'm not guilty, so—"

"You're not?"

"Don't sound so surprised. Of course I'm not guilty!" Her breath caught. "Is that what you think of me? If so, why on earth did you ever propose?"

"Because I love you!" He caught her to him and held her close to his heart.

"Well, if you love me, let me go! Trust me to handle my own problems in my own way."

He watched her flounce toward the beach house without a backward glance, then kicked a nearby boulder.

"Ow!" He hopped on one foot and watched her stiff back as she climbed the steps.

How did things go so wrong, so fast?

McCall regretted her impetuous words the moment they left her mouth and even more after walking the rest of the way home alone.

She walked into the immaculate kitchen and opened the refrigerator door. Nothing appealed to her. Dragging out a half-empty bottle of wine, she trudged listlessly to the rack of glasses and took one down. Tonight she didn't notice the quality of the crystal or admire the deep burgundy of the wine.

She looked down at the more-than-half-full bottle. Tonight, she would get drunk. Drown her sorrows, so to speak. She glanced over at the closed sliding door. No one would know the difference, anyway.

The bottle was cool against her lips when she turned it up and swallowed way more wine than she'd intended. Coughing and gasping for breath, she staggered to the sink and set the bottle on the granite counter. Leaning over the sink, she prayed she wouldn't lose her dinner along with the slug of wine. While she was at it, she also prayed for a future with Alex.

Couldn't hurt.

When she finished the bottle and Alex had yet to appear, she decided she could take a hint and went to pack. She could always spend possibly her last day of freedom doing her laundry.

Trying not to have a major pity party, she trudged up the stairs and dragged her suitcase from the closet. Alex never had helped her clean the bedroom like he'd promised. And what a pit it was! Clothing strewn all over, the result of lust and the furious coupling that followed.

She plucked a pair of her panties from the ceiling fan and threw them into the suitcase.

One of her best bras hung drunkenly from the floor lamp in the corner. Tears filled her eyes when she remembered how Alex had been overcome with lust at seeing her sitting in the chair, reading, in her undies.

She folded the bra and tucked it neatly into the pocket of her suitcase. "Good thing I didn't take him up on his proposal," she muttered. "It would've been the shortest marriage in history."

The tears had her searching for a box of tissues. Lifting her underwear and skirt from the spot she'd flung them on her first day, she was hit by the pungent aroma of overripe fruit. Her skirt was firmly stuck to something brown, shriveled and sticky. "Oh, ick." She peeled off the vile thing, and then folded her skirt, soiled side in, and tossed it in her suitcase.

"What in the world . . . ?" Her skirt had been covering a basket of decaying fruit—and something else bizarre as well. What appeared to be a condom was tied in a neat little bow around a tacky statuette of an overendowed topless woman in a G-string. Her tiny chubby feet were taped to a card. In a bold scrawl were the words *Happy Birthday, you dog. I expect you to use all of this during your vacation. Call me when you get back to town. Jack.*

Use what? She cautiously peeked into the basket to find the fruit was resting on a bed of wrapped condoms. What may have once been a flower lei encircled the basket.

"Hmm." She shrugged. "Wonder who they were for?" She glanced back at the decayed fruit. "And how long they've been here." Seeing the condoms brought thoughts of Alex and how much she missed him. Blinking back fresh tears, she gathered her toiletries from the bathroom and zipped them into the side pocket of her suitcase.

Did she dare spend the night alone in the bed she'd shared with Alex? A glance at the clock made the decision for her. It would be well into the morning by the time she got back to Houston. She didn't want to risk driving alone at night in her piece-of-junk car. It would be safer to leave bright and early the next morning.

She cleaned the kitchen thoroughly again, keeping an ear open for the sound of Alex's step on the deck. It didn't come.

With a heavy heart, she climbed the stairs and into the big cold bed to wait for dawn.

* * *

Derek rolled to his side and looked out over the Gulf. In the gray light of day, the whitecaps of the waves were barely visible. After a restless night, he'd come out here to his deck to wait until a reasonable hour to go to Mac.

Leaving her last night had been the hardest thing he'd ever done. But he knew they both needed space. Space to figure out what was important. Space to realize they belonged together.

He suspected she felt ill-matched, with her jaded past. He considered it proof of the strength of his love that her participation in the world's oldest profession didn't matter to him. As long as he was her last customer.

He opened his eyes to glance at the thin gold watch strapped to his wrist and realized he must have dozed off at some point. After brushing his teeth, he jogged down the beach, anxious to hold and kiss Mac again.

His steps slowed. He needed to tell her who he really was— should have done that long ago. It was stupid to withhold his identity. By the time he'd been with her fifteen minutes, he'd known she could be trusted.

Decisions made, he increased his pace. He also wanted to learn everything there was to know about his future wife.

McCall let herself into her little house and threw her keys onto the scarred coffee table while she sorted through her mail.

Walking toward the back of the shotgun-style house toward her bedroom, she stripped, leaving a trail of clothing. Her almost painfully neat home looked barren to her now. Barren.

She covered her abdomen with her hand. She'd told Alex the truth, but a tiny part of her hoped she was wrong. She'd give anything to be pregnant with Alex's baby. She'd always have a part of him to love.

Shoving those morose thoughts away, she fell back on her serviceable corded bedspread and vowed to buy something frilly and feminine. Sensual. Assuming she was still a free woman when the next white sale rolled around.

Tears burned her eyes at the thought of Alex never seeing her home.

Above her, the ceiling fan lazily stirred a breeze to waft over her nudity. Her nipples puckered at the coolness, causing a fresh spate of tears.

Some wild woman she'd turned out to be.

"Mac!" Tired of knocking, Derek let himself into the quiet beach house. He ran to the bottom of the stairs. "Mac?" Taking the stairs two at a time, he didn't realize how much he wanted to find her sound asleep on the big bed until he saw it was neatly made. A quick check of the bathroom confirmed it.

She was gone.

Shaking fingers brought up Jack's home number on his cellphone screen. He hesitated only a second before pressing the CALL button.

His friend answered on the second ring.

"Jack! It's Derek. I need some info, buddy."

"Shoot. Hey, what did you think of my gift?"

"I loved it." More than he could know. "I need her name and address."

"Whose name?"

"The hooker."

"What hooker?"

"Jack, don't toy with me, buddy! I don't have time. I fell in love with the hooker you gave me for my birthday and I have to find her but I don't even know her full name! I—"

"Whoa!" Jack's voice boomed over the tiny phone. "Back it up a minute. While I would love to take the credit for it, I don't have that kind of imagination. I didn't buy you a hooker for your birthday. Who is she?"

I didn't buy you a hooker for your birthday. Jack's words echoed in Derek's head, causing a terrible ache to build in his temples. He sank to the edge of the bed, his knees suddenly weak. "That's what I'd like to know," he said in a quiet voice.

"You're kidding, right? Didn't you see the fruit basket I left on the dresser up in my room?"

Derek looked up at the basket of rotting fruit. "Yeah, it was great. Thanks, man."

"Well? Did you use all of them?"

"The fruit?"

Jack's laugh echoed over the miles. "No, you moron! I tucked about three boxes' worth of condoms in that basket. Didn't you look under the fruit? And did you check out the rack on that doll?"

Memories of Mac, standing in the shower, water dripping from her magnificent breasts, filled his mind. "Yes," he said. "They were spectacular."

"Well? You said you met a woman. I'm not looking for locker-room gossip, but just answer one question. Did—"

"Hold on a minute, Jack, I have another call." He switched over. "Summers."

A few minutes later he clicked back to Jack. "Jack? Sorry about that. It was my legal counsel. The court date of the fund-raiser from hell has been moved up to tomorrow. Seems the judge's wife is pregnant and he wants to take some time off. I'll call you when I get back in town. Bye."

The judge's wife was pregnant. With all his heart, he wished he'd impregnated Mac during their brief time together. Right now it seemed to be the only way she'd come back to him.

Jack walked into the steak house a few minutes after the hostess had seated Derek. "Hey, big guy," Derek said. Jack's smile was infectious while he heartily pumped Derek's hand

and slapped his back. Derek smiled back at his good friend and cardiologist and reclaimed his seat in the plush, red leather booth.

"Well, you look tan, but I can't say you look rested," Jack said as soon as the waitress placed their drinks in front of them and left. "I'm not a shrink, but you know I'm available if you want to get anything off your chest." He took a sip of his drink. "So, who's the woman?"

Derek shook his head, horrified at what felt suspiciously like tears burning the backs of his eyelids. "I haven't a clue," he said in a thick voice.

"Wow. We all knew—well, hoped—you'd fall again. But, damn, you look like this has really cut you off at the knees. You say she's a hooker?"

Derek shrugged, wanting to howl his frustration. "How the hell should I know? She could be anyone! Who did you rent your house to this past week?"

"No one. Wait, my brother-in-law had a key. Maybe he gave it to someone."

"But you said you wanted me to pick up my present before the next renter got there."

Jack nodded, his Irish setter–red hair standing on end. "That's right. But mostly I just wanted you to get out of your slump and get laid. Renters were secondary. They were due there tomorrow, but as things turned out, they canceled. You could have stayed and made whoopee with your mystery woman for another week." He grinned over the rim of his glass. "Welcome back to the land of the living, my friend." Jack sighed at Derek's scowl and reached into his pocket. He punched a number and put his tiny cell phone to his ear. "Tuck? It's Jack. Say, did you let anyone use my beach house this past week?" Jack's gaze met Derek's hopeful one and he nodded. "You did? Who was it? What? That's bullshit! We're family!" His eyes narrowed. "You're not fucking around on my sister, are you?" He relaxed back against the booth. "So who was it?" He sighed. "Yeah, I understand. Yeah. Right. Bye."

"Well?" Derek leaned forward, praying for a break.

Jack shook his head and took another drink. "Sorry. Client confidentiality. His hands are tied."

"Can he give his client a message?"

Jack pulled out his phone again and hit REDIAL. "What's the message?"

"Ask him if his client's name was Mac."

Jack greeted Tucker a second time without even saying hello. "Was your client's name, by chance, Mac?" He put his hand over the receiver and asked Derek, "And this Mac is a girl, right?" He grinned when Derek threw his napkin at him.

"Tell Tucker to tell Mac that I meant everything I said and to call me." Derek rattled off the number to his private line and cell phone, which Jack dutifully repeated.

Jack slipped the phone back into his pocket and leaned forward. "So what exactly did you tell her?"

"Exactly?"

Jack nodded. "Yes, exactly."

"Okay," Derek said, feeling suddenly optimistic. Mac would call. "I took her hands, like this, and said"—he grabbed Jack's hands in a bone crushing clench to prevent his withdrawal—"I love you. I can't live like this. I'm not ashamed of our love. I want to marry you."

Their waitress dropped their fresh drinks along with her tray with a resounding crash. She stood, eyes wide, mouth open, then turned and ran toward the back room.

Jack glared at Derek, who laughed uproariously, and threw some bills on the table. "Thanks a lot, Derek, old boy. Now you've ruined my favorite hangout."

McCall ran her sweaty hand over her drab gray skirt and nodded at her attorney that she was as ready as she'd ever be to face her accusers. If she was exonerated, she would buy a complete new wardrobe.

"Remember," Tucker told her, his hand on her arm to guide her through the throng of reporters, "answer only direct questions and only then with a yes or no. If even one tiny word of their question is not true, then it's false. Got it?"

She nodded and he held open the courtroom door for her. "I heard the big man himself, Derek Summers, is going to grace us with his presence this morning," he told her. "I subpoenaed him, but thought for sure he'd find a way to wiggle out of it."

"Maybe if I talked to him, told him my side of it, he'd drop the charges?"

Tucker gave a humorless bark of laughter. "Yeah, right! Derek Summers is the Ice Man—what do you think? I'm your lawyer and I'm telling you to steer clear of him."

Gritting her teeth, McCall drew a calming breath and wished for about the zillionth time that Alex were here to give her his strength and love.

And there he was.

He was talking to an older man who sat behind a long, rectangular table, but she only had eyes for him. He looked beautiful. Even more handsome in the tailored gray suit, pale blue shirt and red tie than when he wore shorts and a T-shirt.

While he spoke, he looked around the courtroom and straightened his tie. She knew the moment he spotted her. His hand froze at the knot of his tie. His gaze met hers and the other inhabitants of the courtroom faded away.

She smiled and rushed toward him. Behind her, Tucker called her name, but she maintained eye contact with her beloved Alex and kept walking.

The older man at the table grabbed Alex's arm, but he shook him off, his gaze never leaving her.

Finally she was within touching distance. Why wasn't he embracing her? It didn't matter who initiated the hug. What mattered was that he'd come for her. Together, they could get over anything. Endure anything. She reached for him, only to have his hands stop her with a firm grip on her shoulders.

"Alex? I—"

"Who are you?" he asked in a cold voice.

"It's me, Mac." At his continued hard stare, she laughed. Okay, she'd play along. She held out her hand. "I don't believe we've been formally introduced. I'm McCall Lindsey."

He released her shoulders to clasp her hand, a muscle ticking in his jaw. "Derek *Alexander* Summers. Of the Summers Group."

His last sentence was barely audible over the roar in her ears. Tears burned her eyes as she looked at his beautiful face, set in a grim mask, through a gray haze.

Everything went black.

10

McCall applied another liberal coating of sunscreen and leaned back in the deck chair with a sigh. She'd thought coming back to the scene of the crime, the beach house, would be cathartic. Instead, it had opened up her emotional wounds to bleed all over again.

The criminal charges had been dropped when McCall's immediate supervisor was revealed as the real culprit. Unfortunately, Alex—*Derek*—didn't seem to notice. How on earth could he have accused her of being a prostitute? Thoughts of their time together flashed through her mind and she had to admit it might not have been much of a stretch.

Some wild woman she'd been.

But the lies hurt the most. She'd hidden her identity at her lawyer's advice. Alex—*Derek*—hadn't trusted her enough to tell the truth about himself.

She groped for another tissue and wiped her leaky eyes. Good thing she hadn't accepted his silly proposal.

A jogger made his way down the beach and she wished for

the millionth time it was Alex, coming to beg her forgiveness and sweep her off her feet.

It was hard not to admire the lean fitness of his tanned body, the long, even stride of his legs as he closed the distance, then ran past her section of beach without a sideways glance.

She slumped back and closed her eyes, hoping the soothing sound of the surf and the warmth of the sun would ease the icy ache in her heart.

Coming back to Pleasure Beach was a waste of time. But when Tucker's brother-in-law had offered the house to her for the weekend, free of charge, she'd grabbed at it like a drowning woman.

Maybe it wasn't a mistake. Maybe she needed time to heal. Maybe she needed closure.

Derek's stride ate up the distance from his beach house. His muscles tightened painfully with each yard closer to Jack's house. He'd run by there every day since the trial ended. He snorted. What did he expect, that Mac would be sunning herself on the deck, just waiting for him to get his head on straight and come back to her? How pathetic was that?

Clenching his jaw in determination, he focused on the large seaside boulder in the distance and refused to glance over at Jack's place.

The charges against Mac, being false, were dropped. He heard she'd even been offered her job back with Sunshine International. He also heard she'd refused.

Hank thought they would face a lawsuit from Ms. Lindsey. Didn't happen. In fact, it was as though she'd dropped off the face of the earth.

After licking his wounds for a while, Derek had headed to the modest house McCall rented in the Heights. Empty. The next-door neighbor told him Mac was in the process of relocating and had put everything in storage. No, she hadn't left a forwarding address.

What good was amassing a fortune if you couldn't use it to find one small woman? His best people were on it, but so far had turned up nothing. Nada.

He told himself, for about the millionth time, as he turned around and headed back toward his house, that he'd have to be patient. What they had was real. She would contact him when she was ready.

In fact, he'd been telling himself that very same thing for more than two weeks now. How long did she plan to hold a grudge?

Jack's place was coming up on the right again. Did he dare open himself up for more disappointment by checking for her one more time?

You betcha.

His steps slowed. Was someone on the deck? He veered to the right until he was within a few yards of Jack's deck. There was definitely a person on the deck, and it was definitely a woman.

His heart clenched. *Don't get excited just because she looks like Mac. Could just be your imagination playing tricks—wishful thinking.*

He stopped at the bottom of the steps leading up from the beach.

The woman sat up and glanced around, then untied the top of her bikini, revealing very familiar breasts. He'd know them anywhere.

Mac turned onto her stomach, her face turned away from him.

He made his way cautiously up the steps, not stopping until he stood above her, his shins almost touching her hip.

While he watched, she reached down, then brought up a tissue to wipe her eyes and nose. Maybe she missed him as much as he missed her.

Soundlessly, he retraced his steps until he was safely back to the shore, then took off toward his own house at a dead run.

It might be his last chance. Time was running out. He had to move fast.

He was going to marry a wild woman.

McCall clutched the top of her electric-purple bikini close to her sunburned chest and crawled off the chaise.

The cooler air of the interior sent a shiver across her flushed skin. She must have fallen asleep out on the deck. The sun had already set.

Not bothering with the light, she made her way toward the stairs. Maybe a long soak in the whirlpool tub, by candlelight, might ease her aching loneliness. She could pretend Alex was there with her.

"Get used to it, Mac," she whispered as she rounded the curve of the stairs. "This is the first day of the rest of your life."

She paused, one foot on the next step, and stared at the faint glow coming from the master suite. Didn't she turn off all the lights last night when she finally succumbed to sleep?

Inching her way to the door, her steps slowed to a stop. Afraid to breathe, lest it be a figment of her wishful imagination, she took in the sight before her.

Candles adorned every surface. A silver ice bucket sat beside the bed, a large bottle of champagne nesting in the ice. The sultry breeze from the Gulf lazily stirred the air, redolent with the fragrance of the millions of rose petals that covered the big bed and surrounding floor.

It was gorgeous. Spectacular.

But the most gorgeous, spectacular thing of all was the sight of Alex, lying on his right side, one hand propped beneath his head, wearing nothing but a smile.

"I thought you'd never wake up," he said in a husky voice. "It's getting kind of hot in here with all these candles."

"Well, let's get rid of them then," she responded. She leaned over and blew out the candle nearest her, her gaze locked with his.

She dropped her top and blew out another candle. Then another.

She wiggled out of the miniscule bikini bottom and blew out a third candle before climbing on the bed of petals.

Never breaking eye contact, he licked his fingers and snuffed out the two squat candles on the nightstand next to him.

She blew out the remaining candles and crawled to him until she nestled against him, heart to heart. She slid her arms around his neck and pulled his mouth to hers for a soft kiss.

"Hi," she said against his mouth.

"Hi, yourself." He deepened the kiss, then broke the connection to cover her face with soft, tiny kisses. "I've missed you," he whispered next to her ear.

Tears blurred her vision, burned her nose. "I've missed you, too, so much," she assured him in a choked voice.

His hands skimmed her bare back and hips. The heated throb of his erection beat against her abdomen. "If I can't make love to you again soon, I think I'll explode."

She laughed and wiggled closer. Yes, this was definitely a glorious, wonderful dream. Right where it all began. "If this is a dream, I don't ever want to wake up," she said with a sigh.

Against her, he stiffened, then pulled back, clasping her face in his hands.

"I love you, Mac. This is no dream. I've gone crazy since I last saw you in the courtroom. No one would let me near you." He kissed the tip of her nose. "Then you were nowhere to be found."

"You looked for me?" What had she done in her entire pathetic life to deserve a love like she felt for this man?

"Of course I looked for you! I was frantic. Then Jack convinced me to take some time off to regroup, plan the next move of my search."

"Funny, Jack was also the one who suggested to Tucker that I use his beach house to rest up before I relocated."

Derek chuckled. "I think we've been had."

McCall grinned up at him, tears of happiness in her eyes. "Not yet," she said as her hand closed around his erection.

To her surprise, he grabbed her wrist. "Not yet, sweetheart. I want to do this right, and when you touch me like that all I can think of is burying myself in your wet heat over and over again." He set her away from him and reached over his side of the bed. "I intend to do this right."

He rolled back to her and took her hands in one of his. "McCall, I love you. I think I loved you from the first time I saw you stretched out on this bed, allegedly for my pleasure." He dipped his head and kissed the tip of her breast. "Can you forgive me for being so stupid?" He glanced up through his lashes and gently kissed the other nipple.

She could only nod, her throat too clogged with emotion. If he wasn't going where she hoped he was going with this, death by broken heart was a definite possibility.

"I'm still holding that job open for you."

"Job?" Her voice squeaked. She was an idiot. Of course he wasn't proposing. He'd done it before in the heat of the moment, and she'd turned him down. Whatever gave her the idea he'd ask her again? A secure job and warming his bed, at least occasionally, were about all she could hope for. . . .

"Mac?"

She blinked. "Hmm?"

"Aren't you going to put me out of my misery and say something?"

Her eyes widened at the ring flashing fire in the minimal light of the bedroom. The princess-cut diamond was the size of a small skating rink. She must have missed something.

"Could you repeat . . . that, please?"

Instead of repeating, he slid from the bed. Her heart sank.

He reached to trace her cheek with the tip of his finger. "Like I said, I want to do this right." He held out the gargantuan diamond ring. "McCall, would you give me the pleasure and honor of accepting the position of my wife? I mean—ah, hell! Mac, I love you. Will you marry me?"

A hot tide of relief washed over her, beginning at her toes until she was sure she had a full-body blush going. "Yes!" she croaked.

He vaulted back onto the bed to pull her into his arms for a fierce hug, then slid the ring onto the third finger of her left hand and kissed the knuckle. "Thank God," he said in a shaky voice. "I was so afraid you'd turn me down, after the things I said. The things I did." He shook his head. "The things I thought! Mac, how could I have been so wrong?"

She laughed and snuggled deeper within his embrace, admiring the way the stone of her new ring caught the light. "It's partially my fault. In my pathetic attempt to be a wild woman, I sent out all the wrong signals and played right into the misconception."

"But I'm a great judge of character," he argued. "How could I have been so wrong? I look back now and realize only an idiot would have mistaken you for a hooker."

"I always thought I had a talent for reading people. I thought you were struggling to make ends meet." She hid her burning cheeks against his chest. What a mistake!

He laughed again. "How did you come up with that? I told you I owned the beach house down the way."

"No, you said you were *staying* there. Big difference." She framed his face with her hands, forcing herself to drag her gaze away from the rock on her hand. "Let's not argue about it. The point is, we're back together. I'm sorry if I misled you in my feeble attempts at being a wild woman. But I don't regret it. I had a marvelous time . . . and I found the love of my life."

Talking fell by the wayside while they explored each other with renewed tenderness.

Derek covered McCall in petals, then removed them, one by one, with his teeth, licking the exposed skin beneath until she writhed with need. Her movements released the smell of crushed roses.

He knelt between her legs and dragged a silken petal against her sensitized flesh. She quivered with longing, moving her legs restlessly. Attempts to drag him to her were in vain.

The first hot lap of his velvet tongue made her scream her release.

"I'm sorry," she murmured as he positioned himself between her legs. "I wanted to wait for you."

"I was right with you, babe. Always." He plunged into her, the feeling so right that it took her breath away. He paused. "And, Mac?"

She forced her heavy eyelids open to see him staring down at her with love in his eyes. "What?" she whispered.

"You'll always be my wild woman."

Same Time Next Week

1

"Go, go, go!" the women shouted. Kinsey Carlyle barely heard the chants over the roar in her ears as she gulped champagne punch from the hose attached to a large bottle, tied to . . . a very hunky stripper.

Drinking of any sort, she knew, was totally out of character. Well, for the last three years anyway. Not since the last time she'd tied one on and woke up in Mexico, married to her blind date.

She prayed her weird allergy to alcohol didn't rear its ugly head again during her best friend's bachelorette party, closed her eyes and drained the bottle. Amid raucous cheers, she opened her eyes.

She was eye-to-crotch with the stripper. She blinked, trying to bring all the sequins into focus. Up close and personal, it was a pretty impressive crotch.

Looped. She was definitely looped. She tested that theory with her teeth and found she could no longer feel her lips.

Zachary would be pissed. Her mind swatted the thought

away like an annoying fly. No news flash there. Zachary was always pissed at her these days.

But she would still marry him.

Well, she'd finally say yes to his proposal anyway. Then with any luck she'd have a year or so to get used to the idea of spending the rest of her life with good old, *dependable to the point of boring* Zachary Taylor, D.D.S.

It was what her parents wanted.

No, it was what *she* wanted. Wasn't it? Closing her eyes again and shaking her head to fight off a wave of dizziness, she assured herself that Zachary was what every American girl wanted. With ancestors dating back to the Mayflower, Kinsey was about as American as you could get; ergo, she wanted Zachary. Correction—she wanted to marry Zachary. Want . . . well, want was highly overrated.

"Hey, Kins." Her twin sister slid next to her on the couch. "You okay?" Karly reached to brush a lock of her sister's hair from her forehead. "I was, um, surprised to see you drink anything. Then—"

"Shocked to see me actually having fun?" It was a rude thing to say and Kinsey immediately regretted it. The look on her sister's face didn't help her guilt. "I'm sorry. I know you're just looking out for me." A small laugh ended in a hiccup. "I'm fine, Karly. Really."

"You're not still actually thinking of accepting Zach's ridiculous proposal, are you?" Karly shuddered theatrically. "You'll be dead of boredom within a year."

"Easy for you to say. You're married. What's so wrong about me finally settling down?"

Her sister leaned closer and lowered her voice. "We both know you don't give a rat's ass about Zachary Taylor! You're only considering him because of Mom and Dad." She gripped Kinsey's hand. "Look, I know I disappointed you all when I eloped with Brad, but don't do anything stupid just to try to make them happy."

"I'm not," Kinsey insisted, extricating her hand and moving closer to the sofa arm.

"Whoa!" crowed the bronzed god in a G-string, arms spread wide. His big hands grabbed their heads. "Matching babe bookends!"

Karly broke away first, shoving the stripper until he stumbled back. "Get the hell out of my face!" she shouted. With a concerned look, she turned to her sister. "Kinsey? What's wrong?"

"I think I may be sick—"

Karly swung one shapely leg back and forth as she perched on the edge of the bathroom counter in the lavish suite. Kinsey spit one last time into the toilet and watched her sister's annoying habit, wondering what Karly would do if she grabbed her foot and threw her into the bidet.

Great, now I'm a mean drunk. "Karly, take me home, okay? I don't think I should be driving."

"I can do better than that." Her sister grinned down at her. "While you were heaving, I called the front desk and booked a room for you. Peg said you could use the nightgown you bought her, but she wants it back."

"I can't go out looking like this! Look at me!" Kinsey gestured in horror at her once pristine white suit, now splattered with . . . well, she didn't even want to hazard a guess as to what it was spattered with.

"Not to worry." Her sister hopped down and offered a toothbrush and toothpaste. Kinsey's trench coat was draped over her arm. "Here. Clean up and put this on. Leave your clothes. I'll take them home and wash them, then bring them back to you tomorrow before checkout."

Before Kinsey could think of a reason why that was a bad idea, Karly opened the door and looked back. "You know, sis, I'd use this time to think things through. Maybe have a wild fling. If you marry Dr. Dull, it will probably be the last great sex you have for the rest of your life. Remember that."

Kinsey stared at the closed door. *Remember that*. How could she *not* remember that? Ever since Zachary had popped the question, it was all she'd thought about. Could she really sleep with the same man for the rest of her life? Especially a man like Zachary?

She thought of how devastated her parents had been when Karly ran off with Brad, a totally unsuitable match, in their ultra-conservative opinion. From the way Karly and Brad still looked at each other, Kinsey wasn't sure how unsuitable the match was, at least physically. But sex wasn't everything. Was it?

Trying not to retch again, she pulled her damp clothes from her skin and peeled them down. Ick. The lace bra was soaked, too.

In white high-heeled sandals and a white lace thong, she rinsed her arms, face and breasts with refreshingly cool water, then peered critically at her near-naked reflection.

The white set off her tan; the heels made her legs look even longer. She scowled at her breasts, which, no matter how much weight she lost, refused to shrink. As a teenager on South Padre Island, she knew most of the horny teenage boys on the beach had been attracted by her overly endowed breasts and blond hair. At twenty-seven, she wanted to be loved for her mind and kept her body appropriately clothed.

Until now.

She slowly reached up to stroke both breasts and was immediately rewarded by the tingling moistness between her legs. Shifting to ease the discomfort, she thought again of never sleeping with anyone but Zachary.

Not that she'd had that many sex partners. But then again,

every single one she'd been with had been more adept, more eager to please, than her possible fiancé.

The trench coat gently abraded her skin when she slipped it on, allowing it to hang open while she reached into the inner pocket. Her fingers closed around Zachary's ring, still in her possession despite numerous decisions to return it. She examined it under the harsh fluorescent lights.

The ponderous weight of the gaggingly tasteful ring weighted her hand. Four flawless carats. Eighteen-karat gold. She'd yet to try it on.

And couldn't bring herself to do it now.

The lingering dampness between her legs reminded her of the night Zachary proposed. And her disappointment.

She wanted to love Zachary. Her parents loved Zachary. He was handsome, had a thriving practice. She would be "well taken care of," as her mother was so fond of saying.

So when he'd popped the question and she hadn't known what to say, she'd allowed him to make love to her to take his mind off the fact that she hadn't answered him.

She'd hoped he'd be such a proficient lover that she'd be thrilled and anxious to become his wife. Didn't happen.

Foreplay, for Zachary, appeared to be divesting her of her clothes at the speed of light, squeezing her breasts like they were ripe melons, then jumping her bones. Or, as her sister said, sex by the book: Fit tab A into slot B, repeat as necessary.

That hadn't taken long either.

Have a fling. One last time.

"Oh, don't be ridiculous!" she told her reflection, dropped the ring back into her pocket and tightly belted the trench coat. "Go get some sleep." Maybe the alcohol made her feel so restless, so . . . horny. Things would be better in the morning.

The bachelorettes were busy with the latest antics of the stripper when she slipped out the door of the suite, clutching the card key her sister had handed her on the way out.

Thunder rumbled as she pushed the elevator button and waited for its descent. With a *ding*, the polished brass doors slid open and she stepped inside.

"Great," she mumbled, pushing the button for the fourth floor. "Only sixty-two floors to go." She checked her shoes for stains. What a night.

Her sigh brought a generous whiff of a delicious aftershave. She wondered who had occupied the elevator before her and if he was married, shifting again at her moist discomfort.

No doubt about it, a month was entirely too long to remain celibate. Even the smell of a stranger's aftershave got her hot.

Aroused and restless, she stepped back to lean against the corner of the elevator, and to wait for her floor number to appear above the door.

The space was already occupied. And it smelled wonderful.

Hard arms surrounded her to prevent her fall as she attempted to leap forward.

"I—I'm sorry!" Heat seared her cheeks and she tried desperately to remember if she'd actually been touching herself. "I didn't see you there!"

"My pleasure," came the deep, rumbling, Texas-accented voice above her head.

His arms tightened when she tried again to step forward, and she craned her neck to look up at her companion. Way up.

At almost five-foot-one—five-foot-five in her stilettos—Kinsey knew she looked much taller, due to her long legs. This guy was *tall*, no matter what the length of his legs. Easily six-foot-four or maybe more.

His head of full salt-and-pepper hair belied the youthfulness of his face. Chiseled cheeks, dark, full mustache, firm lower lip. The cleft in his chin made her salivate with the desire to lick it.

Realizing she was staring at his mouth, she raised her gaze to his eyes. *Oh, wow.* Brilliant blue, fringed with a double row of long eyelashes, they made her own baby blues pale by comparison.

She shifted within his embrace. It was then that she noticed his hands had somehow found their way beneath her coat. Calluses abraded the tender skin of her rib cage.

They stood, eyes locked, for a moment, before he began to back away.

Suddenly it was extremely important that she not leave his warmth. His safety. His sexuality.

"Don't," she rasped, her hands sliding up to his shoulders. "Not yet."

His nostrils flared a nanosecond before his mouth lowered to hers.

He paused, his lips so close to her own that she felt their warmth. His breath mingled with hers.

"This is crazy," he mumbled.

"Yes," she agreed on a sigh and closed the distance.

Whether it was the man, the champagne, the gentle rumble of thunder in the distance combined with the smooth motion of the elevator, or hormones, she knew instantly that she could *not* leave him. Not now. Not tonight.

The bristle of his mustache brushed against her upper lip, causing her to open her mouth wider for his entrance.

Either instant chemistry or a jolt of thunder caused electricity to zip through her body from her mouth to every fingertip and toe.

He groaned into her mouth—the sound causing delicious vibrations—and gathered her impossibly closer.

He wore blue jeans, the rough denim setting off sensations on her bare thighs, the large buckle at his waist a distinct barrier to what she sought.

Never breaking lip contact, his hands skimmed her body, leaving a trail of fiery need.

Lungs burning, she gasped when he finally released her mouth to slide nipping kisses down her throat to her breast. There, he licked and suckled, his hairy upper lip brushing against the ultrasensitive nipples until she had to bite her lip to keep from screaming her pleasure.

While he suckled her, his hands delved into her panties to find her wet and wanting. One hard thumb brushed back and forth across her distended nub, causing stars to dance before her eyes.

Her breath hitched in her throat and she knew her climax was near. Against her breast, his hot breath came in hard pants.

Ding!

Kinsey scarcely had time to jerk her coat tightly around her before the doors whooshed open. In front of her, the man straightened up and drew her close against his aroused body as an older couple stepped onto the elevator.

One large hand snaked beneath her coat to toy with her nipple while his other arm remained wrapped securely around her, hiding their activity from the other passengers.

Wet and wanting, Kinsey surreptitiously brushed her dampness against the straining denim.

On the fifth floor, the elevator stopped and the couple stepped out.

As soon as the doors closed, his mouth was on hers, hungrily devouring her, his hands caressing her breasts.

The elevator stopped again and she stepped away, taking great gulping breaths. It was her floor. She reached for his hand.

"It's time to get off." She flashed her card key and smiled her most wicked smile. "Literally."

2

Marcus Wallace numbly followed the blond goddess from the elevator. Well, maybe *numb* was the wrong word. At least one part of his anatomy was throbbing with life.

He'd thought her the most beautiful woman he'd ever seen when she'd stepped into the elevator. Now, flushed with arousal, she'd elevated to breathtaking status.

What the hell was he doing? It was insane. Possibly dangerous. Absolutely compelling. Irresistible.

Though he'd never believed in fate, it was the only conclusion he could come up with for why, at this low point in his life, an angel appeared.

With her sexual glow and tousled blond hair, she looked more like a fallen angel.

He looked down, admiring the partially exposed breast revealed while she used her card key. Could she be a prostitute?

"Listen," he began, "about tonight—"

"Shh." She held one slim finger against her kiss-swollen lips. "Let's just enjoy each other. Tonight."

"But I don't even know your name! I—"

"Shh," she said again, rising on tiptoe to brush her lips against his, her hand brushing his eager cock. "No names. No strings. Just for tonight . . . okay?"

In answer, he lifted her from her feet and walked into the suite while kissing her. With one booted foot, he kicked the door shut and let her slide down his aroused body.

"Let's get you out of these clothes." She reached for his calf-roping belt buckle.

"If you're undressing me, I need something to occupy my hands." He slipped her coat from her shoulders and let it fall to her feet. What he saw took his breath away.

Clad in nothing but a white thong and what his brother called fuck-me high heels, her body held shapely hips, a narrow waist and a rack that would put most centerfolds to shame. She was every young man's wet dream. Some older men, too, he thought ruefully.

The blush that tinged her cheeks reassured him. Hookers probably didn't blush. That, plus the way her small hands shook, told him she wasn't a professional.

He captured both her hands with his left one and raised them to his lips. Watching her face, especially those wide blue eyes, he licked and kissed each slim finger. Her nails were short and unpolished, which seemed more erotic than the long, blood-red lengths many women sported. More personal. More sensitive. Erotic.

Her breath caught and became shallow. Beneath his thumb, her pulse fluttered.

He dropped her hands and cupped her breasts while she resumed work on his belt buckle and button fly. His jeans hit the carpet with a soft thud and the chink of change. She grasped the elastic waistband of his silk boxers and tugged, then stepped out of her panties and shoes while he ripped at the snap front of his Western shirt until they faced each other.

Naked.

He'd never thought much about his height until he saw his erection jutting near her breast. Damn. Would they even fit together? Could he hold her up long enough to sufficiently fuck her?

He ran his hands over her silky skin and groaned. There wasn't enough time in the universe to sufficiently fuck her.

But he'd do his damndest.

"Here," she whispered. "I want you to take me here first." She led him to a wingback chair by the fireplace and pushed him until he sat with an ungraceful plop.

The leather was cold against his bare butt, but he immediately forgot everything when she climbed up and straddled his lap.

Her damp sex brushed his cock, her heat radiating against his skin, eliciting a drop of moisture to pearl on the engorged tip while he fumbled with the condom.

Her hands were cool where they cupped his cheeks, her lips sweet as they brushed his, once, twice, then settled into a lingering kiss.

It was more than he could stand. And not nearly enough.

Blood roaring through his veins, he was more alive than he'd been for a long time. Taking charge, he deepened the kiss and flexed his hips. His sex entered her tight, hot core at the same time his tongue entered her sweet mouth. Teeth clicked.

She broke the kiss and arched back, giving him access to her breasts. Her nipples tasted like champagne, giving him an insatiable thirst.

She rode him hard, giving as good as she got, until their shouts of climax filled the sitting room of the suite.

Damn. He'd wanted to last longer. For her. For him. But she got him so damn hot. . . . Next time. He'd prove himself next time.

"Mmm," she purred, and kissed her way up his neck where she licked his earlobe. Deep within her, his sex stirred with renewed interest.

She leaned back, blue eyes wide. "Again?" she asked with wonder in her voice. "So soon?" By her *cat that ate the canary* smile, he could tell she relished the idea. "Why don't we take a bath?" she suggested as she rose from his lap, one foot on either side of his hips. This action placed her shockingly bare feminine lips directly in front of his face. He gently blew on the damp skin, which caused her to clamp her legs together from knee to crotch, then grasp his shoulders in a momentary effort to regain her balance.

The idea that she could possibly be modest after what had transpired between them was funny, so he laughed.

It felt good. The first honest laugh in too long. Then, careful not to upset her balance, he leaned forward and placed a tender kiss on the fragrant folds. Unable to resist, he swiped the swollen bud with his tongue, tasting her passion.

Her knees wobbled, but she climbed off his lap and almost ran to the bathroom door. "I'll start the bath!" she called, then disappeared.

"I'll be right there," he assured her, unsure if she'd even heard his reply, and reached for the phone. "Hello? Yes, this is Marc Wallace, in room . . ." He stretched and grabbed the card-key folder from its resting place on the bureau, ". . . four-ten. I'd like a magnum of champagne, please. Right away. Yes, that would be fine."

He glanced at the foil wrapper on the floor. He'd only carried one. "Oh, and could you throw in a box of condoms? No, doesn't matter what kind. And add some fresh fruit and a large bowl of whipped cream in crushed ice, please. Thanks.

"Oh, yeah." He rubbed his face, pushed his normally reserved libido away and headed after his latest lover. "It's gonna be an interesting night."

Kinsey settled into the churning water and sighed. Perhaps she'd been impetuous for the first time in her life, but damn, it felt good. One jet gently fluttered her still swollen labia. It felt interesting, so she spread her legs a bit wider to get the full effect.

Oh, yeah. She smiled and sighed. She could definitely get used to this.

She picked up the sponge and trickled water across the tops of her exposed breasts. The effect, combined with the warmer water jostling beneath, was taking her from relaxed and sated to aroused at the speed of light. What was taking him so long?

The bubbles relaxed her somewhat and she sank lower, one hand stroking the most intimate part of her. Her parents had made no bones about masturbation being a sin. Karly had been doing it for years, of course, before she and Brad were married. But Kinsey was the "good twin" and strived for parental approval, even when they couldn't possibly know.

Until now.

Tired of waiting, she began caressing her breasts. The peaks immediately pebbled and she tried to lick her nipples, like she'd seen on cable, but found it impossible. Still, it felt amazing to gently stroke and squeeze.

She closed her eyes and again let one hand slip beneath the water. With her legs still spread, she was able to stroke without changing position. Her fingers rapidly learned each delicate fold. What felt good. What felt better.

Her breathing became shallow. Eyes closed, she moved her hand faster, relishing the feel of warm water against the swollen, sensitized petals each time she moved her fingers.

"Oh-oh-ah!" Her back arched, raising the tips of her breasts out of the water to be kissed by the cooler air, in what had to be classified as a world-shaking orgasm.

A strangled sound drew her attention and she opened her eyes.

He stood at the open door of the bathroom, eyes wide, mouth working, with easily a world-class erection.

Embarrassment at being caught in such a private and intimate act heated her cheeks. Maybe he'd think it was from the heat of the steam.

He sat on the top step, close enough for him to stroke her breasts, but far enough away that she couldn't reach anything fun on him.

His fingertip drew a lazy circle on the tip of her right breast before rubbing back and forth across the tip. Lightly. Any lighter and he wouldn't be touching her at all.

"Do that again," he commanded in a low growl. "I missed the beginning."

Kinsey swallowed and chewed the edge of her lower lip. "I was just, um, I mean—"

"You were masturbating while you waited for me." His slow grin caused her to squirm in the warm water.

"No!" She shook her head, damp curls sticking to her cheeks. Irritated, she spit a piece of hair away from her mouth. "I was just—"

"Masturbating. I want you to do it again. I want to watch you." He seemed to make himself more comfortable on the step. Her eyes widened when she peeked over the edge of the tub to see his large hand close around his rigid penis. "Please." Their eyes met. "Do it," he commanded.

Unable to break away from the vivid blue of his stare, Kinsey reached below the churning water to stroke her open lips. After the first awkward moment, her muscles relaxed, her movements becoming less controlled.

Warm water caressed her with the silken heat of a lover's tongue. She broke eye contact and closed her eyes to center her mind on the delicious sensations flowing through her body.

To imagine *his* tongue . . . down *there*, doing *that*.

Lightning flashed behind her eyelids. Her breath hitched, uterus clenched. Her climax came so suddenly and fierce, she had to clutch the edge of the tub to keep from sliding beneath the water.

Beside her, the stranger's bicep bulged. His strokes became shorter. Harder. Faster. A great shuddering groan shook his broad shoulders.

Kinsey peeked over the rim. Yep. Him, too.

She felt for the washcloth and averted her eyes while he cleaned himself up, and wondered what the protocol was for this type of situation. Would he step into the adjoining clear-glass-enclosed shower so she could grab a towel and make a run for the relative safety of the bed? And if he did take a shower, did she have the stamina to leave the room without at least checking out his, well, his, uh . . . package one more time?

Eyes closed, she debated with herself while the shower turned on. Before she could come to any conclusive decision, the decision was made for her.

Work-roughened hands gripped her beneath both armpits, effortlessly lifting her from the water. Before she could form any kind of response, she was standing in the already steamy shower enclosure. It grew immediately smaller as he stepped in and closed the door.

"My turn," he said, reaching for the soap.

"But I—"

"Shh." His mustache brushed her lips when he whispered, "It was your idea, darlin'. Remember? No words. No strings. Just this." His lathered hands came up to stroke liquid heat all around each breast, setting off tingles clear down both legs to her toes.

"Do you like that?" His voice was more a vibration against her mouth than actual speech. Against her belly, his erection gently thumped her skin, a reminder that their tryst was far from over. *Thank you, Lord!*

She took a deep breath, pushing her breasts more fully into his soapy palms. Blindly reaching for the soap, she lathered up a froth and reached for his most obvious part.

A growl came from somewhere deep in his throat.

"Shut up and kiss me," she whispered against his mouth.

3

_____

While the man paid the room-service waiter, Kinsey leaned against the bathroom doorway, wrapped securely in the hotel's plush white robe, and tried to remember when her legs had taken on the consistency of wet spaghetti.

She glanced longingly at the king-size bed and wondered if her new lover would mind if she took a quick nap. For maybe two or three days. Just enough to recharge her batteries. Who knew sex could be so wonderful . . . and exhausting?

Someone, probably her stud muffin, had turned back the covers to reveal the welcoming smoothness of the silken sheets. She sighed. If she weren't so exhausted, she could come up with some pretty hot fantasies as to what she'd like to do to him on those sheets. As it was, after their sexual gymnastics in the shower and the thorough full-body massage he'd given her on the pretext of rubbing in the scented oil, she just wanted to crawl between the divine-looking sheets and conk out.

The man hung the DO NOT DISTURB sign on the doorknob, closed the door and clicked the locks. He then rolled the cart close to the side of the bed.

Evidently he had no plans to sleep in the immediate future.

She watched as he opened what looked to be a huge bottle of champagne and set it on the nightstand. He uncovered the dishes, then poured two flutes of bubbly. With a fluid movement, he whipped his towel from lean hips and slipped between the sheets.

But not before she caught a glimpse of a firm backside that made her want to see more.

With a renewed interest, she walked to the other side of the bed and smiled shyly at the hunk reclined before her. She must have done something right in her life to deserve a last fling like this.

He reached to dip a plump strawberry in a huge bowl of whipped cream, and offered it to her.

She shook her head, suddenly hungry, but not for food.

His intense gaze burned into her. "Lose the robe," he growled.

With any other man, she would have felt embarrassed, or at least a little shy. But, for some reason his heated gaze empowered her. Excited her beyond belief.

Slowly untying the belt, she felt every loop of the soft terry cloth as it slid sensuously over her heated skin. Every greedy little follicle luxuriated in the gentle friction.

At last, naked, she hitched her leg onto the side of the mattress to join him, only to be stopped by his hand on her forearm.

"Not yet," he said. He extended a glass of champagne. Their rims gently clinked in the silence of the hotel suite. "To tonight. And to infinite delightful possibilities."

Resisting the urge to squirm beneath his rapt gaze, she could only nod and take a sip of the cool wine.

"Are you still up for fantasies?" he asked.

Gazing at the tent his arousal made in the sheets, she was amazingly ready for any and everything he could dream up. "Absolutely. What did you have in mind?"

"Games."

"Games?"

He nodded and gathered up several large pillows, stacking them as though to make a little throne or bed. One hand patted the pile. "Climb on up, my sweet." At her hesitancy, he frowned. "Is there a problem?"

Shaking her head, she climbed and reached for the edge of the coverlet.

He stopped her with a shake of his head. "Ah-ah-ah. You may not be hungry, but I'm starving." He grinned wickedly and reached for the bowl of fruit. "I plan to eat a big old bowl of sexual fruit salad."

She raised an eyebrow, a heated rush of sexual interest already making her moist.

He grinned and parted her thighs. "And you, sweet thing, are my serving bowl." With that, he picked up two peach sections and, spreading her legs wider, inserted each wedge on either side of her feminine petals.

Her gasp echoed from the high crowned ceiling. The slippery coolness of the peach sections against her hot spot made her want to squirm.

He kissed the inside of each knee and patted her vulva. "Good girl. Stay still. I'm creating a masterpiece."

He dipped a strawberry in the whipped cream and slowly dragged it down the engorged centerfold, between the peaches, then lightly licked the creamy streak. Dipping the berry again, he proceeded to paint each nipple with large, sexy tufts of sweet-smelling cream.

Another dip. He outlined her mouth, careful to keep the fruit from her. After licking her lips clean, he lustily bit into the ripe berry, dribbling the by now warmed juice between her breasts. His tongue carefully bathed away every trace.

She groaned, unbearably aroused, dying to see what he would do next.

With a silver spoon, he dolloped whipped cream until he filled her folds. He then lined up a tidy row of raspberries, which he nipped out with the tip of his tongue and ate with obvious appreciation.

Climbing up beside her, he took a sip of champagne, then licked each breast free of the cream with a thoroughness that left her panting.

"Please." She tried, in vain, to reach his bulging penis. "Now!"

He gave her a mock-grim look and shook his finger at her. "No, pretty lady, not quite yet. I'm still hungry."

Back between her spread legs, his tongue made quick work of the peaches. With a loud suck, he removed each section and licked away any remaining juice. One hand searched the fruit bowl and came up with a glistening cherry.

He smiled and waggled his eyebrows as he swiped the last of the whipped cream from its bowl and slathered her entire genital area.

Large hands held her hips pinned to the cushions while his busy tongue licked every drop of the cream from every little screamingly sensitive fold. And then some.

He peered up at her from her mound, his hot breath making her want to scream and push his face into her. He dangled the cherry between his thumb and forefinger, then licked his way back to her opening.

Had his hands not been anchoring her, she would have bucked off the bed when the cold cherry slid into her aching portal.

He looked up. "I've always wanted to eat a woman's cherry," he said with a gleam in his eyes.

Okay, so she screamed when the pointed tip of his tongue deftly removed the cherry from her and sucked the combined juices of her climax and the fruit from her. She'd shown remarkable restraint up to that point.

Weak with the prolonged arousal and forceful release, her

muscles vibrated. And they still had not actually had sex this time! Well, she thought, she could rectify that in a New York minute.

His head was still buried between her legs. Her hands were limp at her sides, but she was sure they would obey her command to drag him up to her at any moment.

At that instant, he moved up, but only as far as her clit, where he began a sucking that had her screaming again within mere seconds.

Before she could catch her breath from her latest climax, he slid up her body and entered her in one forceful thrust.

Matching his rhythm, her last coherent thought was to wonder if anyone ever died from sheer bliss.

The pink fingers of dawn edged through the draperies when Kinsey woke to find herself alone in the big bed. Sometime during the night, her considerate but insatiable lover had drawn the comforter over her exhausted nude body.

She moved and realized she had sore and sticky places in places she hadn't even known existed. A shower was definitely in order. Maybe in a few minutes. As soon as she could get her arms and legs to function.

The bathroom door opened, spilling diffused light into the bedroom. He approached the bed in his silk boxers and open shirt. His lethal cologne wafted toward her, making her think of all the ways he'd taken her. In the dimness, his teeth gleamed.

"Morning, sweet thing!" His good-morning kiss was enough to wake even a dead woman and have her begging for more. "Sleep well?"

She could only nod, both relieved he hadn't deserted her like a cheap one-night stand and a tad fearful about what he expected her to do by light of day.

After her performance last night, or what she could remember of it, what could she possibly do for an encore?

Amazed to find moisture pooling at this early hour, she scooted to the edge of the bed, dragging the comforter along with her. "I think I need a shower."

"No more erotic baths?" He actually looked disappointed.

He gripped her shoulders and she looked up into his blazing eyes. "Maybe later." With that, she attempted to sidestep him and failed.

"I have one more game before we leave here this morning, ma'am." The cover was tugged from her limp hands. He lifted her back to her pile of pillows and spread her legs.

His kiss stopped her halfhearted protest while he vigorously shook the remaining champagne.

At her questioning look, he grinned and held up the bottle. "Amateur gynecologist. It's time for a very thorough exam and your complimentary champagne douche."

4

Kinsey tried to rouse from the lethargy that had invaded her body ever since her "exam" and champagne douche. At the thought of the cool bubbles shooting deep within her, she wanted to smile again, but found it took too much effort.

Her head lolled to the side of the butter-soft leather seat to get a better view of her driver. She wondered again how it came to be that she was speeding along the coast toward his beach house on South Padre Island, clad in nothing more than her raincoat and sandals.

Originally he'd insisted she make the drive in the buff, but had finally allowed her to wear her coat for modesty's sake.

She frowned as a memory tugged briefly on her mind, then flittered away. Seemed like there was something she was supposed to do today. But in her dream car—a Jaguar—with the top down, brilliant Texas sun shining on her and a gorgeous driver, it was difficult to concentrate on much else.

He turned to briefly smile at her and reached to trace the upper curve of her partially exposed breast with the tip of one roughened finger.

Her heart fluttered within her chest. It would be so easy to fall in love with him.

His companion dozed, providing Marc with an unobstructed view of her right breast when she listed toward him. He tightened his grip on the wheel and tried to adjust his ever-increasing arousal. And he'd thought his sex drive was waning! He hadn't been so horny since . . . well, ever.

It had to be the woman next to him.

She was gorgeous, blond and had a body designed to give a man pleasure.

But he knew it was more than that. While her attributes were outstanding, many women would qualify. Yet he couldn't imagine doing the outrageous things he'd done last night with anyone else.

There was definitely something about the woman that called to him. Sure, the sex was out of this world, but she appealed to him on a deeper level. Hell, he was addicted to her smile, her scent. He'd never felt so alive, so male, as when he was with her.

Damn. He was supposed to be taking things easy this month. That was the whole purpose for this imposed vacation. Could screwing his brains out be construed as taking it easy? Sexual acrobatics like he'd enjoyed last night might kill him.

He looked at her breast, pink-tinged from the sun, and his mouth went dry. The sports car hit the gravel by the side of the road as he stood on the brake, coasting to a stop behind a deserted truck stop.

His health didn't matter, the car didn't matter. Hell, even the potential of getting caught didn't matter. If he didn't have her now, he would surely die.

Kinsey squirmed in her seat, trying to hold on to the last remnants of a delicious dream involving the stranger in the elevator. The car had stopped, but her eyelids were still too heavy to open.

Warm sunshine bathed her breasts, a slightly cooler breeze caressing her hardening nipples. Her coat must have come open, she mused. Someone might see her. . . . She'd close it in a minute. Right now she just wanted to luxuriate in the feeling. And remember all the glorious sensations from last night. Her night of independence.

Roughened fingers stroked her nipples. She purred her pleasure. If this was still a dream, she didn't want to wake up.

"Open the coat," a deep voice said in her ear. "I want to see and touch all of you. Here. In the sunlight."

She felt him part the trench coat and shivered, her body anxious for the pleasure only this man seemed able to give her.

Hot breath fanned her left nipple an instant before the warm wetness of his mouth latched on to it. His one hand gently squeezed as he suckled, while his other fondled her right breast, taking occasional forays between her now-spread legs.

Restlessness built, but her orgasm took her by surprise. She'd never even had an orgasm before last night, thought they were the stuff of female legend. By light of day, she couldn't believe what she'd been missing for all those years. And speaking of light . . .

Sunlight gently warmed her engorged sex. Combined with the gentle strokes of the man next to her, orgasm number two appeared to be coming up soon.

She clamped her legs together. Enough was enough. Although the things they were doing felt glorious, it had to stop. She'd done nothing for him, and besides, they were on the side of the road! How hedonistic she'd become in just a few short hours.

"Shh." His breath tickled her ear. Gentle hands stroked her legs until her muscles relaxed. His arm reached across her and the seat motor purred, vibrating her swollen labia in a *very* interesting manner.

She found herself lying almost flat on her back, the bright Texas sun hot on her face and breasts. The man spread her legs wider, his breath hot on her almost unbearably sensitive folds. His tongue lapped at her and she felt her bones begin to melt.

When he sucked her nub, she screamed her pleasure, arching off the seat. While he sucked, his long finger slowly went in and out of her as his other hand kept stimulating her breasts.

She was wild with desire, whimpering with need. It was too much and not nearly enough.

Her climax left her wrung out, boneless. She couldn't form a word if her life depended on it.

She should reciprocate. And she would, as soon as she could breath in and out without the effort it took right now.

The car door opened and closed. Footsteps sounded in the gravel before her door opened.

She should probably open her eyes. And she would, but it took so much effort. Her trench coat was tugged from her.

"Raise that pretty little bottom for me, sweetheart."

She did and felt the coat slide out from under her. His hands were back, stroking her. No point in protesting. May as well just relax and enjoy it.

Bare skin brushed against her own when he lifted her from the car. When she was finally able to open her eyes, he towered above her, totally naked. Totally aroused.

She lay on her coat, the fragrant grass tickling her hip. Regardless of the fact that they were behind a building, that they were beside the highway should have appalled her. Surprisingly, it was more appalling to think of not having sex with him.

She opened, hoping he could read her body language.

He was a fast learner.

*   *   *

Sated, they dozed. Kinsey awoke when she was placed on the warm edge of the car. She opened her eyes as he spread her thighs and entered her again in one powerful thrust.

They were on the side of the road. They were naked. They were having sex.

No, more than that.

He flipped her over, still buried deep within her, her breasts pressed against the heat of the metal. He pumped harder. They were fucking like wild animals.

And she didn't care.

Marc looked at the woman, now dozing again in the passenger seat, then back down the road. He couldn't possibly be getting hard again. They'd just done it, twice, not more than a mile or two back. And along the side of the road, for God's sake! What had gotten into him? He looked at her again.

She had gotten into him.

He knew he needed to rest if he ever hoped to get his life back together. Yet the thought of leaving her at the hotel room had been unbearable. For some reason, he needed her as much as he needed his next breath.

Yes, that was it. She was part of his healing process. Therapy. That was why he couldn't bear to part with her. His body demanded her. That was why he invited her to spend the weekend at his rented beach house. It had to be.

He saw the exit for Pleasure Beach and downshifted. Maybe a weekend of passion would get her out of his system and complete the healing process.

"Wake up, we're here." The gruff whisper ruffled the hair by her ear. His lips brushed her jawline, the contact feather-light. Amazing how quickly she'd become accustomed to the feel of his mustache. The sound of his deep voice. His touch.

How could she ever go back to Zachary after knowing the thrill of being in this man's arms?

Answer: She couldn't. After agonizing over whether or not to accept Zachary's proposal, the answer suddenly became obvious. Now came the hard part—telling Zachary.

Kinsey glanced at her weekend no-strings-attached companion. She'd worry about telling Zachary later. Right now it was time to let go of worry and all inhibitions and enjoy.

The man walked around to the open trunk and began unloading his suitcases. Kinsey looked up at her weekend accommodations. Way up.

Made of rough-sawed lumber and glass, the beach house boasted two wraparound porches—one on each level—along with a first-floor patio that opened onto a pristine white sandy beach. A tropical breeze ruffled her hair, caressed her face, reminded her of why she'd always loved the beach.

Yet another difference between her and Zachary. He detested the sand, said the saltwater made his skin itch. She gave her head a little shake, amazed that she'd allowed him to influence her life to such an extent.

Before she could open her door, her escort was there with a hand out to help her. She smiled at the old-world charm and stepped out, tilting her face to the sun.

"You're lucky my hands are full, woman, or I'd ravish you again right here." He growled. "In fact . . ." The suitcases dropped to the sand with a soft thud. "Kissing you is a much better way to occupy my time." His teeth flashed white as he lowered his mouth to hers.

Her knees weakened with the passion of his kiss, her arms pulling him closer as she leaned against the warm car door.

"Let's finish this inside," he whispered against her lips.

Cheeks burning, she looked away. "I can't believe the way I'm behaving! Right out in public!"

His laugh rumbled against her breasts, doing funny things to her breathing. "That's not a problem. This is a private beach." He bent to pick up the suitcases, brilliant blue eyes raking her from toes to head, then meeting her gaze. "We can do whatever we want, whenever we want, wherever we want. There's no one to see us."

He turned and walked up the steps to the glass doors. She watched the play of muscles on his firm backside, her mouth going dry when the fabric of his trousers pulled taut as he dug in a pocket for the key.

Panic washed over her.

What was she doing? She'd spent a wild night, living every sexual fantasy she'd ever had—and a few she'd made up as she went along—with a total and complete stranger. Oh, sure, it had been her brilliant idea to not even exchange names. But . . . he could be an ax murderer or rapist for all she knew. Or a serial killer.

An immediate picture of him stabbing a box of cereal had her stifling a giggle as she walked up the steps. She knew, on a deeper level, that this man was none of those things. And although it was far from her style, she intended to use him shamelessly this weekend, and damn the consequences. Like Scarlett O'Hara, she'd worry about that tomorrow.

"Care to join me after we get settled in?" The man nodded toward a hot tub that bubbled merrily on the corner of the deck with a magnificent view of the Gulf of Mexico.

Kinsey grinned. "Absolutely." She looked up through her lashes. "But I didn't bring a suit."

His smile widened. "No problem. Neither did I." He stroked her hair from her face. "Don't look so apprehensive—"

"I'm not! It's just that, well, we really don't know each other that well and—"

"Hey, you're the one who refused to tell me her name. You

wanted to just enjoy each other. No strings. No commitment. Those were your exact words." His eyes narrowed. "Changed your mind?"

Her hair brushed her cheeks when she shook her head. "No. I think our original deal is still the best plan."

"You're sure? I don't mind if you want to tell me your name. Or anything else, for that matter."

"Hey, trying to change the rules before we even begin our weekend?" Her smile felt brittle. This was what she'd wanted. And he was right. Her idea, her rules. "Last one in the hot tub has to cook dinner!"

Marc held up the sheer ruffled apron he'd found in the pantry and wondered at his sanity.

He'd suffered a minor, but nonetheless terrifying, medical warning sign less than a month ago. If conditions did not change, he could have serious cardiac problems. Jack, his best friend and cardiologist, had just given him the green light for resuming normal activities a few days ago, along with news of his enforced vacation.

He wadded up the apron and tossed it back into the pantry drawer. Jack would, in all likelihood, not consider his recent sexual exploits "normal activity."

Maybe it was his recent brush with his own mortality that had him wanting to howl at the moon whenever a certain blonde entered his thoughts, much less the room.

Regardless, time away from the hospital was exactly what he'd needed. With or without sex.

He walked toward the doorway and stopped to watch his date gingerly lower herself into the steaming tub on the deck. Within seconds, he'd shed his clothes and strode across the deck.

How could the most intense pleasure he'd ever known hurt him? And even if it killed him . . . what a way to go!

5

Kinsey closed her eyes and concentrated on the churning water that lifted her breasts, jiggling them in a very intriguing way.

The door behind her slid open and shut. Although she couldn't pick up another sound, she knew immediately when *he* joined her.

She opened her eyes to find him intently watching her. His stare set off a tingle deep within her. She'd never considered herself a particularly sexual being, yet found sexual thoughts constantly with her since meeting this man.

Deliberately keeping her gaze cool, she returned his look. Neither spoke for several minutes.

"I'm glad you agreed to spend the weekend with me," he said, moving closer. "And I know we agreed to keep it anonymous. But . . . tell me your name?"

In truth, she'd been dying to know his name, too. Would that put a crimp in the weekend? Probably not. "Okay, how about this . . . first names only. Can you live with that?"

His mustache quirked with his little smile. "I guess it'll have to do. For now." He reached back and handed her a glass of champagne, then retrieved his own. "To this weekend, my beautiful but mysterious companion and ... endless possibilities."

Their rims clinked. Eyes held as they sipped the cool wine. Kinsey concentrated on not breathing in the tiny bubbles as she drank, then held the champagne in her mouth to warm it before swallowing. "Okay, now that I've agreed, what's your name?"

His eyes looked impossibly blue over the rim of his glass. He took a leisurely sip. "Ladies first."

Should she reveal her real name? Would that lead to other complications, complications she wasn't ready to deal with at this point? She could always make up something. After all, she didn't even bring her purse. He'd have no way of knowing whether or not it was really her name.

She dismissed that thought almost as soon as it came. Then again, she could use Karly's name. As identical twins, they had at one time been one being, so the name was *almost* hers. But what if he called out "her" name during sex? Could she bear hearing another woman's name during such an intimate act? Especially her sister? Nope. Too high on the creep meter.

"It's not a difficult question," he said with a slow smile. "I bet you've known your name most of your life."

"Kinsey." She wasn't the only Kinsey in the world. It wasn't as though she'd told him her entire name. So why did she feel so vulnerable?

"Kinsey? Really?" He leaned closer and she nodded. "You're sure you're telling the truth?"

"I'm sure."

He swept her onto his lap and held her close. "Hello, Kinsey." His mouth brushed hers, his firm thighs pressing intimately against her bottom. "I'm Marcus—Marc to my friends. And you're definitely one of my friends." His lips took possession, his tongue boldly thrusting into her oh-so-eager mouth.

Kinsey clamped her legs tightly closed, willing herself not to squirm on his lap. Wow! The guy—*Marc*—sure knew how to kiss! The combination of champagne, hot bubbling water and hot male was bone-meltingly potent.

"Take me!" she demanded, her lips barely leaving his as she straddled him. "Now!"

All it took was one powerful thrust of his hips. Her climax washed over her in a tidal wave of sensations, almost drowning her in its intensity.

His hips pumped into her, faster and faster. His grip on her hips tightened to the point of pain. To her amazement, a fraction of a second after he stiffened and shouted his satisfaction, yet another wave washed over her, leaving her gasping in its aftermath.

Too weak to lift her head, much less leave the warmth of his arms, she rested her forehead on his collarbone and took deep, shuddering breaths, waiting for her heart to resume its normal cadence.

Marc's hands shook when he pushed a tendril of wet hair from her face. His lips warm—also breathing irregular, she noticed—he strung tiny kisses from her hairline to the tip of her nose.

"Kinsey?"

"Hmm?" It happened again. Her bones had melted. She couldn't move if her life depended on it.

"Last night was amazing. Unbelievable. Earth shattering." She felt him shrug. "Easily the best time of my life. But—Kinsey, are you listening to me?"

"Uh-huh." She snuggled closer.

His hands slid to her shoulders and his grip tightened. He lifted her away, still gripping her shoulders. Drat. Must be important.

She opened heavy lids and blinked sleepily in an effort to bring his handsome face into focus.

"While it was wonderful, I have a confession to make."

That woke her up. "What?" She was almost afraid to hear his answer.

"I'm exhausted! I need a nap."

She laughed and slumped against him in relief.

"C'mon, lady. Let's go take a nap."

"You mean a sleep-type nap?" Although the idea definitely appealed to her, the reality of actually getting any sleep next to such a splendid specimen seemed slim.

"Eventually," he said, then stood with her in his arms, grinning down at her. "I think I saw some body lotion on the bathroom counter. What do you say to a deep massage, then a quick nap?"

She slid down his already partially aroused body until her bare feet touched the warm wood of the deck. She turned and immediately his arms went around her, his hands cupping her breasts. Their erotic reflection winked back at her from the glass doors. Although it was slipping quickly from her to-do list, she felt compelled to ask, "Marc? How about that massage now?"

She watched the top of his head in the glass as he bent to kiss the sides of her neck. There ought to be some sort of law against being so gorgeous. Not to mention sexy.

One of his hands reached to open the door while the other still toyed with her nipple. Before she could draw the next breath, he swept her into his arms again and stepped into the cool darkness of the house.

Her eyes adjusted as he strode through the living room. It appeared to be decorated with a private retreat in mind, judging by the amount of candles, the fireplace and varied textures of the plushly upholstered furniture.

The stairway passed in a blur to open into a huge second-floor room, one whole wall of which was a gigantic curved window. The view of the beach and surging surf was breathtaking.

She scarcely noticed the coolness of the quilted silk bedspread when he deposited her on the big, round brass bed.

"Cool, huh?" He reached for a remote on the nightstand. "Watch this." He pushed a button and a whirring sound filled the room. The curved glass began to part, sliding back into the walls.

The sound of surf hitting the sand echoed against the curve of the opposing wall and bounced back.

It was all so overwhelming, she could do little else besides smile. It was like being in the heart of a giant seashell. Amazing.

Marc stretched out beside her, a bottle of body lotion in one hand. "I promised a weekend at the beach. Since we aren't actually on the beach, I thought the least I could do was bring it to you."

She looped her arms around his neck and pulled his face close enough to brush his lips with hers. "It's great! Thank you so much for bringing me!"

"The weekend is just beginning." He chewed his lower lip a moment, then asked, "Do you trust me, Kinsey?"

With the next heartbeat, she knew she did and nodded.

His hands slid down her arms to clasp her hands in his much larger ones. She blinked and found her arms above her head, her wrists held loosely in some kind of soft bond. She twisted her head to look. Velvet. Each wrist was secured within a padded red velvet loop that hung from either knob on the headboard. Her heart hammered. "What are you doing?"

"They came with the furnishings." He shrugged. "I thought we might give them a try, unless you don't want to, but I thought maybe . . ." He leaned closer, his breath ruffling her hair. "Don't be afraid," he whispered. "If you're uncomfortable with it or want me to stop, just say the word."

Oh, she was uncomfortable all right, but loving every minute of it. "Don't stop," she whispered back.

His teeth flashed white against his tan in the semidarkened

bedroom. "The lotion was in a warmer, so it shouldn't be too cold." He squeezed and she watched with detached fascination as a stream of pale cream fell from his fist to draw a line between her breasts, down her abdomen, around her pubic bone, then down each thigh. *Don't move, don't squirm. What's he going to do next?*

The bottle fell to the carpeted floor with a dull thud as each of his big hands spanned her thighs just above her knees and began rubbing in the lotion.

Slow, even strokes took his hands higher and higher. Moisture pooled and it was all she could do to stop from arching toward him when his thumbs brushed her weeping flesh.

When his hands left her she swallowed a whimper, only to all but purr when they resumed the sensual massage, this time spreading the slick lotion carefully over each breast. His thumbs and forefingers rubbed and prodded her nipples into stiff peaks, making them ache for more.

He smiled and blew on them, causing them to draw even tighter. The tip of his tongue flicked over the tips, then his hands continued their path downward. Rubbing, constantly rubbing the lotion into her hot skin, ever closer, ever lower.

At her pubic bone, he paused. He leaned over and placed a tender kiss on her navel, the pads of his thumbs tracing the top edge of her bone. They followed what would have been her line of pubic hair had she not indulged in her first Brazilian wax. Slick and hairless, her skin was a quivering mass of sensation. He carefully rubbed the lotion into her skin, the pads of his thumbs brushing against her swollen flesh.

She gasped and squirmed, anxious to return his torture, eager to touch as she'd been touched. "Please," she said on a breathy sigh. "Untie me. I want to touch you."

His eyes sparkled, a dimple flashed. He slid up her, further inflaming her with a full frontal-body massage. His hands dragged lotion up the length of her arms. At the velvet bonds, he massaged her wrists, eyes locked with hers.

"I want you to touch me, too. But not yet. If you do, it will all be over too soon." He stretched to kiss the inside of each wrist, then slid back down until his hot breath fanned her moistness.

"But I—ahh!" His tongue dragged along her opening, lapping at the proof of her arousal. She groaned.

He groaned in response, setting off wondrous vibrations deep within her.

The pointed tip of his tongue probed, then retreated before she could fully enjoy the sensation. Each thrust went a little deeper. But not deep enough.

Her moans of frustration mingled with the sound of the surf. She felt the pounding of the waves on the shore with each beat of her heart.

His tongue delved deep, swirling within her. Her cry of climax echoed with the surf.

Did anyone ever die from coming so many times? She struggled for breath, then realized she'd clamped her thighs firmly together under the force of her orgasm. To her horror, she'd inadvertently trapped his head. She ordered her thighs to relax, but they seemed to have a will of their own.

He didn't seem to mind. His tongue was still doing almost unbearably exciting things to her nub. When he gently nipped it, wave number two washed over her.

Gasping, she yanked her hands from their velvet prison, then pulled and tugged until he was positioned between her legs, the head of his penis so close she felt it pulse. Her hands gripped his firm buttocks and she pulled as she thrust her hips forward.

He was buried to the hilt; his eyes widened and sought hers. Gazes locked, they began the ancient dance.

Afterward he collapsed on her, his weight a welcome anchor. When their breathing returned to somewhat normal, he rolled to his side and tucked her tightly against him.

He gently brushed her hair from her face and placed a lingering kiss on her temple. "So," he said against her skin, "you're not married, are you?"

6

"Married!" Her attempted laugh sounded forced, even to her. "Don't be ridiculous!" A sudden thought hit her hard, caused her heart to trip. She twisted in an effort to see his face. "Are you?" More scared than she could remember being in her adult life, she could barely force the words from her lips.

His arms tightened around her shoulder and he kissed the top of her head. "Married? Nope." His thumb rubbed the side of her breast. "Never even came close."

It felt silly to be so pleased by his words, but she couldn't help it. She snuggled deeper within his embrace, lulled by the sound of his heartbeat against her ear.

What a wonderful way to fall asleep, she thought as she began to drift off, the sound of surf a gentle lullaby.

Marc felt the last of Kinsey's muscles relax in sleep and gathered her closer, kissing the top of her head. Her hair smelled of flowery shampoo and sunshine.

He willed himself to relax and get some rest. The insatiable woman beside him would wear him out if he didn't get some sleep.

Sleep wouldn't come.

Instead, images flashed through his mind. Some good, like his first encounter with Kinsey. Some fantastic, like every erotic moment they'd had since they met.

Some terrifying. Like the unholy pain crushing his chest as he drove himself to the ER, and the aching, almost useless feeling in his left arm. As a physician, he knew the symptoms of an impending cardiac arrest as well as anyone. He had them all. Funny, though—as he had lain on the gurney waiting for Jack, the thing that scared him most was the numbness of his arm and hand. Very scary stuff for a left-handed surgeon.

Almost as scary as dying alone, with no one to miss you or grieve for you.

Kinsey twitched in her sleep and hitched one smooth leg over his, causing a meltdown around his heart. A heart many had claimed impervious to feeling anything.

He stiffened, trying not to crush her against him. Feelings of any sort were semiforeign to him. Yet when he looked at Kinsey, or even thought about her, fierce possession stabbed him. He swallowed and looked down at her face.

Was this love?

And if it were love, what would happen when the weekend was over? She'd made her intentions very clear. One wild weekend, no strings. He had agreed. Could he convince her to change her mind?

The thought of their relationship—and yes, damnit, it *was* a relationship!—ending with the weekend was unacceptable. Somehow, between now and Sunday night, he had to convince her to stay or at least see him again.

Kinsey woke slowly, sated lethargy deep within her muscles. She reached across the pillow to find nothing but cool sheets and an empty pillow. She traced the indentation where Marc's head had rested, then raised her head and looked around. Where was he anyway?

While they'd slept, the sun had almost set. A fine line of pink edged the water line in the distance. The air from the open wall had taken on a distinct chill.

She sat up, pulling the top sheet around her. "Marc?" Emptiness answered her. Grasping the sheet, she scooted off the bed and padded toward what must be the bathroom.

It was.

Tiny lit candles surrounded a sunken whirlpool tub, its water quietly churning. Gardenias floated in several glass bowls filled with water, releasing their pungent aroma with the warm humidity.

"He can't be far," she murmured. "May as well enjoy the bath while I can." The sheet dropped to the plush, carpeted floor as she climbed onto the pedestal surrounding the tub and stepped into the water.

With a sigh, she closed her eyes. A girl could definitely get used to this.

"Kinsey? Kinsey, wake up, babe. You're turning into a prune." Warm lips punctuated his words. Kinsey smiled and lazily opened her eyes.

"Hi." He sat on edge of the tub, smiling down at her.

She reached for his hand and squeezed his fingers. "Hi, yourself." She stretched and tried to hide her smile at the way his eyes tracked her breasts through the bubbling water. "Where were you? I thought you were exhausted and needed a nap."

"I was, but couldn't sleep." His smile broadened. "I think it had something to do with the sexiness of my bed partner."

She returned his smile. "Really? I slept just fine."

"Thanks." He tweaked her nose. "Are you hungry? The place comes fully stocked, but I don't want to take time to cook on our first night. I figured we could either order out or go somewhere. There's a list of good restaurants by the phone in the kitchen."

He helped her get out of the tub, his eyes busily raking her from head to toe. She wrapped a yellow bath towel securely beneath her arms and smiled up at him.

"In case you haven't noticed, Marc, I'm a little, ah, underdressed to go out to dinner."

He slid his arms around her and tugged her close to nibble her neck. "Oh, yeah, I noticed all right." He pulled the towel from her and captured a peaked nipple between his lips.

Just as her knees were about to buckle and all thoughts of food left her mind, he released her and stepped back, replacing the towel. When he'd tucked it securely, he smiled at her. "While you were snoring—"

"Excuse me? I do *not* snore!" Clutching her towel, she stepped back.

"Of course, my mistake. As I said, while you were sleeping, I went shopping." He reached beside the tub and held up two bulging shopping bags she hadn't noticed. They were from a pricey boutique she'd always dreamed of patronizing. "Let's go inspect your loot." He grabbed her hand and led her into the living room.

A fire blazed merrily in the fireplace. He stopped at a shaggy rug in front of the stone hearth and sat down, pulling her onto his lap.

"My towel will get your shorts all wet," she protested as she tried to scoot away.

"Good point." Before she realized his intentions, he whisked the towel from her and tossed it onto the couch. Well out of reach. "Now stop wiggling or you'll get more than you bargained for, shorts or no shorts." He waggled his eyebrows and grinned. "Most likely, no shorts would be my guess."

Feeling more carefree than she'd felt in ages, she made a big production of getting settled, delighted when he growled in her ear.

"Are you finished, ma'am?"

"For now," she answered smugly.

"Brat." He reached into the first bag and pulled out what appeared to be a bunch of strings. "Here's a bathing suit for you, in case you don't feel comfortable on the beach naked. Although I vote for naked."

"I'm sure you do." She reached for the silken strings of vivid colors. "This has to be just one step above naked. You call this a bathing suit?"

"Yes, ma'am. Saw it on a mannequin myself. Soon as I laid eyes on it, I knew you'd be dynamite in it."

"Uh-huh. A mannequin. Do you by chance remember how the mannequin was wearing it? Because I gotta tell you, it's a stretch for me to even see this thing as a bathing suit." She dangled the multicolored strings in front of his face. "If you don't remember how it goes, I can't see me ever getting the thing on correctly."

His smile gleamed white by firelight. "Well, even if we can't figure out how it goes, we're bound to have a hell of a good time trying to figure it out."

Heat filled her cheeks and she looked away. "What else did you get?"

He stiffened beneath her, as though expecting a physical blow. She shifted to get a better look at his face. The guy actually looked embarrassed. What could he have possibly bought that would embarrass him, especially after the last twenty-four hours?

"Marc? What is it?"

He swallowed. Hard. "Now, keep an open mind, Kinsey." He reached into the bag. "And try to remember how sexy I think you are and how much I want you. All the time. I—"

"Just show it to me, Marc. Please."

He pulled out a short length of filmy, almost totally sheer dark fabric, followed by a scrap of the same fabric masquerading as a pair of panties. Risqué, yes. Sexy, definitely.

"They're lovely." What there was of them.

"They're from a sex shop," he said bluntly.

"Really? I had no idea those types of places carried fine lingerie. They—"

"Have holes."

"Huh?" What was he talking about? It was immediately apparent when he demonstrated by sticking a finger through a large embroidered hole in the crotch of the panties, then inserted an index finger through the tip of each cup on the top. "Oh," she finished in a weak voice.

"Yeah, 'oh.' And it gets better. Check this out." He moved the panties closer to the firelight and stuck his finger through them again. Then she saw it. Around the embroidered hole, there was a pair of embroidered hot pink lips.

She couldn't help it. Laughter bubbled up and erupted in a shriek. At his stunned expression, she doubled over, trying desperately to contain herself. What if Marc was hurt by her hilarity? Wiping her eyes, telling herself to get a grip, she turned to see Marc's shoulders hunched. *Oh, no.*

She touched his cotton-covered shoulder and he turned. Tears of mirth streaked down his face. He took a deep breath, then went off again, deep laughter beaming off the walls. He held up the panties and wiggled his finger. The crotch looked like it was sticking its tongue out. Kinsey lost it, rolling on the floor.

When they'd finally calmed down, she wiped her eyes with the edge of her discarded towel. "Marc, no offense, but what possessed you to buy those things?"

"You," he answered softly, his gaze caressing every inch of her exposed skin. "When I'm with you, or, obviously, thinking about you, I become sex crazed. There's no other logical explanation." He sighed and tossed the lingerie back into the bag. "I'll take them back tomorrow."

"Over my dead body."

"What? But I thought you—"

"I've never had anybody want me the way you want me, Marc." She stroked his jaw. "If you think I would look sexy in them, then I'll wear them. For you. Tonight."

"Tonight is too far away." He loomed over her, yanking at his open shirt. "So is the bedroom." The shirt hit the floor and slid halfway under the couch. "While I was shopping, all I could think of was you. How you looked. How you tasted. How I wanted to make love to you in every room in this house." He shucked his safari shorts, revealing no underwear beneath. "I want to start here. Now."

"Yes," she said against his lips as they sank back onto the rug.

7

Marc rubbed Kinsey's bare shoulder. She sighed and burrowed closer to his heart. "Kins?"

She immediately tensed.

"Kinsey? What's wrong?" He leaned back so he could see her face. "Did I say or do something wrong?"

"No, of course not. It's just . . . well, my sister calls me Kins." She shrugged. "I guess I just wasn't expecting it."

"Would you rather I didn't call you that?" He held his breath.

"No, it's fine. Really. Just unexpected." She settled back against him, one hand petting his chest.

So she had a sister. Were they close? What was their age difference? Did they look anything alike? Of course, he couldn't ask those questions without breaking their agreement. But it was a minor victory that she'd shared that much more of herself.

Maybe by the time his vacation was over he would know all about the mysterious Kinsey. Maybe it would be enough to get her out of his system.

He watched the rise and fall of her breast against his side and gnashed his teeth.

Maybe not.

"Marc?" Kinsey came back in and sat down on the sofa, legs curled beneath her, wearing nothing but his shirt. The woman made his teeth ache.

He cleared his throat and turned from stoking the fire. "Hmm?"

She handed him the cell phone she'd asked to borrow a few moments before. Presumably to check her messages. "Thanks. Um, are all those things from, you know, a sex shop?"

Only in my darkest fantasies. "No. They're from the same place I bought the bathing suit."

She shifted, giving him a brief glimpse of her smooth folds. He'd never had sex with a woman who had no pubic hair. It was erotic as hell. He couldn't imagine doing it the other way again. Hell, he couldn't imagine having sexual relations ever again in his life with anyone other than Kinsey.

He blinked and made a production of replacing the fireplace tool while he absorbed that last revelation. The shock immediately gave way to an intense feeling of rightness.

But, as revelations go, it was big. Maybe even life-altering. He hoped.

Now . . . to get Kinsey to see it that way, too. That might prove to be a major problem. Luckily, problem solving was one of his strong points.

"So," he said as he sat down and oh-so-casually put his arm around her shoulder, "do you want to check out the rest of the stuff I bought for you or will you trust me to pick out something for you to wear to dinner?" He held his breath while she hesitated. She shifted against him and it was all he could do to restrain himself from running his hand up her smooth expanse of leg to play with all that soft skin.

"I think . . . I'll trust you."

She didn't look all that sure, but he jumped from the couch with more than a little relief. If she trusted him enough to wear what he picked out in public, trusting him with more details of her life had to be close at hand.

"Let's take a shower, then get ready and go."

She shied away from his hand and stepped toward the hall. "I don't think that would be a very good idea, Marc. I see that gleam in your eye. I'm hungry. If you get in the shower with me, we both know it will be a long time before I get any food."

"Okay, but make it snappy. I'll lay your clothes on the bed." He stepped to the hall and called after her, "And don't use up all the hot water! I don't know how big the tank is."

Kinsey nodded her thanks to the waiter and sat down, resisting the urge to pull at her neckline. The sundress Marc chose had a built-in push-up bra. On anyone who wore less than a C cup, it would be perfectly modest. On her double-Ds, it was almost illegal.

The sweetheart neckline plunged deeply between her breasts, its edge barely concealing her areolae. The stretchy fabric of the skirt portion—well, what there was of it—was so clingy that even a thong left a panty line. Which was how she came to be sitting in one of the island's more posh restaurants in no underwear. She tried not to think of her sandals as hooker shoes. Even her toes felt exposed.

Did everyone know she was braless and pantyless? If the attention she'd drawn as she walked into the dining room was any indication, they did.

And she'd never actually seen anyone devour something with their eyes until she saw the way Marc looked at her. Her perfume made even her own mouth water; somehow he'd known her taste and bought a small one hundred–dollar–plus bottle of the fragrance she'd been lusting after.

Marc signaled the waiter. She hadn't even picked up her menu. Surely he wasn't planning to order already.

"Yes, sir," the waiter said, approaching their table, eyes glued to her cleavage.

"Would it be possible to be seated in the aquarium room?" Marc asked, discreetly folding a bill into the waiter's hand. "A booth, perhaps?"

"Of course," the waiter said with a smile. "Just give me a moment to prepare a table."

At her raised brow, Marc explained, "They have a huge aquarium surrounded by high-backed, padded booths. It's spectacular. Very secluded."

Oh, she knew how secluded it was, all right. She and her date had dined here on her prom night. She'd bet she could pick out the very spot where she'd lost her virginity, even after all these years. For that reason, she'd always avoided this restaurant like the plague.

Odd—now that she thought about it—that she'd felt only a rush of pleasure at the thought of coming here with Marc tonight.

The waiter returned and led them toward the back, through a padded arch and down a ramp into the center path around the aquarium.

Kinsey braced for the flood of bad memories, but instead found the aquarium breathtaking with its myriad of brightly colored fish. The gentle bubbling of the water soothed her and she realized there was nowhere else she'd rather be at this moment. With this man.

"Do you like it?" Marc's voice was low and intimate, sending shivers up her bare arms.

"Yes, it's beautiful. Thank you. It was a wonderful idea."

He grinned, obviously pleased by her words, and opened a menu.

Their waiter set a basket of hot bread and a vial of melted butter on their table and left as silently as he'd come.

An instant later, she felt Marcus's hand glide along her thigh. He paused briefly before skimming her hipbone to delve long fingers between her legs.

Their eyes met.

The very tips of his fingers danced in and out of her moist folds. Eyes never leaving hers, he whispered, "Close the doors."

It was then that she noticed they were in a privacy booth that had fold-back doors with an internal hook-style lock. She rose on unsteady legs, tight skirt bunched around her naked hips, and reached to tug the doors shut, the fabric of their padded edges whispering against each other.

When she turned, he was standing, the breadbasket on the far end of the booth beside the neatly folded tablecloth, the stoneware pitcher of melted butter in his hand.

He inclined his head, his other hand reaching to help her up on the table.

Cold marble met her heated skin, sending a bolt of longing through her. Regardless of what Marc had in mind, she was more than eager to participate.

Crossing her arms over her chest, she grabbed handfuls of dress and swept it off and over to join the tablecloth.

Her naked back met the tabletop, the coldness causing her already aroused nipples to pucker even more.

Marc stood between her spread legs. He raised the pitcher and let a fine stream of warm melted butter dribble between her breasts, down her stomach. Downward it trickled. Its oily warmth traced her groin, skimmed along the crease of her feminine folds. It took tremendous effort to not squirm under his sensuous assault.

She watched Marc slowly lower his head, and held her breath. Hot hands slicked the butter over her thighs, spreading her wider, opening for the first touch of his tongue.

The tip of his tongue drew lazy circles around the very place that yearned for his touch. Kinsey bit her lip to keep from begging.

Finally, *finally*, the pointed tip of his tongue outlined her opening before lazily lapping every drop of butter from her folds, paying special attention to the hard nub until she grabbed a piece of bread and stuffed it in her mouth to keep from screaming her pleasure.

Marc's fingers replaced his tongue, driving her even higher, her sex at the fever pitch. All during the time, his tongue busily licked and sucked all the remaining butter from her skin.

She came twice before she could get his pants down to his knees. Scooting to the edge of the table, she pushed at his arms. "Hands above your head," she whispered, licking her lips in anticipation.

He obeyed, his heated gaze devouring her, nostrils flared in anticipation.

She poured the remaining butter into her palm. "Oh, no. It's almost gone." Her grin devilish, she looked him in the eye and rubbed her palms together. "Oh, well." She sighed. "I guess we'll just have to make do, huh?"

Marc couldn't have formed a coherent sentence had his life depended on it. Instead, he just swallowed and nodded. He watched the rise and fall of her breasts, her pebbled nipples, and knew she was just as turned on as he was. If she didn't get on with it, he might actually have that heart attack he'd feared.

Her small hands felt hot when they slid up and down his rock-hard cock, gliding in the butter. But their heat was nothing compared to her talented lips and mouth. He groaned and forced his knees to lock in order to stay standing.

When she'd licked every bit of butter from him, plus a little, he could stand it no longer. Gripping her upper arms, he lifted her back to the table and thrust deeply.

"Yesss!" she hissed, pulling him tightly against her while she wrapped her legs around his waist.

She tensed and clenched around his sex. He swallowed her moan of satisfaction. Within seconds, she returned the favor to keep their tryst from becoming public knowledge.

Damp and shaking with suppressed laughter at their ridiculous situation, they finally separated and tidied their clothes.

"I can't believe what we just did," she said as she helped him straighten the tablecloth and replace the basket.

He nodded. "Yeah, it's not like we've been exactly depriving ourselves of sex or don't have a perfectly good bed at home."

Home. A wave of sadness washed over Kinsey at the thought of their weekend drawing to a close. "Speaking of home," she said with forced lightness, "I should probably get back. I have to work tomorrow."

He stared pointedly. "What do you do?" He raised his hand to stop her protest. "It's not like it's a state secret." He leaned closer. "It's not, is it?"

"No, of course not." She chewed her lip, then said, "I'm a kindergarten teacher." Well, Karly was actually the teacher, but it seemed like a better profession to have with a lover than to tell him you were a financial analyst. "What about you?"

His smile was white against his tan. "I'm *not* a teacher."

A slap in the face could not have stung her more. Tears immediately blurred her vision. With a last tug at her dress, she stood and unhooked the doors. The waiter stood directly in front of her, a smug smile on his thin lips.

"Call me a cab, would you, please? I'll be in the bar." With that, she charged toward the bar, not turning or even slowing down at the sound of Marc's voice calling to her to come back.

* * *

Kinsey stirred her mimosa and wondered if she should have turned down the man's offer to buy her another. A glance over her shoulder confirmed she'd made the right decision.

Marc stood in the bar doorway, fists clenched, blue fire shooting straight at her. She'd run, but there was no place to go.

Besides, after her last flamboyant exit, she'd remembered she had no purse and no money or credit cards. No way to pay for the cab she'd so adamantly insisted she'd take.

Marc reached her in less than three strides. "Kinsey," he said in a low voice, his mouth close to her ear. "Please. Come back and have dinner."

"I shared another part of myself with you, Marc—assuming that *is* your name. And what did you do? Blew me off with some flip remark. As if—as if—" To her horror, her voice was choked with tears.

"As if I didn't care? As if what we've shared together meant nothing?" He gripped her arms and pulled her from the bar stool, her breasts pressed flat against his heaving chest. "Hmm? Is that what you were going to say?" His fingers bit into her upper arms. "Who did you call this afternoon, Kinsey? For that matter, is Kinsey *your* real name?"

"Yes," she whispered. "of course it's my real name." She sniffed. "I called to check my messages, not that it's any of your business." He didn't need to know she'd been so lust-crazed that she'd blown off her sister and had to call to make sure Karly hadn't called out the National Guard to launch a manhunt.

He crushed her to him, kissing the top of her head. "What are we doing to each other?" he asked in a ragged voice.

In response, she could only shake her head.

He tilted her face to his with his index finger under her chin. "I know we agreed not to discuss anything personal. We agreed to keep it on a first-name-only basis. I breached that agreement by asking what you did." He swallowed and met her gaze. "I—I'm sorry. If it would help, I can tell you what I do. I'm—"

"It's not necessary, Marc, really." Besides, with his work-roughened hands, swagger, boots and huge belt buckle proclaiming him the champion calf roper of 2001, it was a no-brainer. He obviously made a living with his hands, and if he wasn't a cowboy, he was at least a farmer of sorts. And, judging by the car he drove, a fairly successful one. Of course, she knew he could be one of those types that sank every cent he earned into his vehicle.

She'd never dated anyone who actually did physical labor for a living. Not that she was a snob—it was just the way things worked out. She glanced down at Marc's chapped thumb rubbing small circles on her arm. It was actually sexy as all get-out.

"We only have a few more hours, tops," he said in a low voice, his eyelids hooded. "Do you really want to spend it fighting or giving each other the third degree?"

"No," she said softly. "Can we go back to the beach house? I'm not hungry."

"Me neither. Except for you, sweet thing. Only for you." His lips brushed against her mouth. "Let's go home."

Kinsey sighed in contentment and leaned against the side of the hot tub. "I still haven't used my bathing suit," she reminded him.

"How about next weekend? Can you get away?" He nuzzled her shoulder.

"Yes." Oh, my God, did she sound too eager? "You'll still be here?"

"I have the place rented for the month, so I'll be here for the next three weekends." He kissed the tip of her nose. "Please tell me I won't be spending them alone."

She pulled his mouth down to hers and let him know in the only way they seemed good at communicating that she'd be delighted to share the weekends with him. With only a few more hours to create memories that would last until the next weekend, talking was the last thing on her mind.

8

"Kinsey? Kins! Are you here?" Karly's voice carried through the bathroom door.

Weary from the weekend, the walk from the shopping center at which she'd insisted Marc drop her, and crying her eyes out since she'd let herself into her sister's house, Kinsey stood from the bubbles and wrapped herself in a bath sheet. "Yeah, it's me. Just a sec."

She padded to the door and turned the lock. The door immediately flew open, her sister barreling into her.

"Oh! Sorry. Didn't know you were so close." Karly stomped over to the commode and sat down. "Well? Where have you been? More importantly, with whom? And don't lie to me, Kins. I know your mysterious weekend beach trip and short call to tell me you weren't dead had something to do with a man. And my gut also tells me it was not Dr. Dull. Out with it!"

All their lives, Karly and Kinsey had told each other everything. Yet now, when it felt so damned important, so life-altering, she felt herself wanting to close Karly off. Hold her weekend with Marc close to her heart. Her own sexy and oh-so-personal secret.

But Karly waited and, by the look on her face, would not back down.

"I decided to take your advice—"

"My advice? About what?"

Kinsey cleaned the now empty tub, stalling for time. Karly reached out to grab the brush from her sister. "Would you stop doing that, Kinsey, and *talk* to me? I know you. I know something monumental happened to keep you away all weekend. Spit it out."

"Like I said, I took your advice about having a final fling before I marry Zachary—"

"Oh, my Lord! *Please* tell me you didn't tell Zach you'd marry him!" Karly clutched Kinsey's arm.

"No, of course not." The way Karly slumped against the toilet tank would have been almost comical if Kinsey didn't feel so guilty at hiding things from her. "And you're right. I did meet someone. In the elevator on the way to my room."

"Woo-hoo!" Karly pumped her fist in the air. "Go, girl! I knew you had it in you! So . . . I want, I *need* details! Give."

Karly reached into the cabinet and pulled out her stash of licorice. Both twins kept a stash. It was used to celebrate and commiserate. Karly took a piece and passed the sack to Kinsey.

The sisters chewed in companionable silence. When Karly began looking pointedly at her, Kinsey knew it was time to throw out at least a tidbit of information. Would Karly think she was a terrible person? The thought was a physical pain. The rest of the world could take a flying leap, but if Karly thought badly of her . . .

"What the hell is this?" Karly held up the miniscule red dress between her thumb and forefinger. "And what's all over it?"

* * *

Jack McMillan slipped into the padded booth in the bar at Marc's favorite steak house in Corpus Christi, a scowl on his tanned face. "What are you doing back? I thought you were taking my advice and getting an entire month of rest."

Marc sipped at the sweating gin and tonic, then carefully placed it on the soggy napkin before answering. "I am. Just visiting for the evening."

"Uh-huh. That's why I got the call from my service to meet you here ASAP? There's something going on. I know you." He glanced at his watch. "I have a dinner date in less than an hour. I suggest you spit it out."

"I met someone."

Jack's green eyes crinkled with his broad smile. The new short cut of his red hair made it seem to stand at attention. "Great! About damned time! So, what? You don't need my permission to date, buddy." He waved away the waitress and leaned in. "You do look sort of tired, now that I think about it. You haven't experienced any more chest pains or other symptoms, have you?"

"No! Of course not. If I had I'd have called you sooner than this." He shredded the edge of the cocktail napkin with his thumb. "It's just, well . . . man, this is stupid." He threw some bills on the table and stood. "Forget I called. Tell Mardee I said hi."

"Wait!" Jack grabbed Marc's sports-coat sleeve. "Like I said, I know you. I know you didn't call and ask me to meet you here for no reason. What's going on?"

Marc looked down at the open, freckled face of the man who'd been his best friend since undergraduate days. Jack was right. He had called for a reason. What was the big deal about sharing information on his weekend?

"So, what's her name?" Jack asked when Marc reclaimed his seat.

"Kinsey."

"And where did you meet this Kinsey?"

Pictures flashed in Marc's mind, causing him to become partially aroused at the memory. "In the elevator at the Breakers Hotel."

"The one in South Padre? I thought you decided not to attend that conference?"

"I had, but decided at the last minute to go since I was going to be in the vicinity anyway."

Jack snorted and glared at him. "Marc, that's exactly my point with this enforced vacation! There's a reason it's called a vacation. What the hell made you go to a medical conference?"

"Proximity." He waved his empty glass at the cocktail waitress, who nodded. "Hey, if I hadn't gone, I'd never have met Kinsey." The waitress brought a fresh drink and left. "She's a kindergarten teacher."

Jack's eyebrows rose. "Oh, yeah? Not your typical date. Something you need to announce, big guy?"

Marc frowned into his drink. Was there something more than blistering sex? He would have liked to believe there was. He genuinely liked Kinsey, could possibly be growing to love her. She had to feel something, too. His gut told him it couldn't all be one-sided. "It's too early." He grinned at his friend. "But let's say I'm cautiously optimistic about this one."

"Wow. That *is* big. What's it been? A year since the princess dropped you? More?"

Monica, dubbed by his friends as "the princess," had left her stiletto imprints on his heart almost a year ago to the day that Kinsey had walked into his arms. Marc blinked. "You know, I hadn't even thought about Monica for a long time." At least, not since he'd met Kinsey. "Thank you so much for bringing her up."

Jack spread his hands and shrugged. "Hey, that's what friends are for." He waited for Marc to take another drink, then asked, "So . . . is Kinsey hot?"

The heat zipping through Marc at that question had little to do with the alcohol. "Yep. Definitely. But I didn't call you to have a junior high locker-room discussion about the possible future mother of my children." He set the glass on the napkin. "I need a favor."

"Shoot."

"Do you still have a friend on the police force in South Padre?" Jack nodded and Marc continued, eyes searching the room to make sure no one overheard. "I want an artist's sketch of her. Then some information. I want her last name, where she lives and where she teaches."

"You don't know these things?" Jack asked incredulously. Marc shook his head. "Why don't you just ask the woman? Why all this cloak-and-dagger?"

"Because we agreed to, well, first names only. After I found out she taught, she clammed up. I want—no, I *need* to know why."

Jack shook his head and chuckled. "You sly dog! Although, as your cardiologist, I have to say I'm a little worried about how much rest you've actually been getting. But as your friend, I want to shout from the rooftops that you're finally over your slump! Gimme five!" The men slapped hands and Jack sobered. "Just promise me you won't overdo it. And if you experience any discomfort, I want to know about it. Immediately. Got it?"

"No problem."

Jack looked at his watch and stood. "I gotta go." He clapped Marc on the shoulder, squeezing affectionately. "It sounds like this one may be a keeper. Keep me posted."

Marc watched Jack stride through the doorway, then slumped back in the booth.

A keeper.

Kinsey haunted him. All he had to do was close his eyes to feel her skin, hear her voice. Her scent was forever imbedded in his senses. Was this love? Had he actually fallen in love with someone he had known for only two days?

He pulled his cell phone out of his pocket and stared at it. It would violate their agreement to call her. If he did, she might not show up next weekend. He slipped the phone back into his pocket.

Jack had a reason to worry about him. Kinsey was consuming him from the inside out. He glanced at his watch. Four days, nine hours and fifteen minutes—give or take a few minutes—until he could hold her again, hear her sweet voice, taste her.

He groaned and looked down at the phone again, now once more in his hand. It would take only two punches of buttons to bring up the number she'd called.

Before he could think about it again, Marc did it and slipped lower in the booth while the call went through.

One ring. Two rings. Three, then she answered. It was her. He'd know her voice anywhere.

"Hello?" She sounded slightly breathless and he wondered if he'd interrupted something—like her bath. His vivid recall slammed arousal into him at warp speed. "Hello?" she said again.

Should he answer her? Would she be irritated or angry that he'd called? Maybe she missed him as much as he did her.

"Hello!" she yelled. "I can hear you breathing! Who is this? If you don't answer right now, I'm hanging up." Before he got up the nerve to reply, a distinctive click rang in his ear, followed by empty silence.

He sat for a long time, phone in hand, staring at the display. If he hit REDIAL, he could hear her sweet voice again. But she might think it was a crank call and become frightened. Frightening her was the last thing he wanted to do.

Yet if he identified himself, she might get angry that he'd broken the agreement.

Repocketing the phone, he stood and slowly walked to the door. The night was clear, stars bright. He flicked the locks on the Jaguar and slid inside. The view from the deck of the beach house was probably spectacular. But he wouldn't enjoy it.

Not alone.

The drive from Corpus Christi to South Padre Island was interminable. Exhausted, Marc dragged himself from the car and trudged up the stairs to the deck. Tonight even the sound of the waves hitting the shore sounded lonely. He let himself in and, not bothering with lights, made his way to the master bedroom.

Closing the curtains against the spectacular view, he stripped and climbed into bed.

The sheets and pillows smelled like Kinsey.

Within seconds his erection formed a little tent in the sheet. He glared at the telltale proof of her affect on him. Now that he'd found her, how would he ever get through the week without her?

Taking matters into his own hand, he pumped and thought of Kinsey. Her scent surrounded him. He squeezed and pumped faster. He could see her breasts, taste them. His breathing became ragged. Faster. Harder.

"Kinsey!" Her name erupted from his mouth while something else erupted farther south.

"Say something, Karly." Kinsey wrapped one of her sister's robes around her, trying to ignore the memory of Marc's hands on her body that just telling about him had caused. Karly sat on the deck of the tub with a stunned expression. *Please don't hate me!*

Karly slowly shook her head, a small smile forming on her glossed lips. "I'm speechless. Wow. I can't believe you actually took any advice from me!" She held up a hand. "Not that that's necessarily a bad thing! I'm just surprised."

"I made a terrible mistake, didn't I?" Kinsey twisted the robe belt between tense fingers and dropped to sit beside her sister.

"Don't be ridiculous! You saw something, or, rather, someone you wanted, and went for it. It's about time you acted spontaneously. If we didn't look so much alike, I'd worry we weren't truly related," she joked.

All the ways she'd "gone for it" flashed through Kinsey's mind. Was it getting hotter in here?

"Kins? I asked when you plan to see him again. You *do* plan to see him again, don't you?"

"Um, yes, I do. I mean, I will." She paced to the tub and back. "Next weekend, in fact." At her sister's raised eyebrow, she continued. "At the beach house I told you about. Same time next week. And, I hope, the weekend after that and the weekend after that. But," she shrugged, toying with the belt of the robe, "we'll see how this next weekend goes."

She dropped to her knees in front of her sister. "Karly, I think I really could grow to feel something for this guy. I know I was the one who imposed the limited exchange of information, but now that we're apart, I realize I don't know nearly enough about him."

Karly brushed a strand of hair from Kinsey's face and said, "There'll be time. From what you tell me, he's just as taken with you. Trust me, he'll be waiting for you and just as anxious to be together again as you are."

"I hope you're right." Kinsey stretched and yawned. "I'm exhausted! Great sex really wears you out." The sisters exchanged knowing grins. "Is it okay if I stay here tonight?"

"Of course. Brad is going to be out of town until midweek, so Cassie and I would love the company. You know where everything is. I stuck your clean clothes in the guest-room closet when I couldn't find you at the hotel. Brad parked your car in the garage. Your purse is in the drawer by the bed." She stood and stretched, rubbing the small of her back. "I'm going to get some sleep. Six comes early. Cassie spent the night with a little friend down the block. They'll go to school together and then she'll ride home with me, so sleep as long as you need."

"Thanks." They parted in the hallway. "And, Karly?" Her sister turned to look back at Kinsey. "You were right. Great sex does make a big difference. Regardless of how all this turns out, it's taught me one thing: I can't marry Zachary. I have meetings most of tomorrow, but I'll call him and arrange to meet so I can give back the ring."

Karly ran over and embraced her sister. "Oh, Kins! I know you've made the right decision. Once Mom and Dad think about it, they'll agree. Don't look so worried."

"Easy for you to say. You already faced them down."

"They'd never admit it, but I know they realize I made the right choice for me. They just want you to be happy. And face it, that would never have happened with Dr. Dull."

Kinsey laughed and shook her head. "No, you're probably right. Now, go to bed. Good night." She shoved Karly in the direction of the master bedroom.

Alone in the guestroom, tucked beneath the cool sheets, her body burning for Marc, Kinsey wondered if he missed her even a little.

Four interminable days later, she knocked once and let herself into Karly's large country kitchen. "Hello! Anyone home?"

"Auntie Kinsey!" Cassie barreled into the room, a blur of blonde curls, pink hair ribbons and denim. Her little pink running shoes squeaked on the polished tile a second before she launched herself into Kinsey's arms.

"Hey, brat, where's your mommy? Oh! Hold still, I think I see a spot that needs kisses!" She made loud sucking noises while covering her niece's face and neck with kisses. Cassie shrieked. She was still giggling and squirming when Karly walked into the room.

Kinsey stopped midkiss. "What's wrong?" She let Cassie slide down and took a step toward her frowning sister.

Karly took a deep breath and smiled. "Nothing. It's just so weird." She straightened Cassie's bows. "I've been getting hang-up calls off and on all week. Not a lot of them, maybe three or four." She shrugged. "Ordinarily it wouldn't get to me, but with Brad gone . . ."

"Caller ID blocked?" Her sister nodded. Kinsey patted Cassie's rear end as she scampered from the room. "Thought about changing your number? You know there are advantages to having a husband who works for the phone company."

Karly opened the refrigerator and waved a Coke at her sister. Kinsey nodded and got down two glasses. While Karly opened the cans, Kinsey put ice in the tall tumblers. The sound of fizzing filled the quiet kitchen.

"I just don't want to worry Brad. He hates leaving us as it is," Karly said as they sat at the bleached oak table to drink the sodas. "It's probably nothing. If I make a big deal out of it and get the number changed, he'll freak."

"The caller doesn't ever say anything, just hangs up?"

"That's what is so weird. Sometimes I'm sure I can hear him breathing. It's not an immediate hang-up."

"You're right. That's weird. I still think you should consider changing your number. Brad would understand." Kinsey crunched a piece of ice.

Karly swirled around her ice in the glass. "I'll think about it. So, are you all set for your romantic weekend?"

"I'm not sure how romantic it will be, but . . . Karly, does it mean anything that I've been thinking about him almost non-stop since last weekend?" She sipped her cola, then wiped the sweat from the glass with the pad of her thumb. "It's been a real effort to get through the seminars all week. I'm sure people think I'm brain dead."

"Hey, even brain dead you're still one hell of a financial analyst! Don't sell yourself short. You've just been, well, sort of preoccupied lately." Karly mopped her forehead with the tail of her shirt. "I can't believe how hot it is, and we still have another month of school! I wish I could go to the beach. You're so lucky."

The knot in Kinsey's stomach didn't feel like luck. It was closer to terror. What if what she'd felt they shared last weekend was just an illusion? "Do you think I'm making a mistake, Karly?"

Karly's eyes widened. "A mistake? After what you told me went on last week? Boy, you *have* been celibate too long! Honey, if the sex was that great, there has to be something more. Otherwise it would have lost its appeal before the weekend ended." Her cool fingers gripped her sister's wrist. "You deserve this, Kins. So maybe Marc isn't Mr. Right, but maybe he is. You deserve to find out. I—what the hell is this?" She waved her sister's left hand, the huge engagement ring from Zachary flashing with refracted light.

"Darn. I meant to take that off." Kinsey ripped the heavy ring from her hand and stuffed it in the pocket of her sundress. At her sister's horror-struck look, she explained, "I met with Zachary before I left and tried to give back the ring. I even told him I'd met someone else—"

"Then why is that boulder on your hand? Kins, don't you see? You've actually *lost* ground! At least before, you hadn't worn the thing! What made you change your mind?"

Guilt. "I didn't. Not really." Her shoulders slumped. "Oh, Karly, why am I such a wimp? You should have seen the hurt look on Zachary's face when I told him I'd met someone else. I just didn't have the energy, or the heart, to tell him no when he insisted on putting the ring on my finger."

"And that, dear sister, is exactly how women find themselves married to the wrong guy. You have to be strong. Be honest. Respect yourself and Zach enough to end it. Now. Like I said, Marc might not be the right one, but you owe it to yourself to find out."

Maybe Karly was right. But, then again, maybe she needed to have her head examined for even considering another weekend of sex at the beach. Although great, was it fair to Marc to prolong this . . . whatever it was? She glanced at her watch and stood.

"I need to hit the road or I'll never get there before dinner." She bent to hug her sister. "Thanks for the pep talk. I needed it."

"No problem. Keep me posted!" Karly called to her as she slipped into her sensible, preowned Volvo station wagon. "And for goodness' sake, keep that rock out of sight!"

Even though it was hot, Kinsey opened the moon roof and cranked up the air conditioning for comfort. It was the closest she'd get to a convertible in the near future. With a final wave to her sister with sweating palms, she turned her car toward the beach.

Marc's Jaguar was parked at the base of the steps. She pulled in next to it, noting the disparity of the way the cars went together. Were they like her and Marc? Was she only fooling herself by thinking they might have something more? Taking a deep breath of soothing sea air, she got out and reached for her weekend bag.

Marc met her at the top step, clad in shorts and a barbecue apron. Tan and rested looking, he made her mouth water. Still gorgeous.

As soon as she reached him, he swept her into his arms and swung her around before her feet touched the deck.

"God, I've missed you!" His lips were warm and achingly

familiar when they brushed hers. He set her away from him, his heated gaze burning a trail through her thin, strapless sundress. His nostrils flared. "I'll let you take your bag into the house. If I follow you I know the steaks will burn because I won't be satisfied with a short kiss or two."

Kinsey swallowed what felt suspiciously like disappointment. "I'll be right back. Do you need me to set the table or make a salad or anything?"

Sun glinted off his hair when he shook his head. "Nope. All taken care of. Just put your gear away and sashay that pretty little backside back out here." His voice lowered to a throaty growl. "I've missed you, woman. It was a hell of a long week."

Kinsey nodded and stepped into the air-conditioned interior, almost running to the second floor to deposit her bag in the master bedroom. No point in playing coy. It was a fact that she would be sharing a bed with Marc tonight. And tomorrow night. And, she thought with a smile, possibly all points in between.

Beneath her bodice, her braless nipples puckered against the cotton. No doubt about it, she'd become a brazen woman, as her mother would say. And she loved every minute of it.

With a quick glance in the mirror, she hurried back to the deck. And Marc.

He was turning the steaks, the muscles in his bare back rippling with the movement. She walked up behind him and slipped her arms around his waist.

He immediately stilled. He obviously wasn't comfortable with her familiarity. Cheeks burning, she loosened her hug and began to step back.

His warm hand trapped her arms where they were. "Don't go," he said in a hoarse whisper. "Don't stop. I've dreamed of you touching me all week." He pushed downward on her hand. "Keep going."

Pulse quickening, she began her slow exploration. While her

right hand skimmed the smooth expanse of rippling muscles on his warm chest beneath the bib of the apron, her left rubbed slowly back and forth just above the waistband of his khaki shorts, a finger delving beneath the waistband with each pass.

Her breasts ached with each contact against the burning plains of his back. Moisture pooled. She shifted from foot to foot, achy and restless.

At the last foray of her little finger, Marc sucked in his stomach, the invitation to delve farther blatant—not that she'd have resisted the urge to discover if he wore boxers or briefs.

He wore neither.

Her fingers came into contact with nothing but scorching skin and hard maleness. She and Marc both sucked in air as her fingers closed around the proof of his arousal.

Kinsey closed her eyes and stroked him. Home. She was finally home. Emotion welled within her throat. Tears stung her eyelids. After an interminable week, she was home where she belonged. With Marc.

Marc clenched his teeth and forced his attention to the sizzling steaks. He could sympathize. He was sizzling himself. Kinsey's hand was caressing him, milking him of his resistance. He locked his knees and concentrated on the beef.

He swallowed a groan. The hard little tips of Kinsey's breasts were poking his back. He honestly couldn't remember being this horny as a teenager. The woman behind him turned him inside out with just a smile. What she was doing to him now was lethal.

When she began taking nibbling kisses along his spine, he fumbled for the plate, slapped the fragrant meat on it and, grabbing Kinsey by the hand, headed for the kitchen.

The platter slid along the island countertop. He didn't wait to see if it fell to the floor. With one movement, he swept her from her feet and deposited her on the counter. He couldn't kiss her hard or deep enough. His hands shook. He yanked at the top of her skimpy sundress and was rewarded when her full breasts tumbled into his eager palms.

His mouth latched on to a distended nipple and he suckled until he heard her whimper. Forcing deep breaths into his lungs, he buried his face between her breasts and tried to calm down.

"I've dreamed all week of seeing you like this," he explained, his voice muffled by her flesh. "Just give me a minute to get some control here."

He took a deep breath and stepped back, forcing his gaze to her face. The tenderness he saw there was a gut punch. This was quickly escalating into much more than anonymous weekends of sex play. They needed to take a step back. Regroup.

Regroup, hell. He had to have her. Now. The zipper scraped his skin as he dragged his shorts down to pool around his feet. Reaching beneath her skirt, he grabbed the string that masqueraded as panties and stripped them down her silky legs.

"I can't wait, darlin'," he whispered urgently against her ear. "We'll take it slow next time. Promise." With that, he thrust into her wet heat and sighed. Home. He was home.

"I think you missed me, too," he said in a low voice, its intensity vying with the rolling surf outside and the echo of her own heartbeat in her ears.

Boneless; she was boneless again. How did he do it?

The stone counter felt marvelous against the heated skin of her back. She was still lying down, limp as a rag doll, trying to gather enough strength to sit up, when he gripped each ankle and placed the soles of her feet flat on the counter on either side of his hips.

He quieted her feeble attempt at protest by petting her stomach and gently kissing her swollen petals. Quivers began deep inside and she knew she'd let him do anything as long as these feelings didn't go away.

He dragged his fingertip up one feminine lip, across and down the other. Little dabs punctuated her swollen vulva before lightly swirling up and down and all around. He gently blew against the sensitive tissue while he drew tight little circles around her opening.

Wave number two crashed over her, causing her to cry out in surprised ecstasy.

She whimpered at the cool air marking his departure, but was too wrung out to do much else. He pulled her to a sitting position and peeled her dress off over her head.

The coolness of the countertop felt slick against her hot bottom as he slid her to the edge and plunged into her again. Still limp, she could only drape her arms over his shoulders and hang on.

His breath hot against her neck, he pumped into her boneless body, the friction of his skin against hers erotically pleasant. Her eyes widened in stunned surprise when yet a third wave washed over her.

"Are you okay?" he whispered in her ear.

In response, she could only mumble and nod.

"Let's go for a quick swim before we reheat dinner." He lifted her from the counter and strode toward the deck. She noticed the door was still open as they walked through it. His semierect penis bumped against her hip as they went down the stairs.

The warm ocean breeze caressed her skin, the waves getting louder. Mist from the water moistened her face. The water was satin smooth and warm. Soon she was submerged to her neck, Marc's arms securely around her at her back and knees.

His hands scooped warm saltwater over her breasts, gently scrubbing away any trace of sex. Downward they continued, rubbing the engorged folds between her legs, making her squirm with renewed want.

"Shh," he whispered against her lips. "Relax and let the water hold you up while I love you." He released her and she found herself floating, bobbing gently with the waves. His hands held her hipbones, anchoring her to him, hip to hip. The hard tip of his erection probed at her a second before plunging into her.

The water held her suspended while he surged in and out in lazy movements, warm saltwater following in his wake.

She stretched, luxuriating in the moment. The next moment, his thumb found her exposed nub and pressed with each thrust.

Waves of ecstasy washed over her, surprising her so much that a Gulf wave washed over her. She came up, sputtering and coughing. Marc held her, patting her back, pushing soaked strands of hair from her face.

"I'm so sorry for spoiling the moment," she finally gasped.

In the semidarkness, his smile was white. "You didn't," he insisted. "We came at the same time." He pounded her back as renewed coughs took over. "I'm more concerned with you. Are you sure you're okay?"

"Fine," she wheezed. "Could we please go in now and eat some dinner?"

"Absolutely." He swept her up into his arms and strode toward shore. "We have all weekend. We need to keep up our strength." He bent to brush her lips with his, then continued walking.

It was at that moment that her nagging suspicion became a certainty.

She loved him.

9

Kinsey laughed and ran up the steps the following weekend. "You lose! You cook dinner tonight!" Her smile slipped a bit. After dinner she had to hit the road. Marc wanted her to stay another night, but it was impossible. Besides the fact that she hadn't packed any business clothes, she'd have to get up at the crack of dawn to make the drive from South Padre to Corpus Christi in order to be on time for her first meeting.

For the first time since being hired right after college, she resented her job. She watched Marc climb the steps. She resented anything that kept her away from Marc.

It wasn't just the sex. The sex was great. Fantastic. But it was so much more than that.

The last two weekends, they'd shared their thoughts as well as their bodies and she felt closer to him than she'd ever felt to anyone other than her sister. Thoughts of leaving him made her heart literally hurt.

"Hey, beautiful, why the sad face? Afraid I'll poison you with my cooking?" he teased, his hands cupping her face. His lips brushed hers. "Kinsey, I know we made a deal, but I—"

"Hush! Let's not spoil the weekend with serious talk, okay?" Rising on tiptoe, she kissed his chin, nipped playfully at his lower lip. "I have to leave in a couple of hours."

He scowled and allowed her to lead him into the house. "I thought you taught right here in town. Why couldn't you stay here tonight and drive in tomorrow morning in time for school?"

Because Karly teaches kindergarten in South Padre. I have a corporate job in Corpus Christi. What would he say if she told him that? She couldn't bear to see the accusation in his beautiful eyes. They only had one more weekend after this. It was better to enjoy it to the fullest while it was still possible.

After all, it was the deal they'd made. She'd told him bits and pieces of her life, fusing it with Karly's, but had purposely sidestepped most of the information he'd been willing to divulge about himself. Somehow it seemed easier that way. Plus, there would be no way for her to give in to temptation and look him up later if her stubborn heart kept insisting she loved him.

Marc walked up behind her, his arms automatically going around her bare middle. Their weekends at the beach had been spent like hedonists, naked unless they went outside their private cove. The result was a golden, all-over tan. The thought of ever wearing a bathing suit again was almost heartbreaking.

Marc rolled the tips of her breasts between his thumbs and fingers, gently plucking at them while he nibbled on her neck. "Want to watch a movie after dinner? Or do you feel like going out?"

"Marc." She stopped his hands by laying hers on top of them and looked up at him. "I told you, I have to leave right after dinner." She broke eye contact and stepped toward the kitchen. "I have papers to correct and, um, lesson plans."

"Wow." He walked over to the refrigerator and looked inside. "Kindergarten sounds a lot tougher than what I remember. Probably a good thing I'm old—I'd have never passed kindergarten. Then where would we be?"

She gave a little laugh. "It's not like you necessarily need it for what you do."

Her smile died when he straightened and gave her a narrow-eyed stare. "How's that?"

Oh, no, now she'd insulted him. "I just mean, well, um, I wouldn't think you'd necessarily need much higher education for what you do." Why did she say that? Despite her best intentions, her mouth seemed to have a will of its own.

"Oh, really?" Marc had a fist on his hip. Yep, she'd insulted him. "Why's that?" he asked in a low voice.

"Well, it's not like I really *know* what you do—"

"That's because you chose not to know. Remember? That was the deal." He took a step toward her, and she stepped back, the small of her back feeling the coldness of the island's stone countertop. "What makes you think I don't need an education to do my job?"

She shrugged self-consciously. "Well, it's just that your hands are so chapped. Obviously, you work with them a lot."

He nodded. "That's right. I do work with my hands. Answer my question."

"I, uh, assumed you were a cowboy or farmer or something."

"Big assumption."

"Well, not really. You wear Western-style clothes and boots whenever we go out."

"A lot of Texans do that. They're comfortable." He reached into a drawer, just inside the pantry. "Here. Put this on."

"What?" She looked at the shimmery bit of ruffled pink cloth he'd tossed to her. "Why?"

"Because," he said in a hard, impersonal voice, "our agreement was strictly sex. No strings attached. Nothing personal. If you're leaving right after dinner, I want you to wear this. Put it on. Now."

Hands shaking, she fought back tears as she tied the ultra-sheer apron around her nudity.

"Turn around. I want to see your tits through the apron. Good" he said when she turned. "They're hard and puckered. Tits don't lie. You want me as much as I want you."

He walked to her, put his hands hard on her hips, and turned her away from him, leaning her over the table. "Relax, babe." Tears stung her cheeks, but her traitorous body instantly became moist when he reached between her legs to stroke her folds. "Attagirl, your pussy's nice and wet." The warmth of his breath bathed her weeping sex while he licked her. The tip of his tongue speared her opening. Involuntarily, her legs opened for him.

"Oh, babe, your cunt is so slick and wet for me." His hot breath fanned her sensitive skin.

"Please, Marc," she whispered. She wanted him, especially since it would be their last time together. But not like this.

"Please what? Please stop? Please fuck me? Please what?" He shoved his fingers deep within her. Appalled, she felt her body react, gushing her release over his hand.

His penis drove into her. Harder, deeper, faster. All the while, his fingers pinched her nipple with pleasure/pain.

At some point she became an active participant, bucking and rolling with him. He carried her to the couch and continued pounding in and out of her. At her cries of completion, he jerked her off his lap and laid her over the arm of the sofa to pound into her from behind again. His hands were relentless, stroking and slapping and pinching her to climax again and again.

"I want to fuck you in the hot tub and out on the deck, where anyone passing by on the beach can see us."

Out of her mind with lust, she could only nod and growl deep in her throat, "Yes!"

Hot water surged in and out of her with each thrust. It didn't take long before her cries of completion filled the night air.

Cool air bathed her heated skin. Marc placed a pad from a deck chair on the corner of the railing and plunked her on it, legs spread wide, one foot on each perpendicular rail. Without preamble, he plunged into her again.

They both came at the same time, their cries startling the birds.

Afterward Marc carried her to the bathroom and gently bathed her limp body, then carried her to their bed and stroked lotion onto every inch of her body. Each stroke was punctuated with feather-light kisses.

She roused from her lethargy to return the massage and soon they were both panting.

"Now," Marc grunted in her ear as he tried to roll her to her back. "I need you now!"

"Wait." She reached beside the bed and brought up the can of whipped cream she'd stashed before going to the beach. "Lay back and enjoy."

Air fluttered the partially drawn curtains, adding to the sensation of aerosol whipped cream being liberally applied to his rapidly recovering erection.

He'd been wild with anger and lust when this last episode began. He'd hated himself for what he was doing, but couldn't seem to stop. Then, when she'd joined in, he'd really lost control.

He'd never lost control of anything in his life. Had never felt the myriad of things he'd felt since meeting Kinsey.

His eyes closed as Kinsey's mouth approached his now rock-hard cock. Her tongue gently flicked some of the cream off before she opened wide to devour him whole.

His last coherent thought was to breathe a sigh of heartfelt relief that she hadn't run screaming into the night.

Afterward he fashioned a bikini out of the remaining whipped cream and, amid giggles from Kinsey, proceeded to lick it off.

Her gaze met his. She slowly took the can from his hand, spread her legs and emptied the rest of the whipped cream. "I really do have to go. Soon. But just one more time. . . ."

Marc turned over, murmuring in his sleep. Kinsey slipped from the sticky sheets and pulled the covers over his back.

After a quick shower, she dressed and gathered up her things. When she brushed her lips across Marc's, it sounded as though he whispered, "Don't go," but she couldn't be sure.

What had happened tonight? She closed the back door of the Volvo and got into the driver's seat. She'd never enjoyed rough sex, but with Marc it had been unbearably exciting. She shrugged and started the engine. Maybe she'd experienced latent S and M tendencies. What if *anyone* would have been sufficient for a partner? What if it wasn't love at all?

The white lines of the highway streaked past as the car carried her farther away from Marc and the beach house she'd come to love.

Love.

Did she really love Marc? The impulsive side of her that had emerged since they met assured her it was love. But the practical side argued that it was too soon. Physical attraction can be a powerful aphrodisiac.

She sighed. Maybe she'd never know the answer.

Mark rolled over and shielded his eyes against the morning sunshine. Kinsey was gone. He knew it before he'd opened his eyes.

Of course she was gone. She had to work. Still, it left an empty feeling in the pit of his stomach.

Scenes from the night before flashed through his mind. Their sexual escapades had taken a turn he'd never expected. Had he been too rough?

The encounter on the kitchen table was almost rape, but Kinsey seemed to get into the spirit of it soon enough. Still . . .

He rolled over and retrieved his cell phone from the pocket of his shorts. Without thinking, he hit the number he'd programmed into the memory two weeks ago.

"Hello?" Her sweet voice sounded breathless, a bit husky. She was probably on her way out the door to school. He pictured her delectable body primly clothed as a kindergarten teacher and wondered if anyone suspected she spent her weekends in the nude.

"Hel*lo*?" she repeated, clearly annoyed. He really should say something.

"I miss you," he whispered, but she'd already hung up.

He swung his legs off the bed and stood, stretching to get the kinks out, then padded to the bathroom.

The bathroom smelled of Kinsey's perfume.

He stopped. Simply drawing a breath was painful. What if he'd chased her away with his ardor? He'd tried to tell her how he felt, but she wouldn't listen. Then, when she made the outlandish assumption that he was a cowboy ... well, he'd lost it.

Rubbing the back of his neck, he reached into the shower stall to turn on the water. A slash of color drew his attention to the corner.

Kinsey's sexy little sundress lay wadded where he'd thrown it before their shower last weekend. He leaned down and picked it up, inhaling her familiar scent, aching with his loneliness.

Something fell from the pocket and plunked on his bare toe. That's when he saw it.

A huge diamond blinked in the morning sunshine streaming in from the skylights. He bent to pick it up. An engagement ring.

Doubled over with the physical pain of her obvious betrayal, he sank to the step and willed his heart to keep beating.

A modicum of control allowed him to step beneath the stinging spray, the betrayal ring on his little finger, lest he should forget how he'd been played for a fool.

Cold needles of water slashed his face. Monica's desertion was nothing in light of this. A mere hiccup before the major upheaval.

And, damn! He hit the tiled wall with a fist, the ring spinning to dig into the side of his palm. Neither time had he seen it coming. What did he do, walk around with a sign on his back saying *I'm so desperate for love that I can be had?*

No more.

With jerking movements, he turned off the faucet and stepped out of the shower. Not bothering with a towel, he left a damp path to the bed where he grabbed the cell phone and hit REDIAL.

Seven, eight, nine rings. Then her voice, on tape. "Hi, you've reached us! We can't come to the phone right now; you know the drill. And we'll get back to you."

With a roar of frustration, he hurled the phone against the window. It bounced and landed on the carpet at his feet, mocking his anguish.

Jack. He needed to talk to Jack.

"Mrs. James? Is that your sister?" The tiny girl with a mass of red curls tugged at Karly's jumper and pointed.

"Yes, I'm her sister. Her younger sister." Kinsey grinned down at the adorable little girl, then winked at Karly.

"Three minutes doesn't count, Kins." Karly patted the little girl's head and turned her toward the playground. "Go on and play with the others, Brandi. We only have"—she glanced at her Mickey Mouse watch— "about ten more minutes."

They watched Karly's student skip away. Karly turned back to Kinsey. "Okay. What are you doing here? And don't tell me you were in the neighborhood."

"Well, actually, I *was* in the neighborhood. My afternoon session was canceled. I stopped by to see Mom and Dad, but they weren't home." She sat at the picnic table across from her sister, who watched her intently. "I guess I needed to talk to someone."

"Thanks. Mom and Dad aren't home, so I qualify as the next 'someone' on the list?"

"Don't be dumb. You know what I mean." Her sister nodded, so Kinsey took a deep breath and plunged ahead. "Things have gotten way out of control with Marc."

"Your studly cowboy?" Karly grinned and rolled her eyes.

"I'm serious, here. I think I might have accidentally fallen in love with him."

"'*Accidentally*'? Kins, from what you've told me, you've been going at it like minks for the last three weeks. What did you expect?" She looked out over the playground and blew the red whistle that hung around her neck. "Bobby-Joe! We don't throw sand!"

"Sex isn't love, Kar. You told me that years ago."

Karly shook her head, loosening a few tendrils of hair from her low ponytail. "No, it's not. But when it's all-consuming, like your time with Marc seems to have been, it's easy to mistake lust for love."

They watched the antics of the children for a moment. "He almost told me he loved me this weekend," Kinsey said. "I stopped him." Before her sister could close her mouth and ask why, she told her. "I didn't want to ruin what little time we have left. If we did something stupid like declare our love, it would complicate things." She reached across to grab Karly's forearm. "Don't you see? It was my idea to have a fling, no names, no strings. I can't go back on it. Not this late."

"Why ever not, if you love the guy?"

Kinsey shrugged. "Like you said, in our situation it's easy to mistake lust for love. I still haven't told Zachary that I won't marry him—"

"What! Are you nuts? I thought you decided to tell him to take a hike!"

Kinsey sighed. "I did. But he couldn't make time to see me, then I had that day trip. Next thing I knew, it was time to go to the beach. And Marc." The thought of being with Marc again caused tunnel vision where the rest of her life was concerned.

How could she even contemplate expanding the relationship? It would throw a monkey wrench into her career plans. A career she'd worked hard to build.

"Is it because he's a cowboy?" her sister asked. "Do you think because he doesn't have a degree that he's beneath you somehow?"

"Don't be ridiculous! You know I'm not like that!" Was she? "It's just that, well, I'm not like Mom. I'm not looking for someone to 'take care' of me." She sighed, shoulders slumped. "But I don't want to be the sole support of someone else, either. So . . . yeah, I guess it might have something to do with my decision."

"Your decision to do nothing?"

Kinsey nodded. "It's for the best. In fact, I've just about made up my mind not to go for this last weekend." Scenes from the debauchery on the kitchen table filled her mind, catching her breath in her throat. If his actions had frightened her at first, her reactions had downright terrified her. "Things sort of took a turn for the worst last weekend. It's best to just hold on to the memories and walk away."

"You know I'm here if you want to talk. About anything." Karly stood and blew two short whistles. "Time to go in!" she yelled in her teacher voice.

The sisters hugged. Kinsey stepped back. "Thanks. I'll give you a call. We can talk all weekend." Her eyes filled. "I won't have anything else to do," she said in a choked voice.

"Oh, Kins." Her sister gathered her close as the children stomped past. "I'm so sorry this didn't work out for you."

"Hey, it's okay. It was just a fling, remember?"

"Yeah, but it was my stupid idea and now you're hurting. Next time I make a suggestion, feel free to tell me to shut up, okay?"

"Okay," Kinsey said with a watery sniff.

She watched her sister close the door to her classroom, and trudged slowly back to her car. The beach. She needed to be at the beach. Unfortunately, the beach she wanted to go to was occupied. But the beach that ran along Ocean Drive, back home in Corpus Christi, would do.

Alone was alone, no matter where you were.

"No doubt about it, you need this vacation." Jack leaned over the table to peer intently, making Marc feel like a bug under a microscope. "My beach house is great. The ocean view is spectacular. What the hell are you doing in Corpus, telling me you're ready to come back to work?"

Marc shifted, imagining he felt the heinous diamond of the betrayal ring digging into his hip. "Did your friend come up with anything?" When Jack averted his gaze, Marc knew his worst-case scenario had come true. "Tell me."

"It's sort of what you expected. Her name's not Kinsey. It's Karly. Karly James. And she really does teach kindergarten, at an elementary school not far from the beach house."

"I could live with her name not being Kinsey. But there's more. Tell me." He found his fist clenching and forced his hands to relax on the table.

Jack met his gaze, sympathy clear in his eyes. "She's married, dude. They have a four-year-old daughter."

Jack continued to talk, but Marc couldn't make out the words through the roaring in his ears.

"Marc?" Jack leaned across the table, gripping his arms. "Are you okay?"

Talking was too much of an effort, so he nodded, flexing his left hand against the growing numbness.

Jack's gaze was fixed on something past Marc's shoulder. "Wow. Check out what just walked in." Jack chuckled. "As the saying goes, one door closes and another one opens. Talk about timing! This ought to confirm your belief that there's more than one fish in the sea. And check out that rack! Her cleavage must have its own echo."

Not interested. Nonetheless, he turned, if for no other reason than to compare the recent patron with Kinsey and find her lacking.

Kinsey.

Her skin glowed, her tan golden. She was wearing the red dress he'd bought her, her generous curves dangerously close to spilling over the low-cut neckline. He and Jack weren't the only ones who noticed her.

Before he could react, a tall model-handsome man of about thirty walked up to her and gave her a distinctly unbrotherly kiss. She smiled up at the man, but not the way she'd smiled at Marc. How could she be married to someone else and share the things, *do* the things, they'd done together?

From a distance, he heard Jack's voice, but couldn't make out the words. He saw no one but Kinsey. Karly. Had to remember her real name. Talk. They had to talk. He'd give her a chance to explain before he cut her out of his life.

Before he could force his body to react to his commands, she walked out of the bar, a less than happy expression on her face, arm in arm with the man.

Friday, he waited. And waited. When midnight came and Kinsey/Karly had not appeared, he turned out the lights. Attempts to sleep would be useless, so he sat on the deck and watched the tide.

Then he watched the sunrise.

He still sat there when it set. Numb.

He'd always been a man of action. Why was he letting her get away with this?

Unfolding stiff legs, he went into the house in search of his cell phone.

"Jack? Give me her address. Yeah, I know what I said. Give it to me anyway."

11

Marc stood outside her door, vibrating with the rage that had built as he drove to her home in the pleasant neighborhood. How dare she go back to her ordinary life after she'd ripped out his heart?

The little girl had piled into a minivan with several other giggling girls about half an hour ago. Kinsey had to be in there. Alone.

He rang the bell and waited. After a moment or two, he knocked. Then knocked again. Harder.

From deep within the house, he heard her voice calling that she'd be right there and asking if he'd forgotten anything.

Only to leave her *before* his heart had been involved.

The door swung open. It was her.

He'd hoped Jack's detective had been wrong. But there she stood, wrapped in a bath sheet. Her shapely shoulders had already begun to lose some of the deep, golden tan she'd acquired when she'd been with him.

"Oh! I thought you were someone else!" He'd just bet she

had. She tugged at her big yellow towel. "May I help you?" she asked, all polite as though she had never set eyes on him in her life.

"Surprised to see me?" He stepped into the foyer, forcing her back a step, and closed the door behind him.

"Look, I don't know who you are, but if you don't leave right now, I'm calling nine-one-one."

"Don't I even get a kiss?" He pulled her none-too-gently to him and ground his lips against hers.

She was good. He'd give her that. She was acting out the stranger scene to high hilt. Didn't even respond to his kiss as she'd always done.

"Don't worry, babe," he snarled against her tightly closed lips, "I know we're alone." He grabbed the towel and yanked it from her killer body as his other hand clasped her breast.

She shrieked at the same time a deep voice yelled, "What the hell is going on here! Get your hands off my wife!"

Marc turned in time to see a beefy fist heading straight for his eye.

"Back off, Brad!" Kinsey/Karly commanded from somewhere above him. So she had feelings for him after all. As soon as the ringing in his head subsided, he'd open his eyes.

"I think this may be Kinsey's friend." Friend? Hell, they were more than friends. But why was she talking in the third person?

Her voice came closer to his face. "Marc? Is that you?"

He nodded, pain shooting behind his right eye. Strong hands gripped beneath his armpits and he felt himself lifted to his feet.

"Well, what the hell is he doing here if he's Kinsey's friend?" Huh? Was this man in on it from the beginning?

"What kind of people are you?" Marc asked once he was seated, slumped against the arm of the sofa. Holding his palm over his injured eye, he peeked out at the woman, now wrapped tightly in her towel and the towering WWE wannabe looming behind her, all bristling ego and bulging muscles.

"I think you've made a mistake," she said. "Kinsey is the person you're looking for, right?"

"Right," he said cautiously.

"I'm her twin sister, Karly." She shrugged. "People get us mixed up all the time." The man growled and she looked over her shoulder at him. "Shut up, Brad. You did the same thing when we were dating. Remember? You terrified Kins when she found you in her bed that time?

"This is my husband, Brad James," she told him. "B.J.," she commanded, "shake hands and play nice."

Marc reached out to reluctantly shake the wannabe's hand. "Marc Wallace."

Marc watched Karly and Brad with a wary eye—his good one, that is. They set a plate of sandwiches, a pitcher of iced tea, and glasses filled with ice on the table before joining him.

"What do you do, Marc?" Brad asked, reaching for a sandwich.

"I'm a surgeon. Reconstructive surgery, mostly." He flinched when he touched his eye. "I may need to build a new orbital socket."

Brad grimaced. "Sorry about that. But you have to admit, it looked damning when I walked in."

Marc nodded and winced. "Yeah. I understand." He focused his good eye on Karly, now dressed in jean shorts and a red halter top, feet bare. "I'm so sorry. I don't usually go around accosting women."

She smiled. "I understand. Probably better than most. You're a doctor, huh? Now, why would Kinsey ever think you were a cowboy or rancher?"

He shrugged and looked at his chapped hands. "I guess it's

because I have rough hands." He frowned. "Surgical scrub does that. Plus, I play a lot of tennis and compete in amateur rodeo—hey, I bet I was wearing my calf-roping buckle when we met."

She nodded. "Yep. That would do it."

"Were you at the steak house in Corpus night before last?" She shook her head, and his heart dropped. "Oh, then I guess it was her. She was with someone." He dug the engagement ring out of his pocket. "I found this at the beach house after she left." He gave a humorless laugh. "If I wanted a sign, I sure got one."

"No!" Karly protested, grabbing the ring and tossing it aside. "The guy you saw her with was probably Zach—or Dr. Dull, as I call him. He gave her that ring ages ago and refused to take it back. She never was serious about him. In fact, she was going to meet him to tell him to leave her alone before she had a restraining order put on him."

"But she didn't come to the beach house last weekend. I waited, but—"

"I was afraid she'd do that." Karly's mouth—not nearly as kissable as her sister's, now that he'd had a closer look—turned down. "She was really upset about something that happened the last weekend you were together. Said it would be better to just end it."

The kitchen-table thing, as he'd suspected. His heart clenched. What had gotten into him to act that way?

"It's all my fault." He scrubbed his face with his hands, trying not to wince when he touched his eye. "I need to talk to her, but I'm afraid she won't want to hear anything I have to say."

"So . . . what did you want to say to her?" Karly asked, a little smile playing with her lips.

"Karly!" Brad's hand clamped over his wife's mouth. "Don't pay any attention to her. She's a little, ah, nuts when it comes to her sister. Ow! You bit me!"

"Damn right! And I'm *not* nuts!" She leaned toward Marc, a pleading look in her eyes. "Kinsey's not had the best track record when it comes to romance. I just don't want her to get hurt. She didn't say much about what happened during your last weekend together, but I got the impression it scared her."

Marc hung his head. "Damn. That's what I was afraid of when she didn't show." He met Karly's gaze. "I got a little carried away. She said some things that cut and I guess I wanted to strike back. I—"

"What are you talking about? She said her reactions scared the hell out of her and she thought it would be better for both of you if she didn't go back again. She said you deserved better."

"*I* deserved better? *She* deserves better! Much better than anything I could—"

"Hold on, hold on." Brad held up one big hand. "It sounds to me as though you and my sister-in-law need to talk." He looked pointedly at his wife. "Alone."

"I agree, but how do I get in touch with her? Does she even live here in South Padre?"

Karly shook her head. "Nope. She lives in Corpus Christi." She opened a kitchen drawer and rummaged around before withdrawing a business card. "Here's her card." She reached back into the drawer for a pen and wrote something on the back of the card. "These are her home and cell numbers, if you can't reach her at work."

He stared at the card she handed him. "She's a financial analyst?"

She nodded. "And in very high demand. She conducts seminars, mostly."

"And what if I can't get her to meet with me?" And why should she? She'd made her decision.

"You just leave that to me," Karly said with a smile.

* * *

Kinsey gripped her briefcase handle and juggled the paper-work she'd brought for the seminar for the Wallace Medical Group. All the graphs and pie charts should already have been delivered.

Taking baby steps lest the new high heels she'd bought to cheer her up cause her to slip on the highly polished marble foyer, she approached the concierge desk.

"Excuse me? Hello?" The young man looked up and she swallowed a shriek of surprise at the multiple piercings on his lip, nose and eyebrow. "Could you direct me to the Bluebonnet conference room?"

"Sure," he said in a less than thrilled tone. "It's straight down that hall to your right, almost to the end. You'll see the sign. But it's reserved for the afternoon. Some medical seminar thing."

"Yes, I know. Thanks." She yanked up on the papers, hop-ing she'd maintain her grip until she reached her destination.

The hallway stretched on forever, but finally she spotted the sign proclaiming her destination. The door to the conference room was propped open.

Her new shoes were almost as slippery on the plush carpet, making little whooshing sounds with each careful step. She de-posited her burden and looked around the deserted room. Along the far end, several pitchers of ice water and tea sat next to up-turned stemware. Croissants were arranged on a silver platter, and pats of butter rested in a silver bowl of crushed ice. A glance at her watch confirmed that less than five minutes remained be-fore the seminar was scheduled to begin. Where was everyone?

After placing several stacks of hand-out sheets around the table, she looked at her watch again. It was now five minutes past time to start and she was still the only person in the room.

The first vase of red roses arrived and was placed on the cen-ter of the round conference table. Within ten minutes, twenty more had joined the original.

"There must be a mistake," she told the delivery boy. "I'm scheduled to give a seminar in here. The flowers are filling up almost the entire table!"

In response, he grinned and said, "Oh, no mistake, Ms. Carlyle." With that, he gave a small salute and left the room, closing the door behind him.

That was when she noticed a box, behind the door, wrapped in gold foil with a splashy gold and silver foil ribbon bow. Her name was on the gift tag. She gave it a hesitant shake, then slipped off the top to discover another wrapped box—and the bathing suit she'd never worn at the beach house.

Her hand shook as she unwrapped the smaller box. It held the risqué nightie Marc had bought for her, nestling a much smaller gift-wrapped box. The tag read *Do not open unless/until you are willing to wear these items of clothing. Love, Marc.*

A quick glance confirmed that she was still alone. The hall door was the only opening, so there was no adjoining bathroom. He found her. Did she dare risk putting on the clothing before she began her seminar?

The carpet tickled her feet when she stepped out of her shoes. With a careful watch on the door, she reached under the short skirt of her dress and yanked her thong down her thigh-high stockings. The thong was shoved into her briefcase. Still watching the door, she shimmied into the sheer bottoms of the nightie, since she had no idea how to tie the bikini strings. She'd just straightened her skirt when the door opened and Marc walked in.

He looked so gorgeous, her eyes stung. Her nostrils flared with the heady scent of his aftershave as he slowly walked toward her. Dressed in a charcoal pinstriped suit with a pale blue shirt and red tie, he could have stepped from the cover of *GQ*. As he came closer, she saw the red of his tie was actually millions of tiny painted lips. Against her slick folds, the embroidery of another pair of lips pressed against sensitive flesh. And she smiled.

Marc stopped a foot in front of her with a tentative smile. "Hello, Kinsey." He leaned to brush her surprised lips with his warm ones. "I've missed you." He glanced at the flowers and opened boxes. "Are you ready?"

Oh, baby, am I ever! Her flesh was already weeping for him. But, wait. She had a seminar to conduct.

"I have a seminar—"

"I know." His hand encompassed the room. "This is it. Or rather, I'm it."

She shook her head, telling her heart to slow down, ordering her hormones not to get too excited. "No. It's with the Wallace Medical Group. I'm supposed to—"

He traced the edge of her neckline with his index finger, leaving a fiery trail. "I guess I should introduce myself and let you get on with it, then." He unbuttoned the double-breasted coatdress she wore, exposing her black lace push-up bra and the sheer panties she'd donned. His lips compressed in a tight line while his thumbs brushed back and forth over her lace-covered nipples. His nostrils flared.

Her eyes closed with a sigh. She really should stop him before people started arriving and they were both embarrassed. But it'd been so long since he'd touched her and she missed him so much.

He tugged her dress from her shoulders, putting a stop to her sensual reveling.

"Marc! Stop." She reached out, stopping the downward plunge of her clothing. "I have a seminar to conduct and people will be here any minute."

His eyes met hers, but his hands remained on her breasts, fingers toying with the lace edge of her bra. "Ah, yes. The introduction. I forgot." He smiled into her eyes. "I'm Dr. Marcus

Wallace and I'm the head of the Wallace Medical Group." At her stunned look, he explained. "I found you through your sister and arranged today's seminar. Today's *private* seminar."

"You mean, you're it? You're the only person scheduled to attend the seminar?" He nodded and she tried to wrap her mind around the exorbitant amount he'd had to spend in order to get her all to himself for the next three hours.

"Why didn't you just call me?" she whispered.

"I thought a grand gesture was in order, after the way we parted," he whispered back.

"Oh." She was numb, watching his hands skim her body beneath her dress.

"You put on the panties, I see," he said with a smile.

She nodded. His hands went to his belt.

The suit pants met the carpet with the chink of change and rattle of the gold belt buckle.

He gathered her in his arms, his sex hot and insistent against her ribs. His kiss set off a chain of wild fires that threatened to engulf her.

"I've missed you so much, Kinsey!" he said against her mouth before crushing her lips. "I wanted to wait, to do this right, but I can't wait any longer! I love you!" he growled as he lifted her and plunged his erection through the crotchless panties into her ready heat.

The paneled wall of the conference room was cool against her bare back, its smooth surface a welcome contrast to the hard-muscled heat pounding her. With a cry of joy, she wrapped her legs more securely around his hips and pulled him deeper still. "I love you, too," she whispered in his ear, tears clogging her throat.

Their cries of completion echoed from the tall ceiling. Marc sat in the high-backed chair at the table, cradling Kinsey on his lap, still intimately joined. When she tried to lean back, his arms tightened, holding her close to his heart.

"But, Marc—" she said against his lips as he nibbled hers. "What if someone tries to—come in?"

He concentrated on peeling down the cups of her bra. "Not gonna happen," he told her when he was rewarded by the heavy heat of her breasts in his palms. "I told you." He leaned down to kiss a breast. "I'm your only client." He drew the tip of his tongue over each nipple, then gently blew on the peaks and watched them tighten. He smiled down at her. "Besides, I took the precaution of locking the door." He shifted slightly and grinned. "Thank you for wearing these, by the way. It made things much more expedient."

She buried her face against his collarbone and tried to stop her self-conscious giggle.

"Hey," he said, lifting her chin with the tip of his finger. "Don't be embarrassed. Not with me. Never with me." His lips brushed hers. He reached back to drag the gift box closer. "Now open your last gift, darlin'."

With a curious look at him, she tore open the paper, then stared at what looked suspiciously like a ring box. Did she dare hope?

Sure, they'd only known each other four weeks, but if the feelings of loss and misery she'd felt since leaving him were any indication, those feelings were deep. And lasting. The trepidation she felt while looking at the box was totally unlike the feelings she'd had when Zachary proposed.

If Marc was not proposing, if this wasn't what she hoped it was, how would she disguise her disappointment?

"It's not going to bite, you know." Marc plucked the box from her numb fingers. "I know it's kind of sudden and I'll understand if you tell me to take a hike, but, Kinsey, I love you so much I hurt with it." He took something out of the box, but her tears were blurring her vision.

"I can't imagine living another week without you, much less my life." He held her left hand. "I want to have beautiful babies with you. Grow old with you. So . . . will you put me out of my misery and marry me?"

The gold felt cool against the third finger of her left hand. The large diamond flashed and winked through her tears.

She sniffed and croaked, "Who gets to drive the Jag?"

Jack of Hearts

1

Jack McMillan took another sip of his Jose Cuervo and lime, leaned back in his lounge chair and tried to enjoy the impending sunset over the Gulf of Mexico.

Over. After six years, Mardee told him to take a hike. Just like that, it was all over. Well, okay, maybe not just like that.

Mardee had a point. Had he truly been in love with her, it wouldn't have taken six years to make a decision to commit. His drink sloshed onto his hand. And, sure, maybe he did drink a bit too much, on occasion. But, damn, he was going to miss her.

He glanced at the cordless phone. Would she even want to talk to him? What would he say?

The rumble of a big truck interrupted his ruminations.

He leaned closer to the side of his deck and looked down to see a moving van. After all these years, old man Gooding must have finally sold his beach house. Great timing. Just when he wanted, needed, to be alone. Well, the new neighbors better not expect him to act all warm and fuzzy—in short, neighborly.

He got more comfortable in the chaise and closed his eyes,

letting the sound of the surf soothe him. Maybe things would look better after a short nap.

Bright sunlight woke him the next morning. He knew it was morning because the ice in his glass had long since melted and the inside of his mouth tasted like a sewer.

Jack stretched and scratched his belly, then dragged himself into the beach house for a shower.

It took a moment for his eyes to adjust to the dimness. When he could make out the shape of the spiral staircase leading to the second-floor master suite, he pointed his feet in that direction, trying not to notice how quiet the house seemed. Empty.

While the shower warmed up, he brushed and flossed his teeth, then stood staring at his reflection. He looked like he'd just come off a three-day drunk. He glanced at his analog watch. Pretty close to it. He leaned closer to the mirror to inspect the damage.

Well, all the red added contrasting color to his green eyes. The tops of his ears were burnt, thanks to his new short haircut.

Making a note to slather his head and shoulders with sunscreen before his next trip to the deck, he stepped into the six-head shower and waited to feel human again.

Feeling almost cheerful, he stepped out on the deck with his breakfast, a Bloody Mary. He took a big gulp and winced.

"Breakfast of champions," he muttered, looking out across the water.

He abso-damn-lutely did not have a drinking problem. Regardless of what Mardee thought. His self-imposed leave of absence from his cardiology practice was for a long overdue vacation. And to lick his wounds.

Country-western music, at eardrum-splitting decibels, assaulted his ears. He whipped his head to look in the direction of the sound, then had to wait for his brain to catch up.

Had he not been wearing sunglasses, his eyes would surely have rolled out of his head at the sight.

Golden skin glistened in the morning sunshine; the firm globes of a decidedly feminine backside covered by nothing more than a piece of fat dental floss taunted him.

He fumbled for the table and set his drink down, then lowered himself into his chaise to watch the show.

Beautifully tapered arms reached behind a firm back to untie the floral-print top of the most miniscule bikini he'd seen in years.

No doubt about it, his new neighbor was in fine shape. As a physician, he was trained to appreciate things like that. As a testosterone-laden male in his prime, his appreciation edged up another notch or two.

Her long, dark hair was twisted on top of her head with some kind of clamp, leaving the sexy column of her neck bare to his inspection. Keeping her back to him, she stretched out on her stomach, obviously ready to begin her tanning.

What kind of neighbor would he be, he asked himself, if he didn't at least go over and welcome her to Pleasure Beach?

Decision made, he went into the house and made short work out of making himself presentable. Less than ten minutes later, he stepped onto his deck, more relieved than he cared to admit to find his new neighbor exactly where he'd left her.

Balancing the tray carrying two fat Fuzzy Navels, he negotiated the steps without spilling a drop and soon found himself standing next to the sun goddess, his Hawaiian-print shirt flapping in the ocean breeze.

He cleared his throat. She didn't move. Carefully setting the drinks on a small teak table next to her chair, he cleared his throat again. Still no response.

"Hello." He reached down to tap a firm, sun-warmed shoulder.

The woman jumped up with a shriek and his mouth went dry.

For the fraction of the second before she grabbed her towel, the image of world-class breasts was forever burned into his mind.

"Jack! What the hell are you doing here?"

He pulled his reluctant gaze to the very unfriendly but familiar face of Mardee's sister's best friend. "Royce," he said, hoping his disappointment wasn't obvious.

With a snooty sniff, she wrapped the damned towel tighter around her delectable but definitely off-limits body.

He raked a hand through his spiked hair, idly wondering how he was going to get out of this with his hide still intact. "I still can't figure out what kind of person names their daughter Royce," he muttered, for lack of anything better to say.

"Obviously someone who was determined to have a son." She leaned toward the drinks, then looked up at him. "Are one of these for me?"

"May as well. No point in letting them go to waste."

She took a tentative sip. He watched with detached fascination while the pink tip of her tongue circled her lips to gather the taste and wondered what it would be like to feel that tongue on parts of his body he had no business thinking about when he was around this woman.

Royce St. Claire was a royal pain in the ass. Mouthy and opinionated, she goaded Mardee's sister into doing things she would otherwise avoid.

When it appeared she wasn't going to initiate small talk, or any talk for that matter, he sat down in the chair opposite her and took a long draw from the remaining drink. The peach schnapps mingled with the sweet orange juice to dance around on his taste buds in a delightful early-morning tango.

He watched the rise and fall of her ample bosom beneath the beach towel and thought of other delightful early-morning tangos.

Back, off, Jack! This woman is so not your type, it isn't even funny.

"So are you going to tell me what you're doing here on a private beach?" Damn, that sounded uppity, even to him.

Her thickly lashed violet eyes regarded him over the rim of her drink for so long, he thought she wasn't going to answer.

"I bought this house," she said in a velvet soft voice that clenched his gut. "I assumed that included rights to access the *private* beach."

Embarrassment—the curse of redheads—heated his cheeks. Before he could censor his words, he said, "How did you earn enough money to buy a place like this? You're barely out of college. Don't try to tell me your smutty radio program pays you that well."

Jaw clenched, she set her drink on the table. "If you'd paid the least bit of attention, you'd know I earned my PhD several years ago. That hardly qualifies as 'barely out of college.'" Violet fire shot from her narrowed eyes. "As for my program ... smutty? Tell me, Jack, have you ever even listened to my show?"

"Of course not!" He snorted and took another drink. "I have better things to do with my late nights."

"Ah," she said with a knowing nod. "Masturbation."

Jack choked on his drink and put it down while he wiped his face with the tail of his shirt. "Masturbation? What kind of mind do you have? No—don't answer. I don't want to know." He stood and retrieved his tray. "Forget I asked. In fact, forget you ever saw me, okay?"

"I inherited it." Her quiet voice stopped him at the edge of her deck.

He turned back, not quite sure he'd heard correctly. "What?"

"The money to buy this place." Lying on her stomach again,

back bared to the rays, she shielded her eyes with one hand to see him. "I inherited it."

"From a grandmother or something?"

"Something like that." She turned her face away from him, indicating the conversation was over.

"Right. Well, you're welcome for the drink. I won't bother you anymore." With that, he stomped down the steps, tossed his tray in the general direction of his deck and headed toward the water. Maybe a jog along the beach would clear his head of all the illicit thoughts he'd had since spying Royce's rounded bottom.

His day was a total bust, thanks to his new neighbor. Whenever he tried to accomplish anything around his house to prepare for the next wave of renters, thoughts of Royce's breasts and the curve of her hips had him feeling edgy and restless.

He sat on his deck nursing a beer and a grudge in the dark, until he heard her drive away. Another hour passed before he summoned enough energy to go inside.

Still feeling restless, he showered, then slipped naked beneath the sheets of his round, custom-made bed.

Sleep eluded him.

A push of the button on the bedside remote opened the rounded wall of windows with a soft whir. Sounds of the waves bounced off the curved walls, reminding him of being inside a giant seashell. Always soothing, tonight it failed to work its magic.

He glanced at the radio on the nightstand, then forced his mind to relax. Another glance. What would it hurt to tune in just once and listen to what she might have to say? After all, he *had* formed strong opinions of her without ever catching her program.

He remembered her station was at the end of the dial, but it took a few minutes of searching before her husky voice wrapped around him and stroked his senses. He'd forgotten the depth and sexiness of it. Until now.

"What night games do you like to play?" she asked her radio audience with the voice of a sex kitten, taunting him. "Call me . . . ." She recited the station phone number. Just hearing the smooth enunciation of each number had him hard as a rock.

He listened to each caller, wondering how she kept from laughing at some of the outrageous things they said. Then his breath caught at her reply, his cock growing so hard it felt as though it might burst.

His hand crept beneath the satin sheet. At first he played with his balls, imagining it was her hand fondling him so intimately. By the next call, he was stroking his hard length, then pinching the tip. Before her program ended, he was pumping fast and furious, his hips bucking off the mattress, seeking release.

"Until tomorrow, I wish you love . . . and good mental health." But he knew what she really meant. Her unspoken closing line, said by her husky voice in his mind, whispered, "Keep the sheets warm for me. . . . I'll be in your wet dreams."

Her voice stroked him as surely as if her pouty lips were wrapped tightly around his dick. With a strangled cry, he arched once more, squeezing and pumping until his sheet stuck to him like a second skin. Wrung out, he was too weak to move.

He idly listened to her voice urging everyone to tune in tomorrow, though she really meant for everyone to obey their deepest fantasies. He just knew it.

A smile tugged his lips. Right now his deepest fantasy included having Royce St. Claire in his bed.

If only he didn't have to put up with her attitude.

He was a doctor. . . . Maybe he could drug her.

2

Royce began stripping the moment she walked into the house. Naked by the time she reached her Jacuzzi tub, she turned the jets on full force and lowered herself into the water as soon as possible.

She watched the bubbles jiggle her breasts while the jets beneath her helped relieve a different sort of pressure.

Damn Jack McMillan! Ever since he'd appeared on her deck that morning, he'd filled her thoughts. It was useless to waste this much time thinking about someone like that. He was everything she didn't want in a man or, worse, a potential mate.

Cocky and arrogant as hell, Jack personified the unattainable. Heck, just ask Mardee! Wendy's older sister had wasted more than six years of her life on that man. For nothing. He wasn't the marrying kind. Commitment phobic, he was the male equivalent of eye candy. So why couldn't she get him out of her mind?

She'd deliberately baited her listeners tonight, showing off, probably hoping he was listening. Was he?

Her hand slid beneath the churning water to touch her

aching nub. She deserved to be uncomfortable. She'd turned herself on tonight, letting her mind wander to illicit thoughts of Jack and what she'd wanted to do to him—with him—for six long years.

Her hands skimmed up her torso to tweak her nipples. She arched, aching and empty.

And it was all Jack's fault.

Jack's steps slowed, then stopped altogether. To his left, the surf edged closer to wash over his bare feet. To his right, Royce was preparing her morning sun-worshiping ritual.

He took another step and stopped again, watching the sun glint off well-oiled shoulders. Damn woman was ruining his morning runs. He hadn't had a good workout since she'd begun parking her delectable body on the deck next to his every morning for the past week.

She knew it, he was sure. The blue-balled agony he'd experienced of late had Royce St. Claire written all over it.

Irritated with himself as well as her, he took off again, only to stop and bite back a yelp of pain when his right big toe firmly connected with a rock.

Royce didn't even look up as he hobbled past her deck. Okay, so maybe he was passing closer than absolutely necessary, but, hell, he was injured. The least the woman could do would be to look up to see how brave he was being in the face of what surely would be unbearable pain for a lesser man.

Not that he wanted her to notice.

He dragged himself up the steps and across the scorching hot deck, and was about to open his sliding glass door when her voice floated over.

"You're limping. Are you okay?"

Ridiculously weak with relief for some insane reason, he leaned against the door frame and waited a beat before he answered.

"What do you care?"

"Oh, Jackie," she purred as she rolled over to sit up and look over at him, "don't be like that."

She poured oil into her palms and leisurely stroked it over the tops of her plump breasts. One good tug and her flesh-colored miniscule top would be history.

His cock sprang to immediate attention, the pain in his toe forgotten.

She tugged on her straps, the action lifting her breasts as though testing their weight. "If you promise to play nice, I might be persuaded to share my lunch with you."

With a quick adjustment to his suddenly tight shorts, he stepped over to the railing for a closer look. Good gravy—from a distance the woman looked totally naked. How had he missed that?

"How nice do I have to play?" he asked, praying his voice wouldn't crack with his eagerness.

She stood and wrapped the huge towel around herself, depriving him of a view he hadn't even realized he craved.

"You have to promise to keep your pants zipped." She raised her black-framed sunglasses and trained her eyes on him. "I know you, Jack McMillan. I refuse to be another notch on your bedpost." She walked to her own patio door. "I have a fabulous lobster salad, but it's way too much for me. I'm willing to share it. But that's all I'm willing to share." She waited a beat. "Nod if you understand."

Chagrined to realize he'd been staring at her terry-cloth-covered breasts, praying for another glimpse of a body that made his mouth water, he took a step back. "When and where do you want me?"

Royce stepped out of a quick shower and scrubbed dry with more force than absolutely necessary. *When and where do you want me?* Wow! If he only knew.

The first time she'd laid eyes on Dr. Jack McMillan, the moisture surge between her legs had taken her by surprise. Over the last six years, she'd become rather used to the dampness that just the sound of his name inspired.

His innocent question conjured up a plethora of X-rated, erotic images. Scratch that—nothing about Jack McMillan was innocent. The rascal no doubt knew exactly the effect he had on her, parading around in nothing but a pair of the briefest running shorts every morning for her viewing pleasure.

She could definitely think of a few other things she'd like to drizzle melted butter over and lick off, besides lobster.

Striding into the walk-in closet, she surveyed her meager wardrobe. No doubt about it, a serious shopping trip was in her future. Whatever possessed her to shove such a meager wardrobe into her bag for her move to the beach? Jack. Or rather the possibility of finally snagging his attention. Heck, face it, she'd planned to be naked with him. Or hoped to be. For that, clothing was way down her list of necessities. Faced with reality, though, her sexual fantasy of being with Jack was much safer than actually following through with her plan.

Since it would be harmless to tease and tantalize a bit, her only choice was the decadent red sundress Wendy dared her to buy on her last visit.

After slathering coconut scented moisturizer all over, she slid the sand-washed silk dress over her head and marveled again at the sensual feel as it settled against her heated skin. Loose fitting, it hinted at the curves beneath, but the way it hugged and moved with her body made underwear intrusive. Besides, she'd always loved the way the gentle abrasion, like a lover's caress, made her nipples harden.

She frowned at her reflection in the full-length mirror. The back of the dress draped loosely around her hips, barely concealing the flare of her bottom, while it dipped even more dangerously low in the front. Miniscule spaghetti straps held up the tiny triangle bodice that shielded her nipples. The rippled hemline ended midthigh in front and brushed the backs of her knees with silken kisses.

The knock on her patio door sounded just as she clamped her hair on top of her head for the third time. Shoving her feet into a sky-high pair of strappy red sandals, she headed for the stairs, chiding herself for being so nervous.

Nothing was going to happen. It couldn't. Not with Jack McMillan. But a girl could dream.

Jack's mouth went dry when he saw Royce's long legs appear on the stairway. He watched her stride toward the patio door in her hooker-red, high-heeled sandals and her little wisp of a nothing, fuck-me dress, and all blood headed south. He could not have formed a coherent thought if his life depended on it.

Thank goodness this was Royce, not someone who really mattered or someone he was even remotely interested in on any level other than the purely physical one.

He extended the bottle of white zinfandel to her and managed a grunt.

If she noticed, she didn't acknowledge his caveman behavior. Her radiant smile instilled guilt about the direction his thoughts had been headed.

Then she turned to walk toward the kitchen and her dress gaped, revealing the lush curve of her right breast, the barest hint of the dark edge of a nipple.

Like a dog, he began salivating while he followed the beguiling sway of red silk, his hands itching to rip it from her body.

"I hope you don't mind," she said over the roar in his ears, "but I thought we'd eat in the kitchen. It's so hot on the deck at this time of day."

She stretched across the counter. The deep V in the back of

her dress shifted to the side, revealing the plump curve of her ass. Was her skin as smooth and soft as it looked?

The scent of coconut wafted toward him, making his mouth water as he walked up close behind her. Close enough to touch. What would she do if he ran his hands up under her dress?

At that moment she turned, a wicked-looking corkscrew in her hand. "Would you open the wine while I get the food?"

"Ah, sure." He grabbed the corkscrew and relished the feel of the handle digging into his palm.

"I'm glad you accepted my invitation, Jack," she said from behind the stainless-steel refrigerator door. With a bump of her hip, she closed the door and walked toward him with a sweet smile on her face.

He didn't trust that smile.

"Why?" He took a step back, valiantly avoiding physical contact as she walked by.

"Well, I always felt like you didn't like me very much."

"I didn't really know you."

"Yeah, I know. I was Mardee's little sister's friend." She shrugged a shapely shoulder and he wondered how much movement the tiny straps would take before they gave way. "I know I was sort of a nonentity to you."

"I really didn't think about you one way or the other." It was a blatant lie. Coward that he was, he had avoided Royce like the plague ever since he was horrified to realize the woman gave him an instant boner whenever she was within a mile of him.

Mardee had noticed, but chose not to discuss it. Mardee chose to ignore a lot over the last six years. He knew she, her friends and family all thought he couldn't commit because he was a major player. Hell, yes, he looked and lusted.

In his mind. He'd been faithful to Mardee while they were together.

His hostess bent over the table to straighten a fork. It hit him. He was not in a relationship at the moment. He was free.

Free to pursue the crazed, lustful reactions he'd experienced whenever he was near Royce St. Claire for the last six years.

If he wanted.

3

Royce gathered the dirty dishes and prayed her legs would support her weight. Why did she get weak in the knees just looking across the table at Jack?

Baiting him over lunch had been fun, but she honestly could not recall the taste of a single bite. It had taken all her concentration to keep from squirming under his heated gaze.

Standing now, she was once more in command of the situation. She leaned over the table to retrieve his plate, allowing her breasts to sway slightly beneath the gaping neckline of her dress.

Jack's eyes, riveted to her cleavage, widened. Color flooded his face, tingeing the tops of his ears.

But he didn't move so much as a finger.

Damn! This was much more difficult than she'd imagined when she'd decided to play with him.

She hadn't counted on the constant yearning and restless feelings inspired by just thinking about him.

Why hadn't he made a move? Was she that unappealing? She

leaned closer, feeling the ribbon trim of her bodice scrape along the edge of her nipple.

C'mon, Jack, take it! You know you want it. What good was planning a little slap and tickle if your chosen playmate refused to cooperate?

Still, Jack sat. For all the good it did her, he may as well have been carved out of stone.

Strolling around the table, her erect nipples rubbing the silk with each step, she reached past him for his wineglass, 'accidentally' brushing the side of his face with her breast.

His breath heated her skin, but still he made no move.

She chanced a glimpse. His heated gaze locked with hers. Relief flooded her when she realized he was not totally unaffected.

Steam practically wafted off him.

"Unless you want me," he said in a low, guttural growl, "I suggest you remove your breast from the vicinity of my mouth."

Her breath hitched. This was what she'd hoped for, but was she brave enough to carry it through to the logical conclusion?

"And if I don't want to move it?" Her breathless whisper sent a bolt of disgust through her.

"Drop the strap and find out."

Jack may have interpreted the slow movement of her hand up her opposite arm as seductive, but in reality it was the only way to stop it from shaking.

Finally, *finally*, eyes locked with his, she felt the edge of the spaghetti strap and hooked her index finger beneath it.

An almost infinitesimal tug was all it took. The rounded silken strap fell to her elbow. The triangle patch of fabric covering her nipple followed, baring her left breast to his hungry gaze.

Still he did nothing, his warm breath bathing her distended

nipple, setting off aching shards of awareness throughout her body.

"Tell me what you want, Royce."

She bit back the urge to scream for him to take her in his mouth.

"S—suck it," she finally managed to whisper.

"No."

No? Had he really said no?

Humiliation burned her cheeks.

Before she could straighten away from him and cover herself, his hard hand grasped her right shoulder, anchoring her in place.

One thumb, so much rougher in texture than her own, rubbed back and forth, over her shoulder, beneath the other strap.

"I don't do things halfway," he explained, still toying with her strap. "If I'm going to make the effort to suck a woman's nipple, I want both of them."

With that, he slid the other strap to her elbow, effectively pinning her arms to her sides.

His warm hands closed over both breasts, driving rational thought from her mind, making her weak in the knees. And wet, oh, so wet.

He tugged her closer, urging her to straddle his lap as he covered her lips with his.

She sighed into his mouth. Yes! After all these years, she was right where she wanted to be. Okay, well, almost where she wanted to be.

She'd heard Jack was a great kisser, but great was always open to interpretation. As his tongue slid along hers, his hands sending delicious sensations through her breasts, she decided he'd been horribly underrated.

He sucked and nibbled her lips, dipping back into her mouth occasionally, then made his way downward.

She became spineless, pliable, arching back to give him greater access.

His mouth replaced his hand. His tongue circled her aureola with maddening slowness before flicking the very end of her nipple with the hardened tip.

Every thought, every flicker of sensation centered on that one spot. She scarcely breathed, her heart tripping within her chest.

Finally his mouth covered her aching nipple, drawing it deeply into his wet heat.

She bit down on her lower lip, hard, to keep from keening her pleasure.

Through the damp silk of her skirt, his hardness made the glorious announcement: She was not the only one turned on by his actions.

The realization emboldened her. Unfortunately, her straps restricted her movements so she could not reciprocate by exploring his golden body.

When his mouth moved to her other breast, the explosion between her legs took her by surprise. Before she could stop it, she was in the throes of a full-blown orgasm. Waves of pleasure washed through her again and again until she was limp and weak, hanging in his arms.

He stood, lifting her high, and strode into the living room to place her on the sofa.

After arranging her limp body to his satisfaction, he lifted her skirt. Cool air caressed her moist, heated skin, but she was too wrung out at the moment to move a muscle.

Hot hands skimmed her inner thighs, gently parting her legs for further exploration. Immediately, moisture surged indicating how responsive her body was to him, even in her weakened condition.

He knelt between the vibrating muscles of her thighs, his breath fanning her exposed core.

"I knew it," he whispered against her folds. "I knew you were pantyless." His tongue barely touched her sensitized feminine lips.

He placed a gentle kiss on her opening, then smoothed her dress down into place.

Stunned, she could only gape as he straightened her straps and bestowed a chaste kiss on her forehead.

"Thanks for lunch . . . and dessert." His cocky grin was back. If she'd had the strength, she would have slapped it from his handsome face. "I'll let myself out."

With that, he was gone.

Royce blinked and struggled to sit up. What had happened to make him change his mind?

Jack ran as fast as the iron erection in his shorts would allow, not slowing until he gained the cool safety of his own house and the master suite.

Stripping, he walked into the bathroom and stepped beneath the icy needles of the shower.

He looked down. Obviously, cold showers were an urban legend.

Speaking of legends . . . the hot number next door had been more difficult to walk away from than he'd anticipated. But the look on the little tease's face was worth it.

Just the thought of her sweetly weeping pussy had his cock pulsing with renewed interest.

Maybe he should have taken what she so obviously offered.

Thoughts of his lifestyle, his past, flashed. All his life he'd been overindulgent. He drank too much, and had pretty much nailed anything that moved in his direction.

Until Mardee.

After he'd met Mardee, he still looked, but that's where it ended. After their breakup, his first thought was to get laid by as many women as possible after such a long dry spell. So far, he'd scored exactly . . . nothing. Zero. Hell, until Royce, he'd begun to wonder if his cock still worked.

Just the thought of Royce had the questionable member leaping to life.

Though it was a relief to know he wasn't impotent, why Royce, when no other women had affected him?

He tended to gravitate toward buxom blondes whose chest measurements exceeded their IQ. Although Mardee had been no dummy, she met the other requirements.

When he and Mardee had first met, they'd set the sheets on fire. He frowned. Funny, when he tried to bring up mental pictures of Mardee, all he could see was Royce, her dark hair in disarray from his pleasuring her, eyes shining. Of course, those thoughts brought others: her rosy nipples glistening from his mouth, her flat belly and plump, bare sex, swollen with arousal.

With a growl, he stepped out of the shower and jerked his towel from the heated rack.

"Get out of my mind, Royce St. Claire!" Throwing the towel into the hamper, he stomped into the closet and tugged on his tightest running shorts.

If he couldn't will her out of his mind, maybe he could wear her out of it with exhaustion.

4

Royce watched Jack's retreating back get smaller as he ran down the beach. With a sigh, she dropped the sheer curtain back to her kitchen window and began loading the dishwasher.

A lonely afternoon of tanning on the deck held no appeal. She glanced at her rumpled dress. Shopping was definitely in order, but seemed more of a chore than she was up for at the moment.

A sad smile tugged at her mouth. She could chuck the whole idea of beginning a new life and just while away her days with nude sunbathing and working through every night until the numbness overcame her again.

Numbing her brain with work had been her salvation once. It could happen again.

She looked back at the tiny dot that was Jack. Maybe.

Slow steps took her up to the full-length mirror in the master bath where she let her sundress fall to the tile floor in a silken puddle.

A golden tan kissed most of her body. Her breasts were still firm and full, waist narrow, hips slender. Long legs tapered to slim ankles and feet that were average.

Her eyes narrowed. If she were a man, would she find herself appealing?

Many men had, over the years. Up to and including Gerald, the man she'd found endearing until he'd crossed the line.

As usual, her thoughts came back to Jack, bringing with them the familiar surge of moisture. Her sex looked pouty, slick and bare from her recent Brazilian wax. After the initial pain, the pleasure had been worth it. The air clicked on, blowing a gentle breeze across her dampness, reminding her of the way Jack's breath had fanned the same spot mere minutes ago.

Had she done something wrong? Been too eager? Too easy? Was she too fat? Too thin? Was he not over Mardee? According to Wendy, the split had been a mutual decision with no ill will on either side. Of course, Wendy only knew Mardee's version.

It was unfathomable how any living, breathing woman could agree to ending it with Dr. Jack McMillan.

She touched her damp folds and groaned. Jack. She ached for Jack.

She had to have him. He wasn't totally immune to her. She knew the stirring of arousal when she felt it.

The mere thought of clothing made her nerve endings scream their frustration. She wandered downstairs and filled an ice bucket. With a will of their own, her eyes looked down the beach.

Jack jogged past her house and up the steps of his deck, then disappeared through his sliding door.

Before she could tell herself all the reasons why it was a bad idea, she ran up the steps and threw on a billowy purple silk caftan and, all but tripping in her haste, skipped back down the stairs and out the door.

If Jack turned her down again, there was always her vibrator.

One way or another, she would get satisfaction tonight.

* * *

Jack stood beneath the stinging spray, its icy needles taking his breath away. But not, unfortunately, his erection.

He closed his eyes and willed Royce from his mind, tried to think of baseball. But all that came to his mind's eye was Royce, dressed in a catcher's pad—and nothing else.

"Royce!" he called with a growl.

The glass door opened, cooler air whooshing in around his heated body.

"Yes?" She stood at the open shower door, nude, moisture from the spray glistening her golden, perfect body.

He closed his eyes and took a deep breath before opening them.

She was still there. Still gorgeous. Still sexy as hell. Why was he fighting the inevitable?

He opened his arms and she stepped into the shower and his embrace.

Her sharp intake of breath had him grabbing for the controls to warm the water. Instant steam filled the cubicle. Within his arms, she gave a slight shiver, her hardened nipples erotically rubbing against his chest.

On tiptoe, she nibbled his lower lip, causing a riptide of sensation to tear through him. His heart tightened, warning him this was more than a casual sexual encounter.

Her shoulders were warm and silky beneath his palms. It took all the willpower he possessed to gently pull her away from his willing body.

Questioning violet eyes looked up at him. Her full lower lip shone with moisture. Crystal water droplets hung suspended from her beaded nipples. Self-preservation kicked in. Swallowing a groan of sexual frustration, he croaked, "This doesn't mean anything. You know that, don't you?"

Her brows drew together, creating frown furrows.

"This"—he pulled her against him, flattening her breasts

against his chest—"this is all there can ever be." He palmed her buttocks. "I just want you to know that, going in."

Her lovely eyes narrowed. "Who said I was looking for anything else?"

"It's what you want?"

She nodded, her wandering hands threatening to short-circuit his thought process. "It's what I want," she said with a whisper.

He gripped her waist. "You got it, babe. Spread your legs and hold on."

He lifted her up past his shoulders and then down to impale her. Their gazes met. A slow smile curved her sexy mouth.

She leaned in and licked his chin, then wrapped her smooth legs around his hips. Her inner muscles clenched around his cock, making his knees go weak.

"Do it," she whispered next to his ear.

He didn't need to be told twice.

"Oh, my," Royce said when she could gasp through the desperately needed air wheezing in and out of her lungs. Her heart thundered in her rib cage. Against her back, the cool tile felt slick. Every muscle in her body vibrated. Had it not been for Jack's arms securely around her, she would have collapsed into a sated pile of mush on the shower floor.

Against her ear, Jack's breath still came in harsh pants, his heart beating a furious duet with hers. "You," he said on a breath, "can say that again."

He slid to sit on the tiled floor, holding her firmly on his lap. Warm water sluiced over them from the multiple showerheads.

Royce turned her face into the hollow of Jack's shoulder. "We're going to drown."

"I don't care." His breathing was as labored as hers. "I don't have the strength to move." He reached back to grope for the controls. "Give me a minute."

The water slowed to a trickle. He leaned his head against the shower wall, eyes closed. "I think you killed some brain cells."

"Mmmm." She snuggled closer. "I think it was a mutual massacre."

After a few minutes he shifted and hugged her closer. "Dynamite sex, Ms. St. Claire."

Silence. Damn. What had she done? Attacking Jack in his shower was not part of her master plan.

She attempted to pull back.

"Royce?"

"Look, Jack, while I appreciate your willingness to cuddle, an admitted rarity among men, I need you to just shut up."

5

Jack shifted, the tile floor flattening his buttocks, and looked at the woman he held so intimately on his lap. Now that his heart rate had slowed to something resembling normal, he questioned the sanity of participating in the sexual gluttony that had just transpired. Especially after her last statement.

And that's all it had been—sexual gratification. Regardless of how earth-shattering and mind-blowing, it was just sex.

Just sex.

The ridiculous feeling of tenderness was expected, given how Royce had just rocked his world. If he took her words at face value, it was obviously one-sided. He'd be fine in a few seconds.

"I'm sorry, Jack. This was a mistake. I—"

"Good God, woman, can't you shut up and just enjoy?" Two could play that game.

He knew his words were harsh, but her saying that it was a mistake cut more deeply than he cared to admit. And it was the final straw.

No wonder he'd never liked the woman.

He shoved her away and yanked the towels from the rack, tossing one at her as he stepped from the glass enclosure.

"Don't answer that," he said, wrapping the towel around his hips. "You know the way out."

He spun on his heel and walked out, not stopping until he heard her on the stairs, not relaxing until the soft slide and click of the patio door told him she'd gone.

Weak with relief, and maybe something else he didn't care to identify, he sank to the edge of his bed and waited for the feeling of certainty to come. He'd done the right thing. He didn't want or need a woman in his life right now. Ditto with a relationship.

Especially not with someone like Royce St. Claire.

"Stupid, pigheaded so-and-so!" Royce stomped up the steps of her deck, ignoring the burn of hot planks on her bare feet.

Her nail broke with a stinging pop when she attempted to throw open her patio door. "Damn!"

Sucking on the injured fingertip, she stalked across the room and up the stairs, not stopping until she'd flung her towel in the hamper and wrapped her silk kimono tightly around her shaking shoulders.

Tears of humiliation stung her eyes, burned her nose. She'd gone to Jack, opened herself to him as she'd done to no one else in a very long time. And what had Jack-the-ripper done? Torn out her heart and stomped on it. Brought up all her old insecurities, her feelings of not belonging, not being good enough.

She sniffed and wiped her eyes, then reached for a tissue from the box next to her bed.

Feelings she'd thought were buried bubbled to the surface. They were the past. Her distant past. She'd moved on long ago. Why was it that Jack was able to dredge up all her old insecurities?

Because, despite her best intentions, his opinions mattered.

He mattered.

* * *

Jack threw the steaks on the hot grill, taking satisfaction in their angry sizzle.

With a will of its own, his gaze drifted toward Royce's deck. Her deserted deck.

Where the hell was she? Did she have mind-blowing sex and then just walk away every day? What was he thinking—of course she did! After all, this was Royce. All you had to do was look at the way she dressed, the way she walked, the way she talked. And then there was her radio program.

With a flick of his wrist, he flipped the steaks and ordered his heart to slow down. Here he was, getting all fired up, and she didn't even have the decency to hang around.

Sure, he'd practically ordered her out of his house, but she hadn't had a problem with taking the hint. Disgusted, he shook his head. The woman had practically left skid marks with her hasty retreat.

"Good thing, too," he mumbled, prodding at the sizzling meat. "Saved me the trouble of having to try to get rid of her."

He glanced over at her deck again, then back down at the meat.

"What was I thinking?" He slammed the fork onto the grill tray, vibrating the plate. "How the hell am I going to gag down two big steaks?"

Well, there was only one thing to do. He'd have to ask Royce to join him for dinner.

She'd provided lunch. It was only the neighborly thing to do, to invite her to dinner.

That would be the end. He would owe her nothing.

End it here and now, neat and clean. No muss, no fuss.

The hollow feeling in his gut was just hunger.

Royce rolled over and sniffed, listening to the repeated pounding on her patio door.

At first her heart lifted to think it might be Jack. Then she forced herself to face reality. It wasn't Jack. He'd made his feelings about spending any more time with her, now that he'd gotten what he wanted, abundantly clear.

She rolled over and pulled the pillow tightly over her head. "Go away," she muttered.

Anyone else but Jack wasn't worth the effort to answer the door.

Frustrated more than he thought possible, Jack heaved one of Royce's lightweight patio tables out onto the beach. It felt good, so he followed with the other one and both lounge chairs.

Chest heaving, he regarded the litter of furniture on the beach. "That was stupid." Where was Royce? Maybe she hadn't locked the door. Maybe she was hurt or in danger. If so, he should check on her. After all, he was a doctor.

"Lame excuse," he muttered, "but maybe she'll buy it."

With a gentle pull, her glass door slid open with a soft whisper. He stepped into the dim coolness and looked around her living room.

Several boxes waited to be unpacked amid brightly printed, overstuffed chairs and a coordinated sofa. Brass framed pictures marched along the smooth surface of the wide mantle. Fat, squat candles clustered on one end of a well-polished coffee table, with several magazines stacked on the other end. Even after just moving in, her house seemed like more of a home than his place ever had.

The air smelled faintly of lobster and Royce's perfume.

"Royce?" From his position he could see that the kitchen was empty. He headed for the stairs, then stopped, one hand on the smooth surface of the newel post. "Royce? You up there?"

A sound drifted down the stairs, but he couldn't tell if it was a reply.

He advanced halfway up the stairs. "Royce?"

The sound came again. Definitely human. Definitely Royce.

Without hesitation, he climbed the rest of the way and came to a stop outside the open door of the master bedroom.

The bedspread on the shining brass bed was a jumble of wild colors, some kind of tropical print. In the middle, a small lump moved.

"Royce?"

"I *said*," a muffled voice replied, "leave me *alone*."

He walked to the bed and sat beside the lump. "Believe me, it's a good thought, but for some reason I can't do that."

He lifted the edge of the spread, curiously relieved to see the top of her head. "See, I wasn't thinking and threw two big old steaks on the grill. If you don't come rescue me by eating one of them, you'll be responsible for wasting good meat."

Tear-spiked eyelashes blinked up at him.

"You know," he continued, "there are starving people on the other side of the world."

"Great." She snatched the spread back down. "Send it to them."

Unreasonable anger—what else could it be but anger?—surged within him. "That's it!" He smacked the lump with his open hand, hoping he'd hit her butt. "Is this a private pity party or is anyone invited?"

A brief tug-of-war ensued. Jack won. He crawled under the covers with her.

"You're trespassing," she said, tugging on the spread.

"Not really. I'm a doctor, remember? It was my duty to make sure you weren't injured."

She blinked her unusual eyes and he lost his train of thought.

"Why would I be injured?"

"Huh? Oh. Well, you didn't answer your door."

"That doesn't mean anything."

"Well, maybe not in Houston, but at the shore we're a little more neighborly. If someone knocks, you answer the door. If the phone rings, you answer it." He dipped his head closer to hers. "Do you see a pattern here? It's called being civil."

She jerked to a sitting position, the movement pulling him forward. His face was planted between her breasts. Before he got the chance to enjoy it, her hands clamped on his shoulders, shoving.

"Get off me!" She took advantage of his momentary sensory overload to scoot back another few inches beneath the bedspread.

He looked at her, eyes narrowing with irritation. "I'm not doing anything. You knocked me off balance."

"You most certainly did do something," she countered with a jut of her chin. "You took advantage of my vulnerability to try to make another move."

"Your vulnerability? What vulnerability? You about knocked me down. It wasn't my fault."

"No one asked you to crawl into my bed."

He could feel the muscle in his jaw tick. "That's right. No one did. Sorry to bother you, Ms. St. Claire."

He had one foot out of the cocooning spread when she said in a quiet voice, "You weren't going to make a move?"

"Honey, when I make a move, you'll know it."

"I will?" She sniffed and wiped her eyes with her fingertips, smearing her eye makeup.

He nodded and reached to gently wipe the dark smudges with the pads of his thumbs. "Yep. First I'd get really close. Like this." He scooted until their knees touched. "Then I'd lean forward and kiss you. Like this." He brushed her nose with his lips, then trailed tiny kisses down to nibble on the edge of her mouth. "More?"

She nodded and sniffed. "Yes, please."

His mouth settled on hers, his tongue dipping to taste her

sweetness. She opened wider, her tongue shyly stroking his, her arms sliding up to encircle his neck.

He moved closer, guiding her onto his lap. Her legs wrapped around his hips, the movement parting the thin robe. With a groan, he hauled her closer still, reveling in her dampness pressed so intimately against his burgeoning arousal.

"Then what?" she asked in a breathless whisper.

"Then I'd help you take this off." He stroked her robe from her shoulders, then yanked until the belt gave way, and tossed the garment aside. "And I'd lay you down, like this."

He scooted her up to recline against the pillows, kicking the bedspread away. His breath caught. "You're so beautiful," he whispered, surprised to realize he meant it. He arranged her, his hands moving constantly, petting her. "Let me look at you." He stroked between her legs, rewarded by the moisture he found there.

Her slick feminity glistened with her arousal, her plump pink folds begging to be kissed. He dragged a finger along her opening and watched her sex bloom and weep, his erection straining his shorts to the limit.

Her hands shook when she pushed at his shorts, urging him to get naked, too.

He was definitely a willing participant.

In a flash, his shorts and briefs hit the far wall and he eagerly reached for her. It wasn't until the hard tips of her breasts branded his chest that he remembered protection.

She opened languid eyes and blinked up at him, obviously questioning the halt in action.

"Protection," he explained. "Hold the thought."

He kicked at the impossibly tangled bedspread. The damn thing was strangling his ankle, but he should be able to reach his discarded shorts.

He couldn't.

With a lunge, he lurched for the shorts, just out of his reach, and landed with a thud on the plush carpeting.

Carpet fibers abraded his bare butt. Embarrassment seared his face.

Royce propped up on her elbow and looked over the edge of the mattress at Jack, sprawled in all his naked glory, now kicking furiously at the bedspread surrounding his feet. Laughter bubbled up and, despite her best intentions, escaped to echo from the walls.

Jack had the body of a god. It was lust-inspiring to just look at him, sprawled before her, but it was also one of the funniest things she'd ever seen. Who would have thought Jack, superstud, could be such a klutz?

He looked at her and for a moment she thought he might be angry. Then he grinned, white teeth flashing in his crimson face, and flipped the spread over his head.

His action set off more peals of laughter. Royce rolled to her side, holding her stomach, tears of mirth streaming down her cheeks.

Jack peeked out. "Do I still need the condom? Or have I totally blown the mood?"

She wiped the tears away and smiled down at him. It would be so easy to fall in love with this man. No. No way. Jack McMillan was a major player. Mardee was living proof of how futile a relationship with someone like Jack would be. *Sex. All I wanted was a chance to have a fling with him, to get him out of my system, once and for all. It's just sex. It's all it can ever be.*

Jack stood up, the bedspread falling to his feet. He was truly magnificent.

Warmth spread through her again. If sex was all they could have, it was fine with her.

She smiled and shoved the sheet from her suddenly heated

skin. "Why don't you bring some condoms back to bed with you? We'll see what we can do about your insecurity."

He bent to retrieve the foil packets while she admired the view.

Maybe down-and-dirty sex would exhaust her enough to let her sleep on one of her few nights off. If they did it right, it might even succeed in pushing more tender thoughts regarding Jack from her mind and heart.

6

Jack quietly closed Royce's door and considered banging his head against the wall until he came to his senses.

"Stupid, stupid, stupid." What was it about Royce that made him go temporarily insane with lust whenever he was near her?

After Mardee, he'd sworn off relationships. Too much work. Yet here he was, practically foaming at the mouth whenever he so much as thought of Royce. And the idea of her with anyone else sent his blood pressure into stroke range.

Still, he'd wanted nothing more than to pull up the covers around them and cuddle her all night long. Of course, that meant nothing. The sex was just so damn good, and he'd had such a long, dry spell.

It couldn't happen again. If Ms. Royce St. Claire, PhD, wanted another tumble, she would just have to come to him. Preferably on her hands and knees.

Preferably naked.

Damn! He looked at the steaks, stacked on the plate next to the grill. He prodded one with his index finger. Cold.

Grabbing his remote phone from the deck chair, he punched in the number he'd just refused to call.

His breath hitched at Royce's sleepy-voiced hello.

"Stay where you are. We forgot something."

Within minutes, the steaks were steaming hot.

So was Jack.

Royce had just enough time to freshen up and mist with the perfumed body spray she kept by the bed before Jack's steps sounded on the stairs.

By the time he appeared in the doorway, she was stretched out naked beneath the sheets, every cell ready for round two.

What was he carrying?

Dressed in just a pair of running shorts, Jack approached the bed, his smile white in the lingering sunset.

He placed the tray on the bedside table and whipped back her sheet. Cool air puckered her nipples. From the way his body tensed and his gaze swooped to her breasts, Jack noticed.

"We forgot to eat our dinner," he said in the husky voice she loved.

She began to sit up, but he placed a halting hand on her shoulder.

"No, stay right there," he ordered. "Allow me."

For the first time, she noticed he'd cut up their steaks and what appeared to be a huge baked potato. Several small bowls, with serving spoons, surrounded the single dinner plate.

After dropping his shorts by the bed, his naked hip nudged hers. She made room for him, temporarily forgetting the mouth-watering aroma wafting from the plate in favor of a different kind of hunger.

He swirled a piece of meat in the first bowl, then nudged her mouth open for the first delectable bite. While she chewed and tried not to moan, he licked a speck of sauce from her lower lip, then swirled his tongue around her mouth before swooping down to a kiss.

He drew back and licked his lips. "Good, but not quite the level of satisfaction I was looking for."

He reached for another bite, this time of potato, and another bowl. His skin short-circuited her thought process with its gentle rub.

Coolness from the sour cream laving her nipple made her gasp. He popped the bite of potato in his mouth then licked the sour cream from her breast.

"Much better," he murmured, feeding her, then repeating the process for himself.

It was both heaven and hell, trying to remain still while remembering to chew and swallow, when her entire body quivered with pent-up sexual frustration.

When he reached beside the bed again and brought up a bowl of strawberries and whipped cream, she'd taken all she could.

It was time to give as good as she got.

She relieved him of the bowl and set it on the nightstand. Then, with strength that would surprise her personal trainer, she neatly flipped Jack to his back and straddled him.

Beneath her, his erection twitched. She bit back a smile.

"My turn," she said in a breathless whisper and reached for the bowl.

The strawberries were cool on her fingertips. In slow motion, she bit off the tip of one, squeezing it to let the juice trickle down her chin. She shuddered as it left a trail down her neck, between her breasts, and around her navel, and then tracked coolness between the juncture of her legs.

Jack's heated gaze followed the juicy trail.

"Look at me, Jack." Their gazes met. "I'm all sticky." She leaned down, her breasts swaying so close she could feel his excited breath, which beaded her nipples into aching tips. "Lick it off," she demanded.

For a macho type, he certainly was quick at following orders.

His warm hands bracketed her rib cage, lifting her high against his chest.

An impossibly hot, velvet-soft tongue lapped the juice from her chin. His five-o'clock shadow gently abraded her neck while he followed the sultry sweet path.

Her breath hitched as he laved circles around each breast, then followed the juicy trail down around her belly button. His hands tightened to lift her higher.

She squirmed against the pressure of his mouth while he licked the last traces of the fruit from her folds.

Then he turned the tables on her. Twisting to place her back against the body-warmed sheet, he knelt between her legs, spreading them wide with his knees.

He reached for the fruit bowl and smiled a smile that could only be interpreted as pure sex.

"I listened to your show," he said, dragging a huge strawberry through a pile of whipped cream.

"You did?" Why was the man talking instead of helping her ease her lustful pain?

He nodded, still smiling. "It inspired me."

"R—really?"

"Uh-huh. Gave me all sorts of ideas."

"Oh?"

He leaned down to brush her lips with his. They were cool and tasted like strawberry jam. She ran her tongue around her lips and he groaned.

He dotted cream on the tip of each breast then licked it away. She arched her back, shameless in her desire for more prolonged contact.

He chuckled and dipped the fruit into the cream again.

"Know what I'm talking about?" She shook her head, practically mindless with need. "You don't?" He pulled a mock frown. "Think, Royce. You discussed it at length on your last show."

She wracked her brain. There were so many callers and she'd had such a hard time keeping her mind on the words instead of on Jack. Impotence? That couldn't be it. Premature ejaculation? Definitely not. She squirmed again and arched her back. Why did he want to discuss her show now, of all times?

Jack *tsk*ed and shook his head. The sun, dipping low across the gulf, cast a golden glow across his magnificent chest.

"I guess I'll just have to refresh your memory," he said, scooting back enough and bending so he was at eye level with her exposed femininity. "So pretty," he whispered against her folds, causing her hips to buck off of the bed. "So moist and eager. But not quite ready."

The guttural sound coming from deep in her throat surprised her. Almost as much as the cool touch of the tip of the strawberry and whipped cream on her vagina.

He teased her for a moment, sliding the tip of the berry in and out of her opening, the tiny outer seeds creating a friction that lodged her breath in her lungs.

Every nerve ending focused on the spot receiving his undivided attention. In and out. The delicate scrapings sent shivers coursing down her arms and legs. Her fingers and toes tingled.

He tossed the berry aside, eliciting a moan from her at its absence. She needn't have worried. His hot mouth replaced the cool fruit, his tongue taking up where the berry left off. In and out it plunged, dragging along one side, then the other. Deep within her, he moved his tongue in inflaming little circles.

Her multiple climaxes surprised her, washing over her like a tidal wave, one right after the other, drowning her in satiation.

She may have screamed.

* * *

Jack could stand no more. When her juices filled his mouth, he'd almost lost his barely held composure. He wanted to be buried deep within her when he came.

He fumbled for a condom. He knew he'd placed a pile of them right by the edge. He almost wept with relief when his hand finally closed around the little foil packet.

The damn thing couldn't roll on fast enough. Finally, he paused, his cock throbbing with eagerness at her slick opening.

Their eyes met.

"Royce," he said through gritted teeth.

"Jack," she said on a breath.

He plunged into her. The shapely legs he'd lusted after for so long wrapped around his waist, clinging, pulling him impossibly deeper within her heat.

"Royce!" he shouted, inhaling great breaths through his nose in his effort to prolong the sensations.

Her body began its inner clamping which spelled the beginning of the end for his endurance.

With a window-rattling shout—it may have been her name again—he drove deeper into her willing body and shuddered his release.

When his heart began beating again, he became aware of her drawing agonizing little patterns with her fingernail on the still sensitive skin of his back.

With Herculean effort, he immediately rolled away, lying on his back with his arm thrown over his eyes. A sexual encounter had never affected him like that. Totally wiped out. Maybe he was getting old.

Beside him, Royce snuggled closer, wedging her shoulder against his ribs, her arm slung possessively across his still clenching abs.

"Jack?"

He peered from beneath his arm. "What?"

"That was . . . unbelievable."

He could only grunt in response.

"Jack?"

"Hmm?"

"You like me, don't you? At least a little bit?"

Uh-oh. What was it with women? Best to play dumb. If she was half as exhausted as he was, she'd doze off before they could engage in any "meaningful" conversation.

"What do you mean?"

Beneath his arm, she shrugged. "You called my name. Twice."

"You said mine, too. Twice."

She sat up; his side felt suddenly cold.

"Wasn't that what you wanted?"

There it was. The problem with sleeping with smart women. They were determined to analyze everything you said and did.

"Of course," he said, reaching for his shorts. He tugged them on as he stood. "I wanted to make sure you knew who you were screwing."

7

Royce lay watching the lazy shadow of the ceiling fan, biting her lip until she was sure Jack had let himself out of her house.

A tear trickled from the corner of her eye and traveled around until it pooled in her ear. Tears were too good for Jack McMillan. Heck, right now castration was what he deserved.

Why hadn't she seen it coming? His rolling away from her and covering his face should have been the first giveaway. She was trained to spot these things. His body language had practically screamed his emotional distance. Yet, she'd persisted.

Another tear escaped. She deserved every miserable rotten thing he heaped on her. After all, she knew his reputation. Knew of his commitment phobia. Had it daunted her in her quest to finally grab the gusto with Jack-the-ripper? Nope.

She glanced at the remains of their impromptu feast and groaned.

She'd never eat a steak or a strawberry again.

Jack lowered his emotionally charged body into the churning hot tub and popped the top on his first beer of the day. It wasn't emotions charging his body, he told himself—it was just the aftershocks of mind-blowing sex. That was why his hands shook and his knees were weak. He wasn't used to so much sexual activity in such a short span of time. He was out of shape.

He glanced at Royce's darkened house and wondered what she was doing, what she was thinking after his less than stellar exit line.

Did he really think she'd had so many lovers that she needed to be reminded of whose cock was in her? He snorted. After all, it was Royce he was talking about here. Of course she did. Didn't she?

He took a long draw of the cold beer and let his head rest on the side of the tub, concentrating on the soothing sounds of the surf. Tonight it didn't work.

He set the beer aside. He of all people should know the dangers of drinking while in a hot tub. He dared another glance at Royce's house. Still dark.

Maybe she was in her whirlpool tub. Women liked to bathe after sex. Maybe she didn't know the peril of mixing alcohol with heat and had a heart attack.

Fear lanced through him.

He was a physician, after all. It would be irresponsible of him not to go check on her.

Royce arched her stiff back and let the churning bubbles of her tub work their magic. On a side table, one fat candle flickered a low glow across the room. She idly watched the wisps of steam rise from the water.

Dreams were like that, she philosophized. Insubstantial wisps. Sort of like her dreams of a future with Jack.

She closed her eyes and willed away the tears.

After playing the part of fast and loose for so many years in an effort to capture Jack's attention, what had she expected?

Still, the pain hung there, lodged in her chest, when she thought of his parting words.

Relaxation techniques she'd learned years ago finally worked. The tenseness eased from her body a millimeter at a time until she lolled her head against the bath pillow and drifted off.

Jack eased up Royce's stairs, thankful he'd had the foresight to leave her door unlocked.

From the master bath came the distinct sounds of a whirlpool. His heart clenched.

He paused in the doorway.

Royce reclined in her tub, her head relaxed against an inflatable pillow, dark hair piled high on top of her head, a few escaping tendrils sticking to the sides of her neck.

"Royce?" Was she unconscious or merely asleep?

He rushed to the tub and lifted her limp hand, his fingers seeking her pulse. It beat strong and sure. Weak with relief, he sank to the edge of the tub.

Within seconds, she opened her eyes. After a start, she settled lower in the tub.

"What are you doing here?" she asked, her mouth scarcely clearing the churning water. "Didn't you say all you had to say earlier?"

His cheeks heated with shame as much as the steam rising from her bath. "Ah, no. I mean yes. Shit." He raked his hand across his close-cropped hair. "Royce, I'm sorry. I shouldn't have said what I did."

"But you meant it." Her voice was quiet. Flat. Devoid of emotion.

"What? Hell, no! I don't know what got into me. Can you forgive me?"

She tugged a towel from beneath his leg and stood, wrapping as she rose from the water. Depriving his hungry eyes of the sight of her body. A body he knew intimately and already craved again.

"You need to leave, Jack."

"Not until you say you forgive me. Or at least that you understand."

"Sure." She shouldered her way past him and walked into the bedroom.

"What's that supposed to mean?" He trailed behind her, his fingers itching to rip the towel from her and stroke every inch of her gorgeous, responsive body until he forced her to admit . . . what? That she'd truly forgiven him? That she wanted him every bit as much as he wanted her?

Or did he need her to tell him he meant something to her? Something more than hot sex—a willing, available and able cock?

Shit.

She turned a cool eye on him while he all but vibrated with a need he refused to identify.

"It means," she finally answered, "I understand."

"You understand?"

She nodded and reached for the ugliest purple robe he'd ever seen. "Jack, I've known you for more than six years."

"So?"

"So, I also know your . . . shall we say, limitations?"

"What the hell are you talking about?" He stalked toward her, but stopped before he got close enough to reach out and touch her.

After pulling the ugly robe around her, she reached under and pulled out the towel. "Jack, you're the poster boy for commitment phobia." She walked back past him and tossed the towel into a tall wicker basket in the bathroom.

He stood in the bathroom doorway, blocking her path with a hand on each side of the door frame. "Is that what you're after, Royce? Commitment?" Good God, what would he do if she said yes?

"From you?" She snorted and pushed past him. "Hardly."

"Then what is it that you want?"

"You mean other than your body?" He nodded. Her mouth flattened into a grim line. "Just your respect, Jack. While we're together, I expect—no, I demand—your respect."

"You got it." She sidestepped his advance.

"That means," she continued, "for the duration of our time together, I expect you to be faithful."

"I can do that." Hell, all other women paled beside the hellion standing before him anyway. It would be a piece of cake to be with just her. He reached out to stroke the tip of her breast through her robe with his index finger. A surge of satisfaction shot through him when her nipple immediately puckered beneath the purple silk. "What about after that?"

She shrugged and stepped back, breaking contact. "After I'm through with you, I don't care what you do." She glanced back over her shoulder. "I thought I asked you to leave."

"What if I'm not ready to go?" He advanced until he had her backed against the railing at the top of the stairs.

He snagged the belt tie and dragged it from her voluminous robe. The garment fell around her slight frame like a giant purple tent, only touching her shoulders.

Bending his knees slightly, he gathered the silk in his hands and straightened, raising the robe until he'd bared her to her bodacious breasts.

With a flick of his wrists, the robe fluttered down into the great room.

Royce's chest rose and fell more rapidly with each breath, but she didn't break eye contact.

Interpreting her body language as a positive sign, he reached down and let his trunks fall to the carpeted landing with a soft thud.

His knees weakened when he closed the distance and gathered her in his arms, the feel of her back against his palms like warm silk.

Easy, boy. He closed his eyes and breathed in her unique scent, willing his body to take it slow and easy.

Against his chest, her breasts flattened, the erect nipples sending shock waves of arousal through his extremities.

He swallowed a groan.

She stretched to lightly kiss his chin. He shivered.

"I thought you were leaving," she whispered.

"I will. Soon." He nudged his erection between her legs.

Marveling at her fine bone structure, he lifted her until she perched on the railing, her breasts at his eye level.

She tensed, her hands gripping his shoulders. "Jack. Get me down. Please. I'm not kidding. We're going to fall."

"I've got you, babe. Don't worry." He laved first one erect nipple, then the other, with the tip of his tongue before taking the morsel deeply into his mouth.

He began sucking and she must have forgotten her fear, because she arched her back and gave that sex-kitten growl from the back of her throat that always drove him wild.

Pulling her legs around his hips, he aligned his cock with her opening and plunged into the welcoming heat.

She screamed and tensed.

It took a moment for his passion-fogged brain to register that her scream was not from pleasure.

8

Jack's heart skipped a beat. Royce was falling. He clutched her to him. Her arms closed around his neck with viselike strength.

Still buried deep within her, he stepped back, away from the danger. He was closer to the stairstep than he thought.

Cool air surrounded his heated body seconds before his back met the hard edge of the carpeted stairway. Instinctively, he curled around Royce, taking the brunt of the fall down the steps.

Downward they plunged. Pain shot up and down his spine as it connected with each riser. *Keep your head forward so your fool brains don't get bashed in.*

An eternity, or seconds, later, the back of his head met the hard surface of the tiled floor.

He heard Royce's distressed exclamation right before the world went black.

Time was meaningless. He had no idea how long he'd been out. From the way Royce was crying and clutching him, he suspected no more than a few minutes.

A tentative move of his head elicited a groan.

Royce shrieked and released her grip on his shoulders. His skull bounced on the hard tile, doing nothing for his headache.

"You're alive!" She leaned close to peer through tear-spiked lashes. "Are you okay?"

He rolled to his side and sat up, arching the kinks out of his back. "I appear to be in one piece." Rubbing his neck did nothing to alleviate his headache. He rubbed the bump on the back of his head. "No thanks to you."

She sat back on her heels. When had she put on a robe? "Me? You were the one who had the bright idea of having sex on the handrail. We're lucky we weren't both killed."

She tossed his trunks to land on his lap.

"When did you have time to grab these? On our way down?" He bit back a wince as he shoved his leg into the bathing suit.

"Don't be ridiculous." Despite her harsh sound, she reached to stabilize him while he pulled up his trunks. "When I saw you'd been knocked out, I ran up and got them when I got my robe. Excuse me, but I thought I was doing you a favor by protecting your modesty from the ambulance drivers."

"Ambulance?" The word scarcely passed hip lips before a siren sounded in the distance.

She nodded and walked to the window. "I called nine-one-one. They're on their way."

"Why'd you do that? You should've known I wasn't seriously hurt. My God, you're a doctor." Deep down, he knew she'd only done it in an effort to help, yet the knowledge did nothing to quell his irritation.

"Yes, I'm a doctor—but a PhD. I wasn't qualified to—"

"Can you take a pulse?"

"Of course I can."

"Do you know how to check pupil dilation?"

"Yes, and I did, but—"

"Then you should have known I was all right!" He stalked

toward the door but had to grab hold of the edge of the sofa when a wave of dizziness washed over him.

She appeared in front of him and pushed him down none-too-gently to the soft cushions. "Just sit here a minute and let the EMS confirm you're all right." Her hands fisted on her silk-covered hips. "And what about a possible fractured skull? Or broken bones? I had no way to tell about those things, not to mention the possibility of internal injuries."

A knock sounded on the patio door a second before a young man, dressed in white with a red EMS logo on his shirt, stuck in his close-cropped head and said, "EMS. You called?"

"Come on in," Royce directed, tying her belt tighter. "Here's your patient. He knocked himself out when he fell down those stairs." She pointed at the staircase, then the tiled landing. "He hit his head when he landed there."

The young man dropped his bag and knelt before Jack as two others appeared at the door with a gurney.

A few minutes later the attendant dropped his stethoscope into his bag and ripped the blood-pressure cuff from Jack's arm, the sound echoing in the quiet room.

"Everything seems fine, Dr. St. Claire." He leaned closer to Jack and spoke a little louder, sending shards of fresh pain through Jack's temple. "Do you want to go get checked out at the hospital, Dr. McMillan?"

"No, I don't," Jack all but growled. "And stop shouting. My head hurts enough as it is." He stood.

The attendant put a steadying hand on Jack's elbow. He shook him off.

"I'm fine."

"Why don't you hop on the gurney and let us at least give you a ride home?"

"I live next door," he answered through clenched teeth. "I'm perfectly capable of walking the entire ten feet on my own."

"Do you think he should be alone tonight?" Royce asked, earning a glare from Jack.

"Does he have a way to contact you if he needs you?"

"Last I heard, the phones work," Jack grumbled. "Hell, at this distance, two tin cans and a string would do."

After Jack promised to take it easy and Royce vowed to keep a close eye on him, the paramedics left.

Jack leaned against the doorjamb and cocked his finger for Royce.

She didn't exactly trust the gleam in his eye, so she stopped just out of reach. "Did you decide to stay here tonight?" She knew he was, in all probability, fine and wasn't sure she'd have the strength to resist if he reached for her during the night.

He shook his head and winced. "No. I'm going home to take some kick-ass pain relievers and get some sleep." He gave her the once-over. "I know if I stayed here, that wouldn't happen."

He reached out to pull her by the lapels of her robe until they were breast to chest. He let his hand slide across her breasts to her waist. "Gimme a good-bye kiss."

She stood on tiptoe and brushed a chaste kiss across his lips.

He growled, grabbed her hair on both sides and hauled her mouth back to his for a much deeper, harder invasion.

Her knees took on the consistency of melting rubber just as he broke the kiss. He rested his forehead against hers for a moment, then tilted up her face to look eye to eye.

"Rest, hot stuff," he said, brushing his lips across the tip of her nose. "We're not through yet." One of his hands slid down to grasp her buttocks, the feel intimate and erotic through the thin silk barrier. "Not by a long shot."

With a light tap on her fanny, he turned and let himself out.

She watched his progress, absently rubbing the spot he'd tapped. If she'd known for sure he was unhurt, she would have dragged him up to her bed and had her wicked way with him all through the night.

She smiled at the thought. Who would have thought Royce St. Clair, terminal goody-two-shoes, could get so down and dirty? Maybe it was Jack's fault. He seemed to be the only man capable of wringing that kind of passion from her.

Shortly after going to bed, she threw off her covers and strode to the desk in the corner. If she wasn't going to sleep or make love, she may as well catch up on her reading.

Naked and needy, she couldn't concentrate. Her vibrator held no appeal. At least not when she knew what she craved slept just on the other side of the wall next door.

She opened the balcony door, the cool night air caressing her bare skin, the sea air calming her, and grabbed a pad and pen from the desk before padding outside.

The all-weather chaise pad felt scratchy against her bottom. A quick glance confirmed that the beach was deserted. The glow from her bedroom gave enough light to see what she wrote. Clothing was definitely optional.

Sexual mores and the modern male's inability to commit. A comprehensive study by Royce St. Clair, PhD.

She tapped her pen on the arm of the chaise before writing:

Test Subject One: a successful thirty-six-year-old cardiologist. Never married. One less than serious relationship that lasted six years. High libido for a male his age. While his peers settle down he becomes more sexually aggressive, copulation a way of life.

Feeling pretty sexually aggressive herself, she went on to list the various ways they'd had sex and catalogued the ways she intended to use him in the very near future.

An hour later, she closed her notebook and struggled not to squirm in frustration. It was a bit daunting to realize her latent sexuality. The various ways to copulate she'd listed surprised even her.

Tossing the notebook in the direction of the desk, she headed for the shower.

Her tiled stall now seemed big and lonely. Closing her eyes, she worked her shower gel into a rich lather and let the bubbles slide down her body, pretending they were Jack's hands or tongue.

Frustrated beyond belief, she grasped the handheld showerhead, spread her legs and let the pulsing rhythm of the water ease her aching need. On fire, she didn't admit defeat until the water ran cold.

Stepping out of the shower, she gave a cursory swipe with her towel, and headed to bed.

With her every nerve ending on alert, the sheets scratched her nudity. Her nipples felt almost raw against the top sheet. She reached for her coconut body balm on the nightstand and scooped out a dollop. The coolness immediately soothed her heated skin where she smoothed it over and around her breasts. Cool relief streaked downward, along with her hands. Past her navel, swirling over her hips, down her outer thighs to her knees. Then back up, ever so slowly, inching up the inside of her thighs toward her core. Dare she?

Needy and achy, she shifted restlessly, spreading her legs wider, her hips lifting from the sheet. Searching. Longing.

Her thumbs flicked the swollen nubbin. With an indrawn breath, she arched up off the bed, her breasts tingling.

Jack. Jack, I need you. Her finger slid deeply within her wet passage. Not enough. *I want, I need you, Jack.* Another finger joined the first. She keened her need, arching rhythmically now. Her right hand slipped through the layer of balm to rub and pinch her nipple. Harder. Faster.

Behind her closed eyelids, she saw Jack, his heated gaze locked with hers while he pleasured her. She pinched her nipple to the point of pain, imagining his teeth taking her, his tongue laving her. Deep within, her fingers pushed her harder, faster, toward her peak, her thumb constantly flicking her engorged nub.

She reared off the bed, shrieking and crying Jack's name when her release finally came.

Her hands absently petted while her inner pulsing quieted.

Jack, she thought as sleep claimed her, *come back to me*.

Jack flopped to his back and bit his lip to keep from crying out at the pain galloping down his spine.

A few experimental manipulations after he'd come back home confirmed he'd done no serious injury. But, damn, it hurt. All the soft tissue along the spine was probably bruised all to hell.

The hot jets of his tub or the hot tub on the deck would probably work wonders, but he was too sore and stiff to make the trek.

Blindly groping along the nightstand until his hand closed around the rapidly warming bottle of beer, he rolled to his side.

With the longneck poised mere millimeters from his mouth, he stopped. Was he thirsty for beer? Did he really think alcohol would make the pain more bearable? Maybe Mardee had a point. He knew he didn't have a problem with alcohol. But that didn't mean he wasn't well on his way to one.

With a groan, he set the bottle back on the ledge and fell back against the pillow.

Okay. Admitting you *might* have a problem was the first step. What was he going to do about it?

For that matter, what was he going to do about the riot within his body whenever he was near Royce?

* * *

Royce finished oiling up the next morning and cast a glance toward Jack's silent house. Usually he was out on his deck stretching before his morning run by the time she came out. Not today.

Maybe she should go check on him. After all, he would come to do that for her. Wouldn't he? It was the neighborly thing to do.

While her mind warred with her heart, Jack's sliding door opened and he stepped out.

Relief washed through her. More glad to see him than she cared to admit, she called, "Good morning! Glad to see you're among the living."

He mumbled something and rubbed his arched back. The man obviously had no idea what his partial nudity did to her each morning.

"What?" She shifted on her chair, hoping to catch a better view of all those rippling muscles.

He walked to his railing and braced his arms on the edge. "I said, 'Barely.' My back is killing me. I feel like someone pounded on me with a two-by-four."

She winced. Her weight no doubt contributed to his pain. Had he not shielded her with his body, she'd be the worse for wear this morning, too.

"Anything I can do to help?" Dang. She hadn't meant for her voice to sound so suggestive. Must be the early morning. She hadn't used her voice much yet. She cleared her throat. "I mean, do you need anything?"

He shoved his sunglasses on top of his head and grinned at her. "I can think of a whole list of things you could do for me to make me feel better." White teeth flashed. "But we'll have to wait until I get some of the kinks worked out of my back."

Heat surged to her chest and cheeks. "Maybe I didn't mean it the way you took it."

He winked. "And maybe you did." He tossed a towel onto

the railing. "But right now I'm going to take a long soak in the spa."

His back gleamed in the sunlight as he stiffly lowered himself into the water. With his sunglasses again lowered to shield his eyes, he turned and said, "Wake me up if I'm still here when you're ready to go in. I don't want to drown." He settled back, arms stretched along the lip of the tub.

Two hours later, hot and restless, she looked over to find him in exactly the same position. "Jack," she called, wrapping her towel around her, feeling oddly exposed. "I'm going in now. Jack?"

No answer.

With a shrug, she stepped into the coolness of her house and waited a beat for her eyes to adjust. She'd take a quick shower and then go check on him.

Her notes fluttered on the top of her desk as she walked by on her way to the shower. Maybe she was wasting her time with Jack, but what else did she have to do these days? Commitment was a foreign word for him. She'd known that from the beginning. But he was a hell of a lover. If physical gratification was all she could have, she'd take it.

Mind made up, she showered in record time and dressed in her sexiest lingerie beneath her only other sundress, a rather plain-looking pale pink cotton print. As soon as she could get her obsession with Jack out of her system, she really needed to buy new clothes.

But for now, less would definitely lead to more.

"Jack?" A cool hand rested on his sun-baked shoulder. "Jack? Wake up," Royce said from somewhere near his ear.

A slow rotation of his head worked the kinks out of his neck. He stretched, opened his eyes and said, "Hi. Must've fallen asleep."

His gaze took a leisurely trip from her shapely bare arm to

her tanned chest, semimodestly covered in another sin-with-me sundress. What would she have on underneath this time? The tub blocked his view from her hips down, so he stood and finished the tour.

Her sundress fastened with little pink flower-shaped buttons that marched down to a midshin hemline. Luckily for him, she'd left most of the buttons undone, revealing a tantalizing amount of tan cleavage and leg for his viewing pleasure.

His bathing suit instantly tightened at least two sizes.

Royce seemed to be enjoying the view herself.

"How's your back?" she asked, one hand shielding her eyes.

"Better." He grunted as he stepped out of the tub to stand before her. "'Course, it would probably feel even better if I could have a massage."

Her slow smile sent a streak of heat through him. "I think that could be arranged." She dragged one fingertip down his chest, past his clenched abs, then paused with it hooked under his elastic waistband. "Why don't you go inside and get comfortable? I'll be right back."

His breath hitched when she dipped her finger inside his trunks, her fingernail grazing the engorged tip of his sex.

Then she turned and left.

9

Royce wiped her palms down the sides of her sarong robe and willed them to stop shaking. She'd formulated a plan of sorts, and reached for the basket of props.

Jack wasn't going to know what hit him.

Shower sounds registered the moment Royce stepped into Jack's house. With a smile, she nudged the deadbolt on the bottom of the slider with her toe. Had she possessed a DO NOT DISTURB sign, she would have hung it out as well.

"Take no prisoners," she whispered on her way up the stairs, and got to work.

Jack turned off the shower and paused. It couldn't be steel drums he heard. He stepped out and towel-dried. It was definitely island music. Coming from his room, along with the unmistakable sound of surf via his open patio door.

Slow steps took him to the bedroom door. His room glowed from possibly hundreds of candles, in every shape and size, set on just about every available surface.

Beside his round bed, Royce smoothed his spare set of red

satin sheets into place. She must have sensed his presence because she looked up and smiled.

"I hope you don't mind," she said, walking slowly in his direction. "I wanted to make you as comfortable as possible." Her gaze took a leisurely trip from his face down his nude body, pausing at his already more than interested cock, before completing the tour.

He wanted to rip off the flowered number and lick her all over.

Their gazes met.

She stepped aside and motioned toward the bed. "Lie down."

He could do that.

He obeyed and wondered what she planned to do with his monster erection, jutting like a tent pole.

When she stood, just staring at it, he reached for the sheet.

"No!" Her hand on his arm stopped the sheet's progress. "I need you naked." At his raised brow, she stammered, "I—I'm going to give you the massage you asked for."

She cast another glance at his erection. "Roll over, please."

It was a bit uncomfortable, but he managed, only to all but leap off the mattress at the first touch of oil being dribbled down his back.

Soft, warm hands immediately began rubbing the oil in, kneading the sore muscles along his spine. He sighed and relaxed. The smell of coconut surrounded him.

Downward she worked, rubbing and kneading the backs of his thighs, his calves, manipulating his ankles. Oil was worked into the soles of his feet, between each toe.

If it were anyone else, he would have drifted blissfully to sleep. But since it was Royce, his body refused to totally relax while images of what else her hands were capable of ran through his mind.

"Jack?" she whispered.

He turned his head toward the sound and cracked open one eye.

Royce stood beside the bed, hands clamped primly in front of her. "Do you want me to leave so you can get some rest?"

He smiled and rolled over, his reaction to her touch springing free. "Does it look like that's what I want?" He reached for her hand, drawing her closer to the edge of the bed. "Besides, you've only done half the job."

She cleared her throat. "Okay. Lie back. Please."

A smile tugged at the sensual curves of her lips. Before he had much time to wonder what her lip gloss would taste like, she reached up and casually flicked a button by her upper arm. The sarong fell to the floor.

His breath caught. Before him stood every guy's wet dream.

"No tan lines." He finally croaked out the first thing to come to mind that wouldn't get him slapped.

She shook her head, smiling as she poured more oil into her hand. "Nope. I wear the kind of suits that let the tanning rays through."

To his surprise, instead of stroking the oil over his eager body, she slid her well-oiled palms over her breasts. A little shimmy followed as she generously oiled herself from silky tanned shoulders to her ankles, then back up. She cupped her breasts, gleaming in the candlelight. His heart tripped.

She took a step closer to the edge of the bed, swirling the tips of her index fingers around her oiled nipples.

Just as he began to reach for her, she poured more oil into her palm and placed her slick hands on his nipples. From there, she left a trail of fire as she headed south, rubbing and stroking along the way. Things were definitely leaping to life.

But she bypassed his eager member in favor of massaging the oil into his legs and feet.

His breathing echoed in the room, drowning out the soft sounds of island music and even the persistent surf while he watched her leisurely oil herself again. Damn, but she looked like she was getting off on touching herself.

Finally—finally!—she poured out more oil and climbed onto the mattress. But wait. She was way too far away for him to reach her.

"Relax, big guy." She rose up on her knees, the tips of her breasts grazing the edges of his knees. "I'm in charge now." She nudged his legs apart by crawling between them. "And I want to do a thorough job," she said, her oiled hands closing around his testicles.

Before he caught his breath, she ran her fingers up and around his penis, dragging the tip of her finger over the head.

"Royce," he said in a ragged voice, "you're killing me."

She laughed and kissed the pulsing tip before pouring more oil.

He watched in detached fascination while her slick palms moved up and down his shaft. Of their own volition, his hips began moving in counterpoint.

Their gazes locked, she leaned down and rubbed his cock between her breasts. The heat of oil and skin against skin was so erotic, he forced his mind to recall baseball scores, chores he still needed to complete on the house for it to be ready in time for the renters. Anything but how much he yearned to flip her over and bury his cock so deeply within her that he'd never find his way out again.

Besides, he didn't want to miss a second of her performance.

She finally stopped torturing him and crawled up the length of his body until their slick chests were nipple to nipple.

"I'm just making sure it's all rubbed in," she said in a husky whisper.

"Well, in the interest of being thorough, I need to tell you there's a spot you missed."

"Oh?" Her voice sounded distracted while she rubbed her chest against his, her gaze riveted on the sight.

"Yep," he said at the same time his hands tightened on her waist and he plunged his well-oiled cock deep within her wetness.

Her widened gaze flew to his, then she smiled and they both sighed.

Sighs soon turned to grunts, then moans.

"Jack?" Royce opened her eyes after a search with her hand touched nothing but cool sheet. "Jack?"

"I'll be right there," he called from somewhere downstairs.

"Are you okay?" she called, sliding toward the edge of the bed.

"Great." His voice, so close, startled her. He stood at the door to his bedroom, magnificently naked, his shoulder resting against the frame. "Your massage worked wonders."

"Good." She pulled the sheet a little higher. "What's behind your back?"

"Toys."

"Toys?" she squeaked.

"Uh-huh." He nodded and walked to the edge of the bed, twisting when she tried to see what he held. "No peeking. Now it's your turn to lay back and enjoy."

"But—" Could she do that? Could she relinquish total control without any sort of commitment? Her gaze swept Jack's already semiaroused body. Absolutely.

She lay back, willing her bones and muscles to relax.

Coolness seared her skin when Jack stripped the sheet from her.

"No hiding," he said at her questioning gaze. "Okay, now spread your legs. And close your eyes." At her continued stare, he reached to stroke her hair from her cheek. "Trust me."

At that moment, she realized she did, indeed, trust Jack McMillan. With her life.

With her love.

Even if he didn't want it.

10

Jack looked at the woman sprawled before him. He'd like to think she would do these things with only him. But this was Royce. Her reputation preceded her.

She'd been an itch he couldn't scratch for six long years. That had to be the only reason she had whatever the hell this effect was on him. It had to be.

He picked up the first jar and dipped his finger into the scented cream. The label called it coconut-flavored body frosting. As soon as he'd smelled it, all sorts of erotic images flashed through his mind of how he'd use it on Royce.

He painted circles around each of her nipples, then licked it off. Tasted like coconut cream pie. He drew lines down her stomach with arrows pointing down, then cleaned them off with his tongue.

She twitched and tried to close her legs, but he was having none of that. Spreading them farther apart, he knelt between her knees and slowly dragged a fingertip full of frosting up the inside of each thigh with arrows pointing at her pussy. Before he realized what he was doing, he'd written the word *mine* on each arrow.

He chanced a quick glance at her face to make sure her eyes were still shut, then made quick work of licking off the evidence.

His cock throbbed with eagerness, but he held back. He was too involved. He'd wanted her too long to quit now.

Pushing up her legs until her knees touched her rib cage, he drew a line of frosting along her opening, licking it off before plunging his finger into her wetness.

Her hips bucked off the mattress. He stroked her buttocks, murmuring endearments until she calmed down. His tongue replaced his finger. Beneath the sweetness of the frosting was something much sweeter. More addictive. The sweetness of Royce St. Claire.

Suddenly voracious, he couldn't get enough. Couldn't get enough of her tender sweetness, enough of her smooth soft skin, enough of her essence when she climaxed. And she definitely climaxed. Over and over.

He crawled up next to her when she lay spent and whimpering, and brushed a strand of damp hair from her cheek.

Fighting down the tender feelings that screamed for him to take her in his arms and never let her go, he brushed a kiss on the tip of her nose.

Her eyes fluttered open, almost black with her passion. Delicate nostrils flared with each deep indrawn breath.

He couldn't resist. He covered her breast with his hand. *Mine.* Beneath his palm, her heart beat wildly.

"Rest," he whispered. "I'll be right back."

At her barely whispered, "No more," pain lanced his heart.

It resumed its normal cadence when she continued to say, "I don't need any more props. All I need is you."

A hot, melting sensation filled him. He had to get away before he embarrassed himself.

"I still have a few fantasies I'd like to try out."

He stood and gently drew the sheet over her, then placed a lingering kiss on her moist forehead. "I'll hurry."

His erection banged against him as he strode down the stairs, a painful reminder of his as-yet-unquenched desire.

Returning to his room, he watched the rhythmic rise and fall of her chest. Could he go through with his plan to fuck her brains out then forget her?

For self-preservation, he had no choice.

"Royce," Jack's voice said from somewhere above her. "Wake up, sweet thing. I need you." She smiled and opened her eyes.

Jack's impossibly erect penis, liberally coated in the coconut frosting, bobbed right in front of her face.

She may have been a late bloomer, but even she knew what he wanted. Although the idea of oral sex with any of her other suitors over the years had all but gagged her, she found she had to exercise considerable control to keep from licking her lips at the thought of such an intimate act with Jack.

In one movement, she rolled over, gripped his thighs and took him into her mouth. The body frosting was interesting, but she was anxious to taste what lay beneath and she impatiently sucked and licked until she felt the clean smooth skin over his rock-hard arousal.

Above her, Jack groaned. Beneath her hands, his thighs quivered. She sucked harder, swirling her tongue up and down, around and around. Just as things were getting interesting and she had to clamp her legs together to keep from squirming, he gripped each side of her head and gently pushed her away.

She watched the crimson head bob, its skin taunt and shiny.

Jack looked ridiculous when he wrapped her sarong around his hips, blocking her view.

"C'mere." He helped her rise from the bed and led her to the little sitting area by the edge of the open patio door.

At her back, the waves crashed against the beach, salty air caressing her still heated skin. Her nipples pebbled, whether from the cool air or arousal, she didn't know. Or care.

She was too eager to see what Jack had in mind.

She didn't have to wait long.

Jack had been busy. He'd rearranged the candles she'd lit to surround the sitting area, and placed what appeared to be a white fur rug half over the chair and matching chaise to flair out onto the floor.

"Straddle the chair, Royce, with your back to me."

"What?"

"Trust me."

The fur tickled her in intimate places. May as well let go of all her inhibitions. Spreading her legs as wide as possible while remaining seated, she gave an experimental wiggle and caught her breath at the feel of the fur stroking her bud and swollen lips.

She watched over her shoulder as, naked again, Jack crawled across the rug until his chest was flat against her back. He reached around and manipulated her nipples, eliciting a moan.

"You like that, don't you?" His breath was hot against her ear.

She could only whimper and moan, arching her neck in an attempt to kiss or lick or do anything to any part of him that she could reach.

Jack urged Royce downward. The fur both caressed and stimulated every nerve ending along her body. Wild in her need for Jack, she tried to pull him around for a kiss, but he resisted.

"Jack! Please! Now!"

"Now? Are you sure?" he asked, his mouth close to her ear, his voice setting off vibrations deep within her.

"Yes!" Writhing against him, shameless in her need, she couldn't think, could only feel.

"Shh." His hot breath scorched her ear. "Easy. Let me help. Relax."

Warmth from the fur was replaced by the cooler air drifting in from the open patio door. It swirled around her, licking her passion-heated skin. In the next instant, soft fur again cupped her breasts as Jack placed her face down on the edge of the chaise, her legs spread impossibly wide.

His large hands cupped the sides of her breasts, stroking. His heat warmed her back milliseconds before he entered her with enough force to topple her from her perch, had he not held fast.

Moisture surged from her weeping sex, drenching them in passion, each forceful thrust a counterpoint to the silken glide of her skin against the warm fur. Her nipples tightened and ached, heavy with her impending release.

She rode the wild surf of passion with him, then let the tidal wave of release wash over her. The next moment, Jack's breath hitched, his magnificent body stiffened and he ground into her one last time.

He tugged, and in her weakened state, she slid to the floor to sprawl across his lap.

"You're killing me, woman," he finally managed to say a while later.

If she could've formed a coherent sentence, she would have replied. Instead, she arched her neck and licked his chin.

He laughed and gave her a brief squeeze. As hugs go, it could have been better, but hope soared through her. It was the first sign of affection he'd given her. Sex didn't count.

"Let's take a quick shower and go out to eat," he said, rising and pulling her up. "There's a great seafood place down the beach." He turned her to face him and bent to look in her eyes. "Or do you have to work tonight?"

A date! Jack was actually standing before her, albeit nude,

asking her to go out in public with him. That had to mean something.

Willing her pulse to a normal cadence, her hands not to shake, she said, with what she hoped was a matter-of-fact tone, "No, I have tonight off. And I'm starving."

She turned and headed toward the bathroom, then paused and looked back. The sight of him nearly took her breath away. It was all she could do not to drag him back onto the bed and ravage him. Instead, she asked, "Is my sundress all right or is it dressier?"

He grinned and walked toward her, intent clear in his eyes. "The dress is fine. But you won't be wearing it for a while, babe."

Royce breathed a sigh of relief as she sank down into the padded booth of the Purple Crab. After their last lusty joining in Jack's shower, she hadn't been entirely sure her knees would support her weight on the short walk to the restaurant. Across from her, the candlelight did wondrous things to Jack's rugged good looks. Maybe she wasn't all that hungry after all. . . .

She supposed dinner was good, judging from how packed the place was, but she couldn't taste a thing except the memory of Jack's kiss.

Snap out of it, dummy! You're acting like a besotted teenager, not a perfectly responsible adult. Her eyes narrowed in concentration, honing in on what Jack was saying.

". . . So, what do you say?"

Uh-oh. Say about what?

"Um, I'm sorry, Jack, I think I may have gotten some water in my ear. I couldn't hear you. Could you repeat that last part?" *Smooth, St. Claire, smooth.*

"I said they have a great patio bar here. They have all kinds of furniture out there, even hammocks made for two. They'll serve your drink anywhere you tell them to. What do you say? Want to share a hammock and a piña colada?"

"Sounds delicious." And she didn't mean the drink.

At least an hour and several drinks later, she found herself impossibly tangled with the sexiest man on the planet in the hammock from hell.

For the third time in as many minutes, she swatted his hands away from the buttons on her sundress.

"C'mon, Royce, don't be a prude." His expert fingers flicked open the first few buttons and delved into her gaping bodice to brush back and forth across her nipple while he nuzzled her neck. "We're at the back edge of the patio; it's dark. No one's gonna see us."

Maybe it was the alcohol. Maybe it was the thrill of exposure. Maybe it was the proximity of the man of her dreams. Something short-circuited her saner thought processes.

The results would go down in Purple Crab, if not Pleasure Beach, history.

11

All it took was placing her hand just so over a strategic part of Jack's anatomy. The man went wild. Suddenly he had eight hands and they were everywhere. All she'd worn beneath her sundress was a lacy thong, which launched out into the darkness to disappear somewhere on the beach.

"Jack!" Her reprimand lacked something, given the giggle. What was wrong with her? She never giggled. "My underwear is not a slingshot."

In answer, he growled and flicked her earlobe with the tip of his hot tongue. Shivers scampered to every nerve ending in her body.

Cool air bathed her from neck to toes, causing her already aroused nipples to pucker even tighter. Jack's hands obviously moved faster than the speed of lust.

"You cold?" There was no doubt where he was focused. "I can fix that."

His hot lips closed over one distended bud, drawing it deep into his mouth. She shifted her weight to give greater access and to possibly ease some of the ache she experienced at his touch.

"Touch me," he demanded against her breast, his voice sending vibrations to her heart. He grabbed her hand and guided it to his spectacular erection. His spectacular bare erection. When had he undone his shorts?

His mouth claimed hers with a groan, his tongue dancing a passionate tango with hers, filling her senses with the taste of coconut and rum.

The next second, he was on top of her, his penis probing her swollen, aching flesh. The hammock swung violently in great lurching arcs.

Her half scream, half whimper was muffled by his mouth. "Shh," he whispered against her lips. "We have to be discreet. We don't wanna get kicked out of here." Jack's speech was definitely slurred. How much had they had to drink? "We'll take it nice and slow. Don't want to rock the boat, er, hammock, and arouse suspicion."

Her arms went around him, partly to hang on and partly to make sure his butt was covered. It was. She let her fingers trail around. Sure enough, he'd simply parted his button fly and freed his erection. The sides of her dress formed an effective shield from prying eyes. Jack was right. If they didn't get too rowdy, no one would ever suspect what they were doing.

The thought made her impossibly wetter.

A sharp pain scraped along the inside of her left ankle. "Ow! What was that?"

"Sorry, my foot slipped through the hammock. S'okay," he assured her, "I can still fuck you without a problem."

Jack must have been drunk. After their respect talk, he never used that kind of language. She meant to push him off, she really did. Instead she found her arms clinging tighter, pulling him closer as he barely flexed his hips, plunging in and out of her wetness in slow, languid strokes.

It was heaven.

It was hell.

The first wave of her orgasm surged over her, taking her by surprise. Jack swallowed her gasp, but her excitement was evidently contagious. His back stiffened, his hips began to jerk, harder and faster with each thrust.

"Jack," she warned, digging her nails into his shoulder beneath his open shirt. "Easy. Slow down or we'll attract attention."

With a grunt, he stopped moving, his weight pressing her deeper within their macramé sling. Soon their heart rates returned to normal. Well, normal for people who'd just experienced orgasmic sex in a public place.

"How are we going to get out of this thing without being exposed?" she whispered, more than ready to go back home to continue what they'd started.

Against her back, his hand jerked, whacking her between the shoulder blades. The hammock swung in a deep arc again. He jerked his foot, causing them to hop against the swaying motion.

She sank her teeth into the cord of his neck to keep from shrieking, wrapped her legs around his, her arms around his neck, and held on.

The hammock took on a life of its own. Back and forth, with an exaggerated hop on each side. Jack's chest pressed against her face, impeding breathing, while he moved both legs and one arm against her.

"What are you doing, McMillan?" she said against his flexing pecs, her urgent whisper rasping her throat.

"I can't get my foot out . . . and my watch is tangled in the webbing by your head."

The next few minutes passed in a slow-motion blur as they jerked and tossed wildly before the hammock executed a few loops before spitting them unceremoniously onto the hard-packed sand.

Somehow her sundress skirt ended up over their heads. Her lungs hurt. Cold sand ground into her back while the ocean breeze whispered along her side. Jack still rested atop her. She couldn't feel him inside anymore, which she guessed was probably a good thing.

Her dress was flipped back, a bright light temporarily blinding her.

"Dr. McMillan! Are you all right?" The maître d's voice floated down to her burning ears.

"We're fine." Jack growled his reply close to her ear, his voice vibrating things deep inside her that had no business being vibrated. "Turn the damn light off, Mike!"

Darkness immediately followed. Jack shoved the man's helping hand away and made a big show of getting up. It gave them the time they needed to right their clothing. Sort of.

Face burning, Royce turned her back to the patio patrons and made fast work of rebuttoning her dress.

"I don't understand it," Mike said, scampering beside them as they hobbled toward the exit. "This sort of thing rarely happens anymore. Not since we redecorated."

"Yeah?" Jack shielded her with his arm as they stepped through the gate to the public beach. "Maybe it's defective equipment."

After Mike assured them he'd check it out, they made their way up the beach.

Royce glanced at Jack's profile and felt her knees go weak. Equipment malfunction. Yeah, right. She couldn't resist. "Your 'equipment' seemed to work just fine from where I was, Jack." With a laughing whoop, she barely avoided his swipe at her derriere, then ran down the beach. He followed at a more sedate pace.

She paused at the steps to her deck, smiling at his confident swagger as he closed the distance between them. He stopped directly in front of her, hands braced on lean, khaki-covered hips, tropical print shirt flapping in the breeze. His bare toes dug into the sand. Even his toes were sexy.

Toes. "Jack! We left our shoes by the hammock."

His arms went around her as though he'd held her like that for a lifetime. She wished.

"Forget the shoes," he said in a husky voice. "I have more important things on my mind."

"Oh?" She looped her arms around his neck, loving the way they fit together, despite the height difference. *Loving him.*

"Yep." He nodded and backed her against the hard wood of her deck pier, his hands busy walking the back of her skirt up around her bare hips. "I developed a major hard-on watching you run down the beach, knowing you were plumb nekkid under that pretty little dress."

She rotated her hips, grinding against the ridge on the front of his shorts. When their interlude was over—and she knew it would be, eventually—she knew she might regret her wanton behavior. But she would rather have regrets about what they'd done than regrets over having done nothing.

She moved her breasts against him in flagrant invitation. "Spend the night with me and we'll see if we can't remedy your condition."

He stiffened within her embrace, then stepped back, breaking physical contact. Emotional contact was obviously long gone.

"I don't think that's a good idea, Royce." He shoved his hands into the pockets of his cargo shorts and took another step back. "I'm still kind of sore and I have a lot to do tomorrow to begin getting the house ready for the next renters."

Suddenly cold, she folded her arms over her chest, rubbing her hands up and down her upper arms in an effort to stave off the feeling of rejection.

She refused to beg.

He turned and walked to his deck. She watched his back, waiting. Without a backward glance, he climbed the steps. Within seconds, the *whoosh* and *click* of his door drifted down to her, bringing home the fact that she was, indeed, alone.

Royce turned over on the chaise and checked the travel alarm clock she used while sunning. According to the dial, it had been exactly fourteen minutes. She took a sip of water and closed her eyes, willing the stiffness out of her body.

Next door, classic rock blasted, punctuated by hammering and assorted tool sounds. How much could he really have to do before the next renters arrived?

She yawned. Sleep had eluded her for most of the night. Damn Jack.

Admitting defeat, she gathered her towel, clock and water and padded into the cool dimness of her house.

After a quick shower, she dressed in a loose-fitting purple print sundress she'd found wadded in the bottom of her box of towels, then turned on the fan in her room and settled at her desk to go over her notes.

The afternoon passed. When the phone next to her rang, she was surprised to see it was almost sunset.

Willing her heart to slow, knowing it wasn't Jack but praying it was, she answered.

"Hello?"

"Hey, beach bunny, how's it going?"

Wendy. Royce exhaled and slumped back in her padded office chair. "Great," she answered with more enthusiasm than she felt. "Did you get my fax?"

"Sure did. That's why I'm calling you, even though you made me promise not to disturb you."

Royce laughed and walked over to the chaise to curl up and talk to her friend. "I should've known you wouldn't keep a promise like that."

"Hey! I haven't been bugging you, have I? I just wanted to touch base and tell you I loved your idea for the book so much that I passed on your notes and preliminary premise to a friend who works for U of H. And guess what? He found a publisher who wants to read it!" At her silence, Wendy said, "Hello? Are you there? Don't you think that's fantastic? Royce?"

She closed her eyes and counted to ten. "Wendy, what have you done? I have no intention of writing a book from those research notes! At least not in the foreseeable future. They're more of a personal journal than research, anyway. Tell him thanks, but I'm not interested."

"Why not!" Wendy's strident voice all but shrieked in Royce's ear. "You told me you had too much spare time on your hands, now that you've gone to summer schedule at the station. I assumed that was why you began your notes."

"It was." Royce raked a hand through her hair and looked out over the water. Even with the door closed, she could hear the faint whisper of the surf lapping the shore. "I don't know, Wen. Maybe it wasn't such a good idea, buying a beach house. Makes me restless."

Wendy snorted. "From your notes, I'd say it also makes you horny. So . . . who's the studly beach bum who's got you so hot and bothered? I know all those notes on your test subject didn't come from your vivid imagination." When Royce didn't answer right away, she added, "Strictly off the record, of course."

"You don't know?"

"Well, at first I thought it was Jack, but then I remembered how much you two detested each other. So I began wondering . . . oh, no! Didn't you watch and learn anything these last six years? Royce, please tell me it isn't Jack-the-ripper!"

"Believe me, I'd love to tell you that."

Silence.

"Is it serious?" Wendy asked in a small, hopeful voice.

Life-threatening. At least, for her. She thought of the last time she'd seen Jack, striding away, his back stiff and straight. "Of course not. Remember, this is Jack. I just wanted to see what all the hype was about."

"And?"

"And what?"

"And was it just that, hype? Or is he as good as his reputation?"

Better. And it was killing her not to be with him.

She hoped her laugh didn't sound as fake to Wendy as it did to her. "Please. No one could live up to that reputation."

Wendy agreed and they talked of mundane things for a few minutes.

"Well," Wendy said, "I'd better let you get back to whatever you were doing when I called. Think about the offer, Royce. I think you could turn it into a blockbuster self-help book. If you won't do it for me, do it for the millions of women out there who are stuck in dead-end relationships with guys who aren't willing or able to commit. Just think about it, okay?"

"Okay, I'll think about it." Wendy didn't need to know that the book, even if she wrote it, would never see the light of day.

After a few more pleasantries, they hung up.

The sun set low as Jack stepped out onto his deck. Against his will, he glanced over at Royce's deserted deck. What did he expect? He'd heard her drive away a little while ago. Probably had to work.

With slow steps, he walked to the Purple Crab and nursed a beer at the bar before sitting at his table for one and eating a fisherman's platter he couldn't taste.

"Dining alone tonight, Dr. McMillan?" Mike stood next to the table, smoothing a nonexistent wrinkle from the starched white tablecloth. "Where's your lady friend?"

"She had to work." The lie flowed smoothly from his mouth. As though he and Royce were an old married couple, comfortable with each other's schedules.

Mike nodded. "Would you care for wine with your dinner?"

Jack held up his half-empty glass of warm beer. "No, thanks, I can't even seem to finish this."

"Would you like something else?"

Jack thought a moment. "Yes, I think I would. Iced tea would be great."

Within minutes he had a sweating glass of tea before him. He watched the droplets of condensation dribble down to form a wet spot on the tablecloth, then tossed a wad of bills on the table and left by way of the patio beach gate. Keeping his eyes trained forward, he avoided the sight of "their" hammock. Funny, just the sight of it in his peripheral vision caused a slight ache in his heart.

Of course there could never be anything between him and Royce. They both knew that. It was that knowledge that made him walk away the night before. That same knowledge was the reason he would not return to her bed.

It was fun, but past time to be over.

And no amount of wishing would change it.

12

Laughter erupted from Jack's deck, cutting Royce to the bone. Nonchalantly, she strolled to her kitchen window and peeked through the curtain. Not that she cared, but she didn't recognize anyone in the crowd. Not even Jack.

A few minutes later, she stepped out onto her own deck for her morning sunbath, frowning at the sound of children.

"Hey, neighbor!" A portly older gentleman called from the hot tub just as she got settled. "How long you here for? Want to join us?"

Renters. "Hi. No, thanks. I live here. Which is why I have to go to work in a little while." It wouldn't hurt to be polite. "How long are you staying?"

"We're only here for today and tomorrow. Our kids and grandkids will be here until the weekend. They wanted it through Monday, but the owner had it rented already."

"Well," Royce said, getting up again and wrapping her towel tightly around her, "have a nice vacation. Bye."

She spent the time until she had to go to the station adding to her growing pile of notes. Jack displayed textbook aversion by running back to Houston. She wiped away a tear. She knew the type. Knew he'd run if she came on too strong.

But the knowledge didn't ease the pain.

After three weeks of strangers traipsing in and out of Jack's house, invading her privacy with their boisterous activities, making her miss Jack so much she ached with it, Royce came to an irrefutable conclusion: She had to sell the beach house. Jack's aversion tactics had won.

It was painfully obvious that the good doctor would not return as long as she was in residence. She could do her syndicated program from any affiliate. And face it, the beach no longer held anything but pain for her.

With a heavy heart, she called the Realtor who'd sold her the property.

Kelly Williams, the *perky to the point of being obnoxious* Realtor, was there within the hour with the paperwork.

"I can't believe you're letting this piece of prime property go!" Kelly shoved the listing contract toward her. "Do you have any idea how scarce houses are in this area? Are you sure you want to do this? I need your initial here." She tapped the paper with a long, crimson nail.

Royce initialed, willing her lunch to stay down. "Yes, I realize it. I just can't keep making the commute every night." Boisterous laughter sounded from Jack's deck. Royce winced, a tight smile on her face. "And I hadn't counted on living next to rental property."

Kelly raised her perfect-shaped eyebrows and inclined her head in the direction of Jack's deck.

Royce nodded. "It's getting worse."

"From what I hear, it's just as bad when the owner is in residence!" Kelly laughed, then gathered all the papers and stuffed them in her briefcase. "I hate to see you go. I know if you'd give Pleasure Beach a chance, you'd love it every bit as much as the other owners. It's truly a paradise." She let out a little sigh and looked out at the water. Perkiness firmly back in place, she said, "I just know I'll have this place sold in a jiffy! How about we go down the beach to the Purple Crab and have a drink on the agency? The Crab makes killer margaritas and piña coladas."

Swallowing around the sudden lump in her throat, Royce shook her head and choked out, "No, thanks, I need to get some of these boxes out of here if I want it to show well."

"All righty, then! I'll just get the sign up and head back to the office to put the listing in the computer."

Royce held out her hand. The Realtor grabbed her in a gardenia-scented hug. "Oh, we're too informal for handshakes down here!" She stepped back and patted Royce's arm. "I'll be in touch!"

Closing the door and her thoughts, Royce made her way to her desk. Maybe some kind of work would help ease the pain.

Jack sat back in the booth at his favorite Houston bar and regarded his friend. Just back from his honeymoon, Marc radiated happiness.

"I hope Kinsey knows what a lucky gal she is to land the most eligible bachelor in Houston," he told Marc, wiping the sweat from his untouched Manhattan.

Marc grinned, teeth flashing white in his tanned face. "I guess I have been talking nonstop about my wedded bliss, haven't I?" He took a sip of his drink. "So, have you heard from Mardee since you've been back?"

Jack shook his head. Not only had he not seen or spoken to his ex, he hadn't so much as thought about her. "Naw, that's history. Whatever we had was dead long before we buried it."

"That why you're not drinking?"

"Nope." He shoved his glass to the edge of the table and motioned for the waitress. "Just not in the mood, I guess."

"Thanks for taking my rotation, by the way. Now that I'm back, you may as well use up the rest of your leave time."

"Trying to get rid of me?" He picked at the sodden cocktail napkin.

"You know better."

They sat in silence for a beat.

"When did you realize you were in love with Kinsey?"

Marc smiled and wiped the edge of his glass with his thumb. "I'd like to say the moment she stepped onto the elevator, but it was probably when she grabbed my cock." He met Jack's interested gaze. "The way I see it, a woman's got to know what she wants and go after it to have the guts to do something like that to a complete stranger."

"Good point."

"True point, my friend."

"But what if, strictly hypothetically speaking, a woman went after what she wanted with someone she knew?"

"Hypothetically speaking, huh?" Marc shrugged. "I'd guess she knows what she wants even more. Takes even more balls to risk getting shot down by a friend." He leaned forward. "Anyone I know?"

Jack snorted and leaned back. "Not likely. Like I said, strictly hypothetical."

"Right." Marc stood and threw a few bills onto the polished tabletop. "Well, hypothetically speaking, a guy who was so lucky shouldn't tempt fate by letting a woman like that slide through his fingers." He gave a two-fingered salute and left.

Jack sat long after his friend left. Shouldn't tempt fate. Did fate bring Royce to him just when he'd needed her most? Maybe he'd always needed her and now was just their time.

Time. He'd wasted a lot of it lately. He threw down his money.

No more. Whether fate or Royce had brought her into his

life, it didn't matter. What mattered was that she stay in it. Until death did they part.

"Royce?" Kelly's concerned pixie face swam through the tears filling Royce's eyes. "Are you okay?" She leaned close, her peppermint-scented breath mingling with her perfume. "If you're not well, we can postpone the closing."

Royce wiped her eyes with the wadded-up damp tissue clutched in her fist. "No, I'm fine. Allergies. Where do I need to sign?"

Her house had sold in record time, even for Pleasure Beach. Less than twenty-four hours after it was listed, an offer was made.

During the closing, she smiled and said all the appropriate things, all the while dying inside.

It was for the best. She and Jack had no future. He wanted nothing more to do with her. He'd made it abundantly clear.

Jack frowned at the SOLD sign posted on Royce's deck, then brightened. She wouldn't need the house after they were married. Not a problem.

It took feeling around two of the three fat ceramic frogs on her deck before he found her spare key. He picked up the champagne and roses and stepped inside.

The comfort that was Royce surrounded him like a balm. He loved her. She was his soul mate. His home. Why had he taken so long to realize it? Now he just needed to convince Royce.

He headed upstairs. Turnabout was fair play. The roses would look better scattered over her sheets and delectable body than in a vase, anyway.

Inside her bedroom door, he reached across her desk to flip on the lamp. Several papers fluttered to the ground. He smiled. The intelligent woman he hoped to wed had obviously been busy during their separation. He stooped to pick up the papers and stopped, his numb brain struggling to absorb what he read.

Sexual mores and the modern male's inability to commit? What the hell was that? It didn't take long to realize who her first "test subject" was. Everything they'd done over the past few weeks was chronicled in black and white. And to think he'd been about to beg her forgiveness and pledge his undying love. When pigs flew!

Two hours after signing away her hopes and dreams, Royce trudged up the deck. Jack's house was quiet and dark for a change. She'd be glad to be away from him and the constant reminder of what could never be, she thought.

She let herself in with the spare key she always kept hidden in her frog trio. She'd promised the new owners to be out by the end of the week, and given them her key so they could begin moving in right away.

A light glowed from her room. Cautious steps took her up the stairs toward the steady beacon.

Her heart tripped at the sight of Jack, standing at the patio door, looking out across the Gulf. Hungry eyes devoured every gorgeous inch of him. She was afraid to hope. "Jack?"

He turned. Fierce and unreadable, he advanced on her.

Her joy evaporated like so many of her dreams when she saw the papers clutched in his fist.

"Jack, I can explain. I—"

"Forget it. You got what you wanted. Tell me, Royce, did you enjoy all the "research" we did?" He stomped to the top of the stairs before looking back. "You had a fax. Good offer. I think you should take it. I hope it keeps you warm at night. Good-bye, Royce."

Numb, she stood, nailed to the floor, unable to speak, cry, beg or even scream. The patio door slid shut.

Jack was gone. Forever.

She should be glad. Jack McMillan was an egotistical, overbearing chauvinist with Neanderthal thought processes. When it came to the opposite sex and relationships, he was emotionally stunted.

And he was the love of her life.

13

Jack leaned back in his leather desk chair and swung his stethoscope around with his index finger while he stared out his window at the top of the hospital cafeteria.

"Dr. McMillan, why don't you call it a day?" Sylvia, his office manager, stood in the doorway, hands on ample hips. "No offense, but you've been about as useful as tits on a bull this week. Why did you even come back? You aren't scheduled for anything for more than two weeks."

She took a step into the office and closed the mahogany and beveled-glass door. "I know you don't have any renters right now," she said in a sympathetic voice. "Why don't you go back to the beach for a while? I can handle things here."

"I'm getting married." The announcement surprised him as much as Sylvia. But suddenly he knew it was true. And he'd move heaven and earth to make it happen.

"What? When? Congratulations!" She rounded the desk and almost smothered him in her motherly hug. "Do I know her? When's the big day?" She cuffed his shoulder. "I can't believe you haven't told anyone! Does Dr. Wallace know?"

"No, Marc doesn't know." His new partner would probably gloat. Newlyweds seemed to love sharing their wedded bliss.

He couldn't wait.

He stood so fast, several files slid to the floor. "I haven't convinced her yet, Sylvia. Any suggestions?" He bent to help retrieve the papers.

She shooed him away. "As if you needed my help! You just go on and get that lady to the altar! I'll handle everything here."

Impulsively, he kissed her rouged cheek. "I'll send you an announcement."

"You'd better. Now, get!"

Royce closed the door of her Galleria area condo and stared at the FedEx envelope. Her contract.

"I should be happy. Jumping for joy," she said, tossing it onto the dining table. "Why do I feel like crying and throwing up?"

Impatient pounding on her door drew her out of her pity party.

With a heavy heart, she walked to the door, not bothering with the peephole. Without Jack, it didn't matter. A serial killer would be welcome about now.

Instead, it was Jack.

They stood for several moments, staring at each other.

"Aren't you going to ask me in?"

Royce braced her arm on the door, gripping the edge. She couldn't just let him waltz in and out of her life whenever he had an itch he wanted scratched. "Why? I thought you said all you had to say last time."

"Thanks, I think I will come in." He shouldered his way past her, then turned and rescued the door from her death grip. It closed with a soft click.

He flipped the dead bolt. "You moved without saying good-bye."

"I thought we'd said all there was to say the last time we saw each other." She took a step back.

"Do you have any idea how hard it was to track you down? The station is very closemouthed about things like that."

"You've been looking for me?" Despite herself, hope blossomed.

He nodded and took another step toward her. "I finally had to break down and call Wendy." He frowned. "I didn't remember her being so opinionated."

"Yeah, well, that's Wendy."

"I didn't come here to discuss Wendy. Or anyone else, for that matter."

"You didn't?"

"Did you accept the book deal?"

"Why—"

"Just answer the question, would you?" He advanced, backing her up until she felt the edge of the snack bar dig into her spine.

She swallowed and straightened. "Yes."

He nodded. The confusing man even had the gall to look pleased. What did he care?

"Good," he said, standing so close now that she could feel his heat along the entire length of her body, smell his unique combination of male skin and mouthwatering aftershave. "It was a good offer. Too good to pass up. You're smarter than that."

He reached up to drag his fingertip along her cheek. It was all she could do to bite back her groan. It seemed like years, instead of weeks, since she'd felt his touch.

"I've missed you, Royce," he whispered. "Did you miss me?"

She could only nod and pray that, whatever game he was playing, he would never stop. No doubt about it, when it came to Jack, she had no willpower.

He reached for something but she didn't care. He could do anything to her, bondage, whatever. As long as he never left her again. She was desperate, shameless in her need for him.

"I only have one suggestion for your book. It has to do with revisions. And the dedication."

"Huh?" He was back within touching distance and he wanted to talk about her book?

He tilted her chin until their gazes met. "I want you to change your conclusions. At least about Test Subject One." Feather-light, his lips brushed hers.

"You do?"

He nodded and kissed her again, this time a bit longer. "Uh-huh," he said, brushing a kiss on the tip of her nose. "You see, this is one test subject who has changed. I love you, Royce St. Claire. I'm over my fear of commitment."

With a squeal, she threw her arms around his neck, but he stopped her exuberant kisses. "Now, about that dedication."

"Jack, do you really want to talk about that right now?" She squirmed against his arousal, but he pushed her away from him.

"We need to shake on it first." He extended his left hand.

She frowned, confused, but if she had to shake hands with him to get him back in her life, it was a small price to pay.

She placed her hand in his.

He drew her closer.

Mouth scant inches from hers, he said, "About that dedication . . ." His breath was hot against her lips.

"What about it?" she whispered, all but quaking in her need.

Something cool and hard touched her ring finger, but she refused to break eye contact.

"I want you to dedicate it to your husband . . . Jack."

"My—?"

"Husband." He raised their joined hands. On hers, a diamond the size of an ice cube glittered beneath the light from her hallway. "Put me out of my misery. Don't let it be too late," he urged. "Tell me you love me. Say you'll marry me."

She ran her free hand down over the bulge in his trousers. "Jack, why don't we continue this where we'll be more comfortable . . . in bed?"

"Say it," he demanded, love shining from his eyes.

"Remember the first time we made love?" she asked, drawing circles on his chest.

"Of course. Now say it." Despite his words of protest, he busily unbuttoned her blouse.

"You asked me to trust you. Repeatedly."

Her breath caught at the feel of his mouth on her neck. Her knees went weak.

"Right. Say it."

"I love you, Jack," she said with a sigh.

"And?"

She dropped to her knees. Her hands on his belt buckle, she looked up and smiled. "Trust me."

Four friends. No limits. Pick your man and get ready to play by Susan Lyons's CHAMPAGNE RULES, available now from Kensington . . .

"So, tell all, Suze." Jenny leaned forward, elbows on the table, pink flamingo earrings dancing. "What's the best sex *you* ever had?"

Around their outside table at Las Margaritas restaurant, three flushed female faces grinned at Suzanne.

It was Jenny Yuen who'd launched the topic, with her description of hot sex in her boyfriend Pete's double Jacuzzi. "It was the best sex of my life!" she'd exclaimed, brown eyes flashing. "I swear, Korean men beat Chinese, hands down."

"Ssh," Suzanne had said, used to the fact that Jenny's personality was twice the size of her petite body, but wishing she didn't always have to be quite so out there.

She wished she'd kept quiet, though, when Jenny turned the question on her.

"I, um . . ." Best sex? Suzanne barely suppressed a nervous giggle. That would have to be with her dream lover.

Jenny rolled her eyes, turned a pink-sweatshirted back to Suzanne, and said to Rina Goldberg, "So, what's the best sex you've ever had?"

"Not with Marty, that's for sure." Tonight, at the Awesome Foursome's regular Monday dinner, Rina had already told them she'd called it quits with the man she'd been seeing for the last several months. Her heart definitely didn't seem broken.

"The best sex," she murmured. Looking like a gypsy with a fringed burgundy shawl over her usual black clothing, she pulled a wayward lock of curly black hair behind a multi-ringed ear as she sipped her second margarita and considered the question.

The others waited, munching from the platter of nachos locos—laden with everything yummy and fattening you could possibly imagine—and working on their own second margaritas.

Rina began to smile, and nodded her head firmly. "Yeah, I know *exactly*. The summer I turned eighteen, I went to a music school in Banff. There was this other student, Giancarlo, from Italy. He was a pianist and he had the most awesome hands."

The others oohed and aahed as Rina described the things Giancarlo had done with those hands, including making her come three times in a row atop the grand piano in a student rehearsal room.

Somewhere during the recitation, a third round of margaritas got ordered for everyone but Suzanne, who had a strict two-drink limit.

When Rina finished, Jenny turned to Ann Montgomery. "Your turn," she said, talking around a guacamole-and-sour-cream laden chip.

"You know I'm a conventional gal." But Ann's eyes were twinkling. "I'm not much into Jacuzzis or pianos. I like big, comfy beds. And a man who wears a tie."

"A tie? Bo-ring," Jenny scoffed.

"Not when there are four of them, all silk, and they're tying you to a four-poster bed."

"Bondage?" Suzanne frowned. "Ann, that's—"

"No, no!" Ann held up a hand to stop her. "I totally consented. And they were tied really loosely. He made slow, beautiful love to me, and all I could do was respond."

Jenny gave a skeptical frown. "I can't imagine you surrendering control to anyone. You're the control freak to end all control freaks."

Ann stuck her tongue out, then shrugged. "Okay, I concede your point. And yes, it surprised me too." She smoothed her short brown hair and straightened her shoulders inside the jacket of her navy suit. "I've never come so hard in my life. It was a little . . . scary."

As Suzanne glanced around the table, she thought how lucky she was to have found these women. They'd met last year at an introductory yoga course. The bonding began when, after the second lesson, they decided food, chat and alcohol were far better tension relievers than contorting their bodies into pretzel shapes. The four didn't have a lot in common, but that made the conversations even more stimulating. Strong ties of friendship had formed, and now the Foursome members were deeply loyal to each other and their Monday nights.

She stopped feeling lucky when Jenny turned to her with an evil grin. "Didn't think we'd forget you, did you, Suze?"

Oh God, after her friends' sexy tales, how pitiful to have to confess that her own sex life ranged between boring and non-existent.

Except for her cave-sex lover.

The thought sent a thrill of excitement coursing through her. She slugged back the last of her second margarita and took a deep breath.

"Remember me telling you how I treated myself to a week package deal on Crete, after my second year of university?" They nodded. "Okay then . . ." She closed her eyes, letting the scene form.

"It's my last afternoon. I'm walking along a beach and this

man comes toward me, and it's like we're both struck by lightning. Immediate chemistry."

She opened her eyes, and saw she had their rapt attention.
"Did I mention"—she paused deliberately—"that this is a nude
beach?"

"Suzie!" Rina gasped, heedless of the salsa tumbling from
her chip to the table.

"Our Suze on a nude beach?" Jenny said.

"We've established the man is nude," Ann said. "So get to
the good stuff. What does this guy look like?"

"Tall, muscled, handsome. Absolutely perfect in, how shall I
say this? Every dimension."

"In other words, he's hung," Jenny said, shoving up her
sleeves and resting her pointy elbows on the table.

"You can say that again! I've never seen—" Suzanne broke
off, then continued in a lower voice. "Yeah, definitely hung.
Anyhow, then, somehow, we're holding hands, walking together, not even talking. Me, not talking. How weird is that?"
She reached for her margarita glass and brought it to her lips,
only to find it empty.

"Go on," Ann prompted, shrugging out of her suit jacket
and leaning forward.

"We follow a path that leads uphill, through scrubby bushes.
There's a zillion pretty little wildflowers dotting the ground."

"Skip the travelogue," Jenny demanded. "Like Ann said, cut
to the good stuff."

"I'm shooting him these sideways glances, checking him
out. And he's getting aroused." She grinned. "What a turn-on."

"Oh man!" Jenny said.

"We come across a cave. We step inside the mouth and suddenly we're kissing. He lifts me up, I hook my legs around his
waist and we make love right there, standing up."

"Oh, my, God!" Rina fanned herself with the fringed end of
her shawl.

"It's fast, explosive." And she'd had an orgasm for the first time in her life. Not just an orgasm, but a mind-shattering one.

"Afterwards, we lie down on my beach towel and explore each other's bodies with our hands, lips, tongues. He makes me come with his mouth and I, you know . . ."

"Give him a blow job," Jenny finished, at the same moment Ann said, "Perform fellatio."

Suzanne felt her cheeks grow hotter. "He stops me before he comes, then he's inside me so hard and fast and deep, and it feels so amazing that I come again before he does." She cleared her throat and fiddled with her margarita glass, almost wishing she'd broken her two-drink rule, even as she remembered the reason she never would.

"Jesus, girl, I didn't know you had it in you," Jenny marveled, reaching for another cheese-coated chip and shoving it into the guacamole.

Suzanne closed her eyes, remembering watching as their bodies joined, separated, joined again. "Did I mention he's black?"

"You mean African-American," Ann corrected.

"Or African-African," Suzanne said. "Or from England. Lots of English people holiday in Greece. No accent, though. Yeah, probably American, you're right." Damn, doing this analysis had thrown her out of the moment, away from Crete and back to the restaurant.

"But definitely gorgeous, eh?" Jenny said. "And hung."

Suzanne nodded. "Yup. He was this delicious shade of dark chocolate and he had short dreads. His face was so striking. A sexy little goatee. His eyes were chocolate too, and sparkly. Vibrant."

"Wow," Rina breathed. "A chocolate man. How yummy."

"He was." Even now, she could remember that taste.

"And of course he was a fantastic lover." Rina sighed dreamily.

"He was a stranger, yet sex with him felt like the most intimate act I'd ever committed. For a moment I even found my-self wishing our lovemaking would create a child." Suzanne gave a shiver. "Is that insane or what? Especially given my, uh, rather traditional feelings about marriage and kids."

"Traditional!" Jenny hooted. "Try archaic. Any woman whose deepest aspiration is to marry Ward Cleaver from *Leave It to Beaver . . .*"